AT HELL'S GATE

RICHARD JOHN THORNTON

To Debbie

Thankyou for you
amazing support

Jo x

7/3/23

THIS STORY IS DEDICATED TO THE ADVENTUROUS
AMONG US.

PROLOGUE

It is purported that the world is now a much smaller place.

Modern theorists boast that more people are in simultaneous transit around the globe than ever before, and that timed duration of routes is being reduced year on year. Locations generally viewed as remote just fifty short years ago are now readily familiar to a considerable proportion of travellers. Ease of accessibility and inexpensive air mileage has enabled millions to satisfy their natural wonder regarding distant lands in the Twenty-First Century.

And it is of course this human whim to progress that has forged the foundations of history and will no doubt influence much of the future.

The eternal quest to consume, confront and identify the unknown.

The desire to discover and perhaps conquer.

However, the appetite for sampling ways of life which are deemed to be far beyond our typical existence is often only partially satisfied.

Equally, such a philosophy can occasionally bring great reward and perhaps even notability among its participants.

But there is also occasion for genuine curiosity to be viewed as intrusive. Indeed, tourism is regarded in some quarters as a distinctly unwelcome facet of our existence.

There are times when those partaking of such supposed foreign delights should perhaps heed signals of caution - although such warnings are invariably implicit and unclear.

It is the more inconsiderate souls among us who typically find themselves helplessly blinded to accepted local codes of conduct.

'When in Rome' is a policy rarely applied by many explorers, yet such unwavering arrogance guides them through their individual journeys, safely affording them evasion of hurdle and hindrance.

But inevitably, there are those members of the unwitting, innocent minority, for whom fortune proves far less favourable...

ONE

Curt Osbourne finished his tepid cup of vending machine coffee and checked the clock on the office wall.

Nearly midday.

Nearly mid-way through yet another tedious, mind-numbing shift at Littleholt Logistics Limited.

Reluctantly sitting up in his creaking chair he grimaced at the soiling aftertaste that coated his tongue and dropped the empty coffee cup into the waste bin under the desk. Idly flicking through a selection of recently printed consignment notes, he wiped away remnants of the drink from the tabletop with the cuff of his smock.

Scrutinising the week's imminent orders, he recognised with a certain pang of concern that the haulage firm collecting for a major Australian customer would be arriving within the hour.

The shipping confirmation seemed complete as he focused attention to the other occupant of the transport office.

'Caroline…have you had the picking list back yet for the Melbourne job?'

The accounts clerk lifted her head from her computer screen and smiled knowingly.

'Not yet Curt, my love! They're sitting on it down there for some reason. I haven't invoiced the customer yet, either. I think the loaders need a kick up the arse.'

'Okay…leave it with me. I'll chase it up.'

Sighing wearily, Curt eyed the clock again judging it high time to assess the progress downstairs.

Wearily pushing himself up onto his feet, Curt shuffled across to the office window which overlooked all four gangways of the warehouse. Affording himself a preparatory glimpse of any possible activity beyond the glass, the thought struck him that the current absence of movement and dearth of bodies reminded him of the deck of some long-deserted ghost ship.

Deciding to descend the stairway of the mezzanine office, he pulled open the door and made his way down to the shop floor. Stepping with purposed caution so as not to disturb his hardy team of operatives during what appeared to be another of their regular periods of rest and recuperation, he reached ground level and scanned the peaceful arena once more.

Slowly but surely, his curiosity was drawn to the sound of familiar voices on the rear yard.

As the chief facilitator of the warehouse material handlers for the past six months, Curt was now in a position of some responsibility. It was a grandiose title for a basic role that required him to ensure that his colleagues were endeavouring to meet the requirements of daily business.

In theory, confirming that orders were compiled on schedule was a simplistic task.

In practice, however, he found himself readily frustrated by the reliable apathy and lack of urgency on display from the warehouse team.

As expected, the usual suspects were found outside beyond the main shutter doors immersed in idle conversation whilst leaning on a polythene-wrapped pallet of goods.

Curt could not refrain from a mild pang of inner amusement and as such, a broad smile preceded his sarcastic bark across the uneven tarmac yard.

'OI! YOU TWO! IT WON'T GET DONE BY STANDING THERE NATTERING, WILL IT?'

Both conversationalists interrupted their private exchange and glared scornfully toward the smirking figure of the supervisor.

Trevor Palmer was not averse to a bout of abusive banter if sufficiently encouraged and his immediate response to the call of his supposed superior was typical. Trevor's precisely formed V-sign was accompanied by a mimed rendition of the favourite two words in his vocabulary.

His partner in chatter, Gary Lockley, proceeded to enjoy the developing spectacle as Curt returned Trevor's silent yet decisive volley.

'It's alright telling me to fuck off, Trev, but I need that Australian order finishing pretty sharpish! I take it is done and you're just discussing which one of you will be bringing the completed pick list upstairs?'

Trevor adopted his typically arrogant standpoint and repeated the abusive physical gesture - this time with both hands.

Gary's amusement at the display resonated across the yard as he continued to lounge across the pallet.

Pleased to see that the bait had avidly been taken by Curt, both warehousemen simply stared in practised glee as their team leader came marching purposefully toward them.

'Getting you two into second gear is like pulling bloody teeth!' quipped Curt, as he drew nearer to the pair.

Trevor's instant retort was barbed and only partially offered in humour.

'I'll tell you something, Curtis, my old mate. Since you got your stripes in the summer you've completely forgotten where you came from! Gone right up your own arsehole you have! And to think we trained you up from a young virgin!'

On reaching the less than dynamic duo, Curt observed Trevor's slovenly appearance. His general attitude and manner appeared to be increasingly bitter and occasionally hostile. Curt was fully aware of the inflexible disposition of his work colleague and was usually astute enough to try and douse the ever-ready negativity.

'Look, mate. Play another record, will you? Have you finished picking the Melbourne order or not? If so, can I have your signed pick list so Caroline can process an invoice?'

Having been sufficiently entertained by the mild verbal joust, Gary opted to diffuse the immediate sense of antagonism.

'Curt…we are actually propping up the very last pallet for Australia and I was just about to line it up with the rest of the order over there…see?'

Following Gary's outstretched forefinger, Curt glanced in the direction of the said consignment positioned neatly in the corner of the yard ready for loading.

'Oh…right…great! I never doubted you. *Either* of you!'

Unfortunately, Trevor's quick-fire temper had begun to bubble beneath the surface.

'Piss off, Curtis! Patronising prick!'

Curt thought about ignoring the highly predictable insult, but instinct compelled him to try and smooth relations as opposed to letting them deteriorate further.

'Look, Trev…chill out, mate. I'm just doing my job.'

'Yeah? What is your job these days exactly?' snapped Trevor, his features reddening by the word.

'My job is making sure that you are doing *your* job. Okay?'

11

'Yeah? A nothing job if you ask me! Fucking promotion! I always suspected you were a suck-off merchant from day one, Curtis! Always in the gaffer's pocket you were! It was only a matter of time before I was proved right!'

As Curt retrieved the paperwork from the top of the pallet and slowly made his way back across the yard, Gary again felt it appropriate to adopt the role of mediator in an attempt to dampen the unnecessary tension between the pair.

'Hey, Curt! Don't you listen to this miserable twat! The load is ready...yes...all done!'

The facilitator was no longer in a sociable mood and confirmed as much with his dismissive response.

'Good! About time! Hope it doesn't rain or you'll have to bring it all inside under cover. The lorry's not due until after one o'clock.'

Trevor was just about to suggest another derogatory viewpoint when Gary decided to steer the conversation away from the workplace.

'Hey, Curt! Don't go just yet. We want a word for a minute.'

The warehouse supervisor suddenly halted his stride once more and against experienced judgement turned back toward his grinning colleagues who had resumed their nigh-on recumbent positions against the pallet.

His natural inclination was to expect further sarcasm though he was prepared to play the game for a little longer.

'Oh really, lads? What on Earth could you ever want to talk to *me* about?'

'It's about what me and Trev were discussing before you so rudely interrupted us...about my fortieth birthday.'

It was only mild interest in the subject that caused Curt to slowly re-convene with his workmates against the pallet.

'Forty? Is that all you are...you old git! And to think you barely look a day over thirty-nine! So, what's this about your birthday?' asked Curt.

'Well...I fancy planning something a bit different to the usual pub crawl. Me and Trev were just talking about the idea of going away for a weekend. You know...a few lads...a few beers...maybe a few women into the bargain? Should be a right laugh, I reckon. You'd be up for something like that, wouldn't you?'

Curt noted the expression of sincere disapproval that had etched itself across Trevor Palmer's unshaven features before offering a cautious reply.

12

'Erm…I suppose so. Not sure. What did you have in mind?'

'Don't know yet. It will definitely be in early January, though. I'm thinking about booking one of those dirt-cheap getaways on the internet. You can fly anywhere from anywhere these days.'

Curt was taken aback by the mention of flights.

'You mean…go abroad? What? Just for a weekend?'

'Yeah! Be brilliant! Everyone's doing it nowadays! My younger brother Ian's been on a few weekend benders all over the place. I was talking to him about it last night. He reckons Prague is the real hot-spot at the moment.'

Trevor's curiosity was pricked sufficiently for him to display another indication of total ignorance.

'Where the fuck's Prague?' he sneered.

Despite being equally uninformed, Gary rolled his eyes before replying.

'I think it's in Yugoslavia…or is it Bulgaria? You know…that decent football side. England always struggle to beat 'em, anyway.'

'England always struggle to beat everybody! Anyway, that doesn't answer the question. Where the fuck is it?' Trevor snorted again.

Curt watched the display of idiocy develop as Gary again conveyed a woefully poor knowledge of geography.

'Not sure. Somewhere the other side of Germany, I think. It's definitely in Europe though. I think so, anyway. Or it could be Russia.'

Curt was becoming intrigued by the concept and dispelled the uncertainty shrouding the geography.

'Actually…it's in the Czech Republic. So, what's the plan, then, Gaz?'

'Haven't really got one yet, mate. It's just going to be a general piss-up really. Our Ian seems dead keen, though. Says I've got to get some names together. He says he'll book it and sort all that shit out on his computer. Got to be a right laugh though, hasn't it? Can't bloody fail?'

Ever the sensible and considerate husband, Curt quietly hedged his bets as Trevor's gaze bore right through him and detected the hesitancy.

'Erm…I'll get back to you, Gaz. Christmas isn't that far away. I don't know how much money I'll have spare come the New Year.'

As usual, Trevor Palmer did not disappoint with his immediate and sour injection.

'What you mean is…you've got to ask the missus if you can go?'

'No…it's not that…but you know…cash is tight. I can't commit myself just yet.'

Trevor was not keen to relinquish the role of willing tormenter.

'Yeah…right…this is how it works…you arrange your pass-out with the wife tonight and then tomorrow you give us the nod that you're in! You're a sad man, Curtis. You need to sort your life out, mate.'

Curt did not rise to the unceremonious and expected challenge, instead choosing to display genuine interest in his colleague's proposal.

'So, who else is invited, Gaz?'

'Oh…there'll be about half a dozen. You…me…our Ian, obviously. Our Elaine's husband, Paul…and no doubt this fat twat here will want to gate-crash as well.'

Trevor smiled at Gary's good-natured commentary whilst never letting his attention wander from Curt, whose enthusiasm for the idea was steadily increasing.

'Sounds like it's already arranged, lads.'

'Oh…we're definitely going. Just don't know where or when, yet. Ian wants to get things organised being as it's getting close. He definitely wants to get it all booked well before Christmas.'

Trevor's smug visage emitted a teasing query, knowingly making Curt feel ill at ease.

'So…Curtis…are you in…or what?'

'Look…I'll check it at home first. It's still a few weeks away, yet. I can't just bugger off and leave the family, you know. She'll likely get the hump.'

'She'll be fine about it. Probably be glad to be fucking rid of you for a couple of days. I know I would be if I was her.' sneered Trevor.

Curt could not resist the opportunity to shut the antagonist up and the ammunition fell readily to hand.

'Oh yeah? What if *you* had a wife to consider, Trev? Be a different story then, wouldn't it?'

Mildly embarrassed by the surprising confrontation, Trevor quickly lifted his weight from his elbows and stood up straight before opting for a most unwelcome dose of self-deprecation.

'Well…I never really bothered, did I? Better off being single, anyway?'

Having assumed a partial victory in this latest verbal joust, Curt brought the jagged conversation to a temporary close.

'Well…the idea is now in my head. So, I'll give you a more definite answer tomorrow. Okay, Gaz?'

'Fine, mate! It'll give us something to look forward to when we come back to this dump in the New Year, won't it? Just make sure the missus' answer is a 'yes'!'

Trevor hadn't quite finished with his personal contribution.

'Hang on a minute…about this Prague…I've heard a lot of these foreign cities are right shit holes.'

Gary attempted to allay his cynical counterpart's undue concern.

'No, no! Prague sounds pretty much alright…even though I haven't a fucking clue about the place. Come on Trev…lighten up. Where do you want to go, then? Blackpool?'

'Well…suppose Prague would be fine. As long as the foreign women like to shag English blokes, who cares?'

Curt studied the evident desperation in Trevor's features, noting the baggy eyes, black stubble, and world-weary expression just as Gary supplied the perfect put-down.

'Well, well, Palmer…aren't those Czech ladies in for a right treat when you turn up on their doorstep unannounced.'

Trevor noted the mockery from his companions and snapped back in typically blunt style.

'Fuck off, Gaz! I'm not the one who needs permission off his missus, am I? Not like this wimp, here. I'm free as a bird, me. I don't need a permit from a wife!'

Curt was not prepared to allow the obvious sideswipe to go unacknowledged and resumed the launching of vocal artillery.

'A man in your position should keep his gob shut about the subject of domestic harmony. Hardly an expert, are you, Trev? In fact, I don't think you've got the first clue about the fairer sex. Do you even know where the hole is anymore?'

Despite the backdrop of Gary's chuckles, the atmosphere between his warring colleagues turned distinctly cooler as Trevor's posture became mildly aggressive and his stubby forefinger was fortified with a hissing repost.

'What the fuck is that supposed to mean, Curtis? Explain yourself! You hardly know anything about my personal life!'

Gary laughed out loud as Trevor edged around the pallet toward Curt.

'You'd better fucking shut it before I land one on you. It's not my fault you like living under the thumb. One more fucking word. Just one!'

'For Christ's sake, Trev! Do you have to try and settle all arguments with your fists?' Gary enquired, still smirking.

'Well…it's that stuck-up twat…he's winding me up, isn't he!'

'You're pretty good at winding *yourself* up, mate!' Curt concurred. 'Just try and have one day off from being an angry short-arsed cock-end!'

Now Gary and Curt found themselves in the grip of unbridled mirth as they observed Trevor's frothing features quickly become deep scarlet with rage.

Having temporarily composed himself, Gary opted to change the tone of conversation once again.

'You ever been abroad before, Curt?'

'Yeah…of course. But not for donkey's years, though.'

'Not on a lads' piss-up like this, then?'

'No. Just package deals. Before the kids came along. Can't afford it nowadays to be honest. A static van in Cornwall is about my limit.'

'Where have you been abroad then, Curtis?' Trevor enquired, having quickly calmed his inner temper.

'Erm…Greece…Majorca…Ibiza…'

'Oh…a real party animal in your past, then?'

'Well, I wouldn't say that Trev...no...'

'Well…you will be when we've finished with you. Your perfect little life will seem very dull once you've sampled the feminine delights knocking around foreign parts these days!'

Trevor's obvious attempt to try and regain the upper hand was music to Curt's ears.

'Oh yeah? Where have you been to, then?' Curt probed.

'Loads of foreign joints…Barcelona…Dublin…'

'What? Dublin? Hardly the height of European mystery, is it?' Gary chuckled.

'Dublin's a brilliant place! Fucking expensive, though. And the Guinness is proper Guinness. Not like the shit we get over here! Real Irish recipe…and real Irish women!'

Curt glanced at a grinning Gary before completing Trevor's self-induced embarrassment.

'Oh really. Got lucky over there, did you?'

'No…well, I couldn't really, could I?'

'Oh? Why not?'

'Well…already had a bird with me at the time, didn't I!'

The trio shared the raucous laughter at hearing Trevor's inconclusive portrayal, which finally served to eliminate the earlier element of friction.

16

Making the most of the frivolity, Gary posed the original question once more.

'So, Curt…are you in on this trip…or are you out?'

'Yeah…it sounds good! Get me a general date. I'll see 'er indoors.'

Trevor shook his head and smiled once again but Curt would not be drawn back into repeating the pointless argument.

'Right then. Our Ian will get the ball rolling and start looking up some accommodation.'

Trevor's attention was suddenly alerted to another attractive aspect of the impending trip.

'Does your little brother still indulge in recreational habits now and again, Gaz?'

'I do believe so, Trev, yes! No doubt he'll share some of his stash with you if you behave yourself accordingly.'

'Fucking hell! How old is Ian these days?'

'He's thirty-two…I think!'

'Christ! He was doing pot at school, wasn't he? He's smoked that much weed I bet he can't remember anything about the last twenty fucking years!'

The threesome shared the joke once again as Curt wrestled inwardly with the concept of time away from his family. In all honesty, it was a prospect that he didn't particularly relish, but on the other hand he felt it might do him good to venture off for a change of scenery even if only for a couple of days.

However, more pressing matters eclipsed the optimism afforded to a possible weekend on the booze.

'Right…I'd better get this list up to Caroline. Thanks for the invitation though, Gaz. I'll get back to you tomorrow so you can give your brother the nod.'

As the facilitator returned to the warehouse office, Gary and Trevor resumed their relaxed posture against the pallet.

Curt had only just moved out of earshot when Trevor announced his dissatisfaction.

'What the hell did you have to go and ask that boring bastard to come with us for?'

Gary's chuckles indicated the expectancy of his friend's disapproval.

'Cos he's been a work-mate of ours for over fifteen years, Trev. That's why. How could I *not* ask him?'

17

'He's no work-mate of mine.' snapped Trevor. 'Not since he took that gaffer's job on and deserted us.'

'You talk like a fucking twat at times, Palmer. You really do. Curt took the opportunity for a bit more money for a bit more responsibility. He's still the same bloke, you know. You're still upset because the company didn't ask *you* to become warehouse supervisor!'

'Huh! I wouldn't do it for all the money in the world. I prefer to be one of the lads than a gaffer's nark.'

'Yes...the gaffer knows that, too...that's why you didn't get asked...dick-head. You don't want to be seen as being all matey with the boss, even though you know deep down he's your mate. You're too stubborn for your own good, Palmer!'

Trevor looked at Gary and adorned an expression of feigned suspicion.

'Hang on a minute! Are you his fucking *dad* or something? Jesus Christ, Gaz! Get this pallet lined up over there and let's get some dinner down us.'

The resonance of Gary Lockley's sudden vocal disdain echoed around the rear yard as he scaled the nearby fork-lift truck, just as the first spots of rain began to hit his windscreen.

'I DO NOT FRIGGIN' BELIEVE IT! TREV! GIVE US A HAND TO GET THIS LOT BACK INSIDE.'

His colleague merely smirked, raised a two-fingered gesture of defiance and continued inside towards the warehouse canteen.

TWO

Despite his personal success and progress at work, Curt found that he embraced home time more avidly than ever before. The sound of the five o'clock siren was always welcome, and the enticing sensation of imminent liberty never seemed to have dwindled over the years.

He enjoyed his job for sure but enjoyed his family life to the point of obsession. The simple daily act of locking the warehouse office and departing for the clock machine always felt novel, yet with this particular evening's departure he found himself with something of a bounce in his stride.

The typically upbeat preoccupation with the journey home was disturbed by a familiarly sarcastic tone that carried across the car park.

'OY...CURTIS...DON'T FORGET TO ASK YOUR MISSUS ABOUT THE BOOZE-UP!'

A smile and thumbs-up was all Curt would willingly muster as he pulled open his driver's door and slung his hold-all across to the passenger seat.

Once behind the wheel, he engaged the radio for some welcoming music. With his favourite sounds duly eclipsing any encroaching weariness, he selected first gear and eagerly merged with the stream of cars filing away from the premises.

The rush hour passage through the outskirts of the city was always frenetic, especially now as the ever earlier Christmas rush had commenced infancy. Yet despite the tardiness of the plodding traffic, Curt found it easy to settle his mind onto more pleasant matters.

The festive period always brought a sense of warmth into any household, and the Osbourne clan was certainly no exception. His two daughters were of an age when every Christmas is still a fantastically wondrous experience and despite the financial struggles incurred in making their annual dreams come true, the paternal satisfaction garnered in seeing his children happy always made the end of year endeavour worthwhile.

Thoughts of home readily fuelled him with a sense of solace and the primitive frustrations experienced by most rush hour drivers never seemed to afflict Curt. The prospect of beholding his wife and children of an evening immediately diluted any negative slant that might try and pollute his generally buoyant mood.

But there was another added dimension to his mental schedule as he navigated a large roundabout and filtered slowly onto the dual carriageway.

Invitations abroad to join a birthday celebration did not confront Curt's safe and ordered routine very often. In fact, never before could he recall being enthused by such a premise and the idea of a weekend away with his friends - and Trevor Palmer - had instigated a most unusual state of inner euphoria.

However, his colleagues' mockery pertaining to his wife Hayley's reaction was indeed causing him some discomfort. She was generally very laid back about most aspects of life but nonetheless, raising the subject of Gary's birthday needed a considerate approach and the moment for revelation required very careful selection.

With these pleasant distractions flowing through his mind, Curt's voyage home had seemed far shorter than the typical thirty-odd minutes that he usually wiled away by singing along to his CD player.

Having left the busy dual carriageway behind, the distant glow of the village streetlamps guided him ever homeward, encouraging his foot to press a little firmer onto the throttle as he weaved toward his little piece of heaven.

Light rain began to fall and be carried on the breeze as shelter beckoned.

The residential estate was a relieving sight as he steered the car through the amber-hued avenues that swayed with the chilly autumnal wind, causing ominous shadows to erratically twitch and dance in the orange pools.

Finally reaching Leyton Close, Curt dropped into second gear and swerved onto the block-paved driveway of number thirty-two.

As he pulled on the handbrake, the engine continued to rattle out an unhealthy sounding din; a troublesome symptom that had begged for attention and subsequently been ignored for some months.

Curt switched off the music and fumed mildly at the mechanical rumblings emanating from beneath the bonnet.

Knowing precious little about the modern combustion engine, he turned the key toward him to disengage the ignition.

'You'll have to wait your turn you bag of nails!' he hissed into the dashboard. 'Christmas is the priority. You can whine all you like. I'm skint until January!'

Sighing with relaxation at having finally arrived home, he retrieved his rucksack from the passenger seat and clicked open the door.

As he set one foot from the car, a beauteous vision took him by surprise. Curt was overjoyed to be greeted by his seven-year-old daughter, Emily. Standing in the half-glow cast by the porch security light, she had positioned herself proudly on the adjacent front lawn to greet her father.

He studied her impish smiling features which were definitely inherited from Hayley. Two long blond pigtails framed her shoulders as she hovered, smiling broadly in her school uniform.

Now Curt felt fully sated.

'Hello, Em! What's this? A hero's welcome, eh? This is a nice gesture. You okay, my love? Give us a kiss!'

Father and daughter embraced in the semi-darkness.

'Hello Daddy!' she boomed.

'Have you got your shoes on, Em? The grass will be damp. You'll catch cold. Your mother will go spare if she catches you getting those new socks dirty.'

Emily did not respond but merely jumped up and down on the spot as Curt hauled himself from the car and shut the door. She instinctively grabbed for his hand containing the keys, causing him to chuckle.

'Yes, yes…I know…I know…you can lock the car. But listen…don't mess about with the switch. Press it once and then once more when the orange lights flash. Okay?'

He stood by the open front doorway as Emily squealed with delight at the magic of remote-control central locking. The car lamps eventually blinked to affirm the task had been completed.

Curt shivered in the brisk wind whilst issuing a final command.

'Yes…well done, Em! Now come on in. It's dark and cold.'

Once inside the hallway, he kicked off his work boots and dropped his bag and coat at the bottom of the stairs. The aroma of cooking assaulted his nostrils as he observed Emily still posturing in the murk of the front lawn.

He shook his head and smirked at the sight of her shoe-less feet.

'Come on my love…come in and watch TV. I need to see Mummy.'

On through the lounge and into the kitchen, the source of the culinary scent was soon apparent. Hayley was just closing the oven door as he entered.

'Hello, darling!' she beamed with wide blue eyes brightening at his sudden entrance. 'I can hear you two out there. What's Emily up to?'

'Oh…nothing…just looking after me. She's just making sure the car's locked for the night. That's all. She likes to do it.'

The reaction of his wife was instinctive and predictable.

'Did she put her shoes on?'

'Yes…of course she did! I think so anyway.'

Hayley planted a kiss on Curt's lips before venturing to the hallway where she discovered her youngest daughter still standing in the porch light playing with the central locking.

She then observed Emily's pair of slip-on black leather school shoes beneath the coat rack.

'Emily! Inside! Now! It's bloody freezing out here! I'm not paying for our central heating to heat the whole street you know!'

Reluctantly bowing to the rigid demands of her mother, Emily skipped back inside the house with a giggle and handed her mother the car keys before bounding onward into the lounge to watch the television.

'Look at your feet! Wet through! Take those socks off, please.'

Hayley returned the keys to the kitchen work surface and filled the kettle.

'You had a good day at work, love?'

Slouched idly at the breakfast bar, Curt glanced up from the evening newspaper.

'Alright, I suppose…you know the score, I'm sure. Same old shit…same blokes…same script. Same everything, really.'

Hayley switched on the kettle before approaching Curt from behind. Placing both arms around her husband's waist, she kissed his neck in order to grasp the rare moment of intimacy.

'That feels nice.' he whispered in response. '*Very* nice, in fact! What about your day?'

'Oh…same as you. Did my shift at the supermarket. Played with all the moaning customers. Filled the same old boring shelves. Nothing enlightening to report I'm afraid.'

The unsuspecting parents commenced a game of kiss and tickle with one another just as an inquisitive head poked itself through the kitchen doorway and reluctantly observed the unexpected spectacle.

Nine-year-old Hannah instantly grimaced at the image of her mother and father locked in loving, playful union and opted to intervene.

'Hello, Daddy!'

22

Curt did not divert from his present course of action, addressing his eldest daughter whilst lightly poking Hayley in the ribs.

'Hello, my love. School alright?'

'Yeah…not bad. Mum…when's tea? We're starving!'

Draping both arms across Curt's shoulders, Hayley yawned and glanced at the wall clock.

'Erm…about an hour I suppose.'

'What is it?'

'Roast chicken and vegetables. That okay with you?'

'Brilliant! Can I have a packet of crisps to keep me going?'

'Go on then…take one for Emily as well.'

'She can get her own.'

'Don't be so mean! Now take one for Emily!'

Mother and father struggled to hide their mutual amusement as Hannah hunched her shoulders in defeat, shuffled across the kitchen floor to the cupboard, retrieved two bags of salt and vinegar crisps and sulked her way back into the lounge.

'Oh, to be so young again.' sighed a smirking Hayley.

Curt withdrew from his wife's gentle clutches, kissed her on the nose and rubbed his eyes.

'I believe it's called growing up, dear. I bet you were just the same with your younger sister.'

'I was not! I was taught to share and share alike!'

Curt sniggered as he opted to end the teasing.

'Okay, love. I believe you! Have I got time for a bath before dinner, then? I could kill for a good soak.'

'Yep! Take your time, love. Nod off if you want. I'll give you a shout when it's ready.'

*****

With the evening meal finally served just over an hour later, the Osbournes convened around the dining table amid a combined contribution of stifled yawns and rumbling stomachs.

Despite the vigorous appetites of all diners, the protests commenced soon after they were seated.

'Mum…I don't like carrots.' moaned Emily.

'Swap you for my cabbage.' quipped her sister.

'But I don't like cabbage either.'

Hayley quickly interrupted the pointless debate with a conclusive request.

'Look girls…just leave what you can't eat. I'm sure your father will happily finish up everyone's plates in the end, anyway.'

Curt observed both his daughters' expressions convey their general dissatisfaction with the outcome before picking up a fork himself and skewering a roast potato.

Hannah's voice then arose once again, but this time to offer a surprising and somewhat pleasing query.

'Anything good happen to you today, Daddy?'

His response was almost automatic.

'No! Nothing good ever does happen at work, love. That's why it's called *work*. I go for the money…not the excitement.'

No sooner had he presented his standard reply the memory struck him regarding Gary's invitation. He didn't really want to broach the subject at the dinner table, but the atmosphere seemed sociable enough.

He glanced briefly at Hayley, whose entire attention at that instant was centred on applying more gravy to her mash.

'Actually, I've told you a little white lie there, Hannah. Something good *did* happen at work today!'

The three female members of the Osbourne family immediately gazed toward Curt in wide-eyed expectation of the imminent disclosure.

'Really?' smirked Hayley. 'Get a pay rise, did you?'

'No…not much chance of that these days! No…I had a brief chat with Gary at lunch time.'

Hayley nodded in recognition as she removed the flesh from a chicken leg with her knife.

'Oh yes…Gary Lockley? How is he?'

Curt swiftly commandeered the gravy boat before continuing with the revelation.

'Well…it turns out he's going to be forty-years-old next January. Can you believe that?'

'Christ! It doesn't seem five minutes since we went into town to celebrate his thirtieth, does it?'

Having successfully drowned the contents of his plate, Curt glanced at his daughters who had now resumed interest in consuming their own meals.

'Well…its funny you mention that, because he's had an idea for a celebration for *this* birthday, too. Just an idea he ran past me this afternoon.'

Hayley was now fully engaged by her husband as she popped a morsel of chicken into her mouth.

'Yes? Go on then?'

Curt inhaled a couple of deep breaths before plundering onward.

'Well…he says…he wants to do something a bit different to just going out and getting drunk. He's mentioned…well…invited, actually…to me and some others…about the lads going away for a weekend. You know…few beers and a laugh.'

He stopped breathing for a second at the idea slowly registered with his pondering spouse.

She stopped chewing her food for exactly the same reason.

It was difficult to assess Hayley's initial reaction as she stared back across the table. Curt quickly tried to fortify the positives of the concept.

'He'll no doubt be having a party here as well for family and friends…you know…for couples...like us, I mean.'

The continuing hiatus in Hayley's reaction was becoming increasingly discomforting, but the eventual response made his inner sufferance completely worthwhile.

An earnest smile was supported by news of a small victory.

'I think that's a superb idea, love! You deserve a break from us lot! I hope you said yes when Gary asked you!'

Now in a state of mild shock at his wife's generous spurt of enthusiasm for the foreign venture, Curt swallowed the ball of food that had been residing in his gullet for over a minute in an attempt to wallow in the unexpected endorsement.

As he analysed the content of her statement, the resulting vibes were intoxicating. By his interpretation, not only was he officially considered a hard worker by his wife, but he was also now about to be deemed husband of the year.

'Well…I didn't say anything concrete to him today…because I said that I would need to check it was okay with you first.'

Hayley shook her head and laughed in genuine disbelief at her husband's claim.

'You did *what*? You daft…soft…sod! I bet the lads at work think I'm a right old battle-axe. I hope you didn't really tell them that. Honestly. They'll think you're right hen-pecked!'

Curt simply offered a half-smile and shovelled more potato into his mouth as Hayley continued to giggle.

'Well...what do you think, love?' he asked again, tentatively.

'No! You go, love! Do you the world of good! Do you know where this men-only party will be taking place, exactly?'

The second wave of pleasurable relief cascaded all around Curt as he once more immersed himself in masculine glory.

'No, no...not yet. I think they're on about booking one of those cheap flights pretty soon, though.'

Now Hayley appeared genuinely intrigued by the new strand of information her husband had attached to the development.

Yet again, Curt's inner fears proved unfounded.

'Wow! Abroad? Brilliant! Its years since you've been abroad, love. I bet its over ten years since we went to Majorca.'

Effectively skewering a sprout, Curt blurted out his attempt to escalate the positive tone of the conversation.

'Yes...well, funny enough, that's exactly what I said to Gaz! It was definitely before Hannah was born, wasn't it?'

'You'd better dig your passport out, then! You'll definitely need to apply for a new one! In fact, that will be your priority!'

Curt nodded in silent agreement before sensibly yet cautiously attaining confirmation of Hayley's final feelings on the matter.

'So...you don't mind, then...if I say to Gary that I'll go along with them?'

With her face now exhibiting an expression of sincere bewilderment, Hayley set down her cutlery, reached across the table and cradled her husband's worried visage in her palms.

'You silly...sentimental fool! Why would I mind? I think it's very sweet that you've even considered me. I'm very touched. And to be honest I'll be glad to see the back of you for a weekend.'

Curt giggled nervously as his attention slowly guided itself back to his dinner plate.

'You know what? That's just what Trevor Palmer said! Thanks, love. I'm glad you're alright with it.'

'Hey...Mister Osbourne...you do actually wear the trousers around here you know! Even if it doesn't seem like it most of the time! You wanna go? You damned well go! I would say *yes* like a shot if I was in your shoes.'

Curt sniggered again as his cutlery wrestled with the other chicken leg.

Hayley was not quite finished with her commentary on the issue.

'Anyway…I bet Trevor's going as well, isn't he?'

'Yeah…you know him. Always up for a booze is our Trev.'

Hayley rolled her eyes as another little thought crept into her head.

'But there is just one condition Mister Osbourne…'

'Anything, dear. Anything.'

'Well…actually…there are *two* conditions. Firstly…no chatting up any foreign ladies. Especially the ones sitting in the windows!'

Curt laughed out loud as both Emily and Hannah simultaneously displayed looks of utter bemusement at their mother's last statement.

'And secondly…and this is the most important…bring me some of my favourite apple perfume from the duty-free shop on your way back.'

Hayley observed fondly as Curt continued to chuckle to himself.

'Okay. I'm pretty sure I can oblige both of those requests. No problem at all.'

A contented silence resumed around the dining table as the family finished eating. Having now placed the matter firmly to the back of his mind until morning, it was Hannah who unexpectedly re-opened the conversation some minutes later as she licked gravy from her knife.

Sensing the burning necessity to appease her concerns about one particular portion of the earlier exchange, she glanced at her father with a furrowed brow.

'Daddy…'

'Yes, love?'

'Can I ask you a question?'

'Of course, my sweet. Fire away.'

The nine-year-old paused thoughtfully before broaching her query.

'Why do foreign ladies sit in windows?'

THREE

The alarm clock didn't annoy Curt quite as much as it normally seemed to do at six each weekday morning. Reaching through the darkness to employ the snooze function, he then enclosed himself back securely under the covers and snuggled up to Hayley.

'Your arm's cold.' she muttered into the pillow, on receipt of his outstretched limb around her upper leg.

'Sorry, love.' he whispered, nuzzling mischievously into the back of her neck.

'Your nose is cold too!' she squirmed, now becoming enlightened to the commencement of a new day with great reluctance. With her speech remaining slurred and muffled, further accusations were made.

'And you've let cold air under the duvet. What were you doing?'

'Turning the alarm off, love. What do you think I was doing?'

A deep sigh of resignation was issued followed by a groan of dispute.

'Not already. It can't have gone off. It can't be six yet!'

Curt simply laid back and stared into the minimal light of the bedroom. The tardiness of the early November dawn indicated a damp stillness beyond the window blinds.

Another dynamic day to confront; another pre-destined dollar to be made.

Then the birthday trip abroad entered his head and within seconds, a secret smile of anticipation grew across his face. He recalled the permission being granted. He revelled in the knowledge of being in his wife's good books.

This was indeed a morning that already differed greatly from the usual.

'You want a coffee making, love?' he whispered across the pillows.

Hayley's reply was definitive yet less weary. It never failed to amaze him how suddenly awake and vibrant she became once it had been established that it would be *he* - not *she* - venturing downstairs first to put the kettle on.

Her responses to the gesture adopted an enthusiastic tone which conveyed surprisingly considered and concise detail.

'Yes, please. In my usual big mug. A nice coffee, though. Not too strong. But not too milky. And not half a cup as normal. And hurry all the way there and hurry all the way back.'

Hayley's demanding monologue was interrupted by the vibration of her own giggles rising from underneath the bedclothes. Then her own reality hit home as Curt pulled himself upright beside her.

'I'd better shift myself to be honest. I'm in work at nine this morning. Can't afford to be dragging my heels. Better get the girl's up for school a bit earlier, too. Hurry with the coffee, love. You're letting cold air in again.' she grinned to herself.

With the final declaration from his wife, Curt perched on the edge of the bed and waited just long enough for the alarm to scream once more before switching it off and meandering downstairs to the kitchen.

As he prepared the drinks, Curt's thoughts turned to work and the probable response to his involvement in the birthday trip. No doubt he had been the subject of discussion for most of the previous day.

Only now, he could contentedly enter the warehouse as the bearer of great news.

*****

He had barely been afforded time to unlock the office door and remove his coat before a familiar plump face appeared behind him at the top of the mezzanine staircase.

Sporting a conceited smirk akin to that of a particularly large and unshaven Cheshire cat, Trevor Palmer adopted a most untypical approach and opted not to utter a word for once as he stood beside his facilitator. Curt instantly knew the precise reason for his colleague's unannounced appearance and in the name of playing the same game proceeded to try and completely ignore him.

Routing through a palm full of loose change, Curt selected a coffee from the adjacent vending machine along the walkway.

Trevor remained in position outside the door with a sense of expectant smugness widening across his features, eventually causing Curt to offer an implicit warning.

'I shouldn't stand there too long if I were you. Smithy is supposed to be in early today. You know how he can't stand you lackeys hanging around the office when you've got work to do.'

Trevor continued to stare without utterance; his rounded face still sporting a broad and distinctly uneven grin.

In a lethargic effort to counter the ridiculous silence, Curt opted to change tactic and lighten the moment by veering onto one of Trevor's favourite subjects.

'Oh, I get it now! Is it Caroline you've come to leer at? I'm afraid she won't be here until eight. So, until then you've just got my ugly mug to admire!'

Retrieving the plastic cup of brown coloured water from the vendor tray, Curt shuffled past Trevor to enter the office and take his seat. Scrutinising the forecast schedule for the day's order of business, he proceeded to switch on his computer whilst tentatively sampling the putrid contents of his cup.

'Jesus...this stuff is horrendous! Fifty pence for a cup of hot piss!' he murmured.

The noiseless colleague beyond the door was now beginning to annoy Curt. He chanced a brief glimpse of Trevor Palmer gurning incessantly at him back through the glass portal.

The irritating seconds passed with the mutual stand-off providing signs of neither victor nor loser. However, the observer's resolve slowly began to weaken, and Trevor finally found himself forced to disclose the reasoning for his presence.

Poking his head through the now open office doorway, he held fast to the frame and leaned into the room.

'Well, Curtis?'

Now in a mood to wilfully torment his companion, Curt opted to oblige with the ensuing charade, hoping that the warehouse manager, David Smith, would conveniently appear and bring a most welcome yet amusing halt to the episode.

'Well...Trev? What do you mean...well? Well...*what*?'

Trevor's arrogant demeanour did not endure for long.

'You know bloody well what. The booze-up! Gazza's birthday! Daft question this, I know...but I just wondered...did you get the say-so off the missus last night...or didn't you?'

Curt chuckled and sat back in his chair as the computer drive slowly booted itself into action.

'Come on Curtis...tell me what I want to hear. She said you couldn't go, didn't she...?'

Curt clasped his hands behind his head and swivelled position to examine the pathetic light of hope in his friend's eyes.

Trevor Palmer could indeed profess himself to be a sad and embittered case at times.

'I bet you haven't slept a bloody wink all night thinking about the row I had with my missus when I got home, have you? I bet you were lying there...wide awake... probably playing with yourself...hoping that I was cowering on the sofa having been thrown into the doghouse. Well...were you?'

Trevor's somewhat dumbfounded expression conveyed more than a little confusion when trying to analyse Curt's subtle yet well founded assault.

'So...does that mean you're coming with us...or what?'

Maintaining an air of indifference, Curt simply stared back and held a dignified, non-committal peace.

Trevor's evident frustration at his colleague's well-honed act was now beginning to simmer towards boiling point.

'Well...did she actually say you *couldn't* go then, Curtis? Did you get the big No-No or what?'

Still the subject of the now mildly enjoyable scrutiny, Curt offered absolutely nothing in response as the feeble inquisition developed itself to a rapid if woefully misjudged deduction.

'You mean to tell me...that your wife...who is supposed to love you, by the way...has refused you permission to go on a break with your mates? AND YOU'RE GOING TO JUST SIT THERE AND TAKE IT?'

It was a struggle to suppress the abiding sense of pleasure that now welled within Curt's core, but to see the shallow figure of Trevor Palmer falsely jumping to such a misguided conclusion was a sight too good not to encourage.

'Jesus friggin' Christ, Curtis. You're even more of a wimp than I thought you were. Gary's gonna be right pissed off about this! You wait until he gets in. He'll be gutted. He'll be up here like a shot. What a let-down you turned out to be!'

Finally, Curt opted to indulge himself in the issue whilst cleverly continuing to dangle the inquisitor over his preferred pit of ignorance.

'To be honest, Trev, I don't really want to talk about it just now. I'm still annoyed. Anyway, I've got more important things to sort out. Okay?'

Trevor folded his arms in another gesture of false presumption.

'More important things? Mind you...I'm not surprised you don't want to bloody talk about it. Embarrassing it is. You should be ashamed. Call yourself a grown man? You're a disgrace to the male species.'

31

Curt was hoping to bring closure to the fruitless dialogue when right on cue David Smith appeared behind Trevor's bobbing form, whose brimming sense of self-entertainment had caused him to unwittingly shift position and fully block the doorway.

Now seated firmly on the front row for a sideshow of mouth-watering potential, Curt simply reclined once again and watched the cabaret unfold.

'Nothing to do at the moment, Mister Palmer?'

Trevor was visibly jolted and turned on the spot as the stern-faced logistics manager of glared at the slovenly obstruction.

'Erm…yes. Morning, David. Erm…'

'Well? If you've work to get on with you shouldn't be bothering my facilitator. No doubt he's very busy, too.'

Trevor's tone of voice rapidly switched from that of eager tormentor to mild mannered underling.

'Yes…of course, David. Erm…just checking that some work is actually about to be put out for us. That's all.'

The sharply suited superior glanced over toward his team leader, who was now staring into his blank computer monitor, happily feigning the act of preparing picking lists for the loaders.

'How long before you can get some work to these lads, Curt?'

Curt rapidly adopted an inner sense of triumph as he scanned his wristwatch.

'Just checking the schedule spread sheets as we speak, David. Ooh…I would say…half an hour at very most…'

Turning attention back to Trevor, the perturbed warehouse manager offered a suggestion.

'There you are, Mister Palmer. Thirty minutes.'

Trevor glared at Curt whilst inwardly squirming on the spot.

'So, what do we do until then, David?'

'I tell you what needs doing. This warehouse is a mess. There is a company insurance health and safety audit at the end of the week. So…I suggest that you and some of the others grab a broom and have a good tidy up. Okay?'

Trevor nodded meekly and was gone in an instant, leaving a highly satisfied Curt in peace to work through his scheduling.

However, Curt's amusement was short lived.

David Smith watched Trevor's descent to the shop floor before finally entering the office.

The subsequent conversation suggested that he was in a far from compliant mood.

'Damned bone idle that Trevor Palmer. You shouldn't encourage them up here, Curt. It's bad for business. I don't want the likes of him moping about upstairs.'

Curt did not look up, instead continuing to scrutinise the invisible data on his PC screen.

'Yes, David. I'll make certain to pass the message on.'

'Is Caroline not here yet?'

A strange question, to which the answer was self-evident.

'No, David. She starts at eight. Every day.'

'Oh yes…of course. How's the coffee this morning?'

'Like ditch water! The same as every other day. Detestable!'

The manager hung up his coat and began to circle the office floor impatiently.

'I'm thinking of investing in some proper kitchen facilities up here. I need to get a quote from maintenance to see if it will slot into my budget.'

'Yes, David. Good idea.'

Curt did not care for the generally dismissive approach of his superior towards others in the department. He held the view that meeting business targets should be viewed as a team effort.

As such, trying to indulge in pleasant conversation with David Smith was taxing and tiresome at the best of times.

'But there's not too much room in here is there, Curt? What do you think?'

'What's that, David?'

'A kitchenette! Do you think there's room for such a thing up here?'

The facilitator opted to try and inject a strand of humour into the exchange as he studied the back of his superior's bald head.

'No, David. It'll be fine. I'm sure we can make room for a sink and worktop. Then we can put Caroline to some good use at last, can't we.'

David Smith did not laugh. He did not even respond with a hint of a chuckle. Instead, he continued to march around the office, eventually moving back out to the landing and fingering his trouser pockets for money.

Then, just as Curt had surrendered any hope that his manager had any sense of humour whatsoever, a low-key comical reply was eventually emitted.

'You know what, Curt. That's a very sexist, yet absolutely brilliant idea. She can chase accounts and make the tea! Multi-tasking, I think it's called. Well done!'

*****

An hour passed before Gary Lockley appeared furtively at the top of the mezzanine stairs and stepped cautiously into the open office doorway.

'Psst...where's Smithy gone? Is the coast clear?'

Curt looked up from his computer screen to greet the expected visitor.

'Ayup, Gaz. I've put some work out for you. I think Reg and Colin picked the first lot up.'

'Yeah! I'm not bothered about that. I want to know where balloon-head is.'

The sound of loud giggling resonated from the far end of the room as Caroline registered Gary Lockley's unflattering reference to David Smith. She turned to wave to the visitor.

'Morning Caroline.'

'Morning Gary, love. Alright?'

'Yeah, sound.' replied Gary, gaining full view of Caroline's ample and shapely legs as she pivoted lazily in her chair.

Bearing in mind their manager's earlier ordainment regarding the whereabouts of warehouse operatives, Curt was anxious to uncover the motive for Gary's presence at the door.

'Smithy's gone to a meeting. Why? Did you need to see him?'

'No, I fucking don't. I want him out of the way cos I want to talk to you.'

'What about?' Curt smirked, knowingly.

'You know what about! My birthday! Are you winding Palmer up or what? You are alright for this trip, aren't you?'

Curt exploded into laughter as he left his seat and walked toward the door.

'Of course I am you fool. Christ almighty! Trev's really taken the bait hasn't he! I bet he's bleeding glad I'm supposedly not going. Bet he's chuffed to bits really, isn't he?'

Relief visibly altered the strained expression on Gary's face.

'So, you are definitely on the trip then?'

'Yes! Definitely!'

'No hassles off the missus?'

'None at all. She's totally sweet about it.'

'That's brilliant! I'm going to keep Palmer in the dark for the whole day, then. I'll just let it eventually slip out in casual conversation that you will being coming after all. Can you imagine the look on his stupid fat face? Then he'll have real reason to sulk!'

Curt tittered at the prospect just as Caroline expressed interest in the plan.

'You lot going off somewhere, then?'

'Yeah. My fortieth birthday bash!' Gary responded, again eyeing the long lower limbs of the accounts clerk as he hung from the door frame.

'Oh great! When's that kicking off, then?'

'January. We're going abroad. Pissed as newts for an entire weekend. You fancy coming along for the ride, Caroline?'

The accounts clerk shook her head slowly as she offered an opinion on the boys' basic strategy.

'You must be joking. Knowing you lot you won't make it on to the plane. Where are you thinking of going anyway?'

Gary's excitement was now fully evident in his features as he unveiled the main aspect of the itinerary.

'I reckon Prague is the current hot favourite.'

Caroline instinctively laughed yet the tone of her reply contained a pang of seriousness.

'What's so funny?' asked Curt.

'Well...if you ever do manage to get out there, you'll have to behave yourselves, you know. The police operate zero tolerance for public offences - especially football-mad drunkards from England taking a wee in bus shelters and throwing up in shop fronts! I bet at least one of you ends up in a cell! It's got disaster written all over it!'

Curt began to feel mildly concerned at Caroline's apparently knowledgeable overview and required some confirmation.

'What? Are you kidding? Are they that strict out there, are they? Jesus!'

Caroline laughed once more at the open-mouthed vacancy of her work companions.

'I'm only winding you up you dopes. You'll have a great time. My parents went there a couple of years ago. They loved it! Bloody cold, though! Especially in January. You'll need to take your thermals with you.'

Curt nodded to his colleague in acknowledging Caroline's comments as only semi-serious.

'Thermal undies? I wouldn't be seen dead in a set. Especially the places I intend to frequent!' winked Gary.

'I don't want to know thank you very much, Gary.' squirmed Caroline as she turned back to her work.

Both colleagues laughed as they meandered onto the outer landing. Curt eyed his weighty opponent waving at the pair from below.

'Anyway, Gaz. Good plan. Say nothing to Palmer. Mum's the word. Keep that idiot down there dangling on a string for as long as you can.'

*****

The shift elapsed with Curt mostly managing to keep himself to himself. He endured the lunchtime break in the loaders' mess room with Trevor Palmer regularly littering the air with several severely ignorant and misguided opinions on the apparent fragility of Curt's domestic situation.

As home-time arrived, Curt convened at the foot of the office stairwell with Caroline and a few of the warehouse loaders, including Gary and Trevor.

Trevor Palmer's incredulous mask of mocking disapproval had been adopted for the entire day. Gary began to smile as the siren signalled all to depart for home. As they strolled through the manufacturing plant and outside past the security lodge, the burning issue of the impending foreign venture reared its head for the umpteenth time.

Unsurprisingly, it was Trevor who wished to convey a parting shot for the day.

'Go on then, Curtis. Off you go. Back home to the gaffer. Back under the thumb...where you belong.'

Curt and Gary smiled and glanced at one another as they fought against the stiff autumn gusts. Entering the car park, Trevor continued to berate his colleague as they separated to their vehicles.

'Have a nice night with the wife then, Curtis. Don't misbehave or swear. And certainly no farting! And finish all your dinner. Who knows, she might even let you have a can of beer if you're a really good boy and do the washing up.'

At the last possible moment before going their separate ways, Gary declared it time to finally put Trevor out of his and everybody else's misery.

'Right Curt…so…I'll nip round to our Ian's tonight then and tell him there's definitely six to book for Prague.'

Although only just within hearing range, Trevor's ears pricked up at the ensuing conversation occurring twenty yards away and frantically requested to know the details of the exchange.

'Are we sorted, are we? Who's the lucky six, then, Gaz?'

Gary smiled at Curt before relaying the final candidates for his birthday jaunt.

'Well…there's me, obviously…and there's you, unfortunately…our Ian, obviously…plus my brother-in-law Paul…and Paul's younger brother Geoff…'

Visibly racking his brain with the mathematical sum, Trevor was quick to signify that a name was missing from the list.

'But that's only five. Who's replacing soft touch?'

'Soft touch? Who do you mean?' sniggered Gary.

'Curtis! Fucking hen-pecked fucking shandy-pants…over there!'

'Oh yeah…' gestured Gary.

Gary turned to Curt as Trevor's infesting curiosity now bubbled without restraint.

'Sorry, Curt mate…I almost forgot. You're coming too, aren't you?'

'Dead right, Gaz! Wouldn't miss it for the world!'

Trevor Palmer's vexation became evident across his face even in the encroaching darkness. His instant change of demeanour was quickly followed by the resounding slam of his driver's door and a frantic screeching of rubber as he departed the premises.

Gary looked across to his newfound partner in crime as he ducked into his own car.

'Think we sorted the fat twat out…don't you, Curt?'

At the welcome sight of Trevor Palmer's sincere and fully disclosed disappointment, Curt Osbourne found himself fuelled with an inner delirium that inspired him not only for the journey home, but for the remainder of the entire evening.

FOUR

'Here's your copy. Just for information. You don't really need it. Just thought I'd commemorate the moment. Give everyone a little souvenir before Christmas.'

'Oh right...cheers, Gaz.'

Curt studied the slip of paper handed to him as he entered the warehouse canteen. Trying to digest the content of the computer readout, he took a seat at the table opposite Trevor Palmer who had already commenced his avid assault on a cup of noodles.

He briefly observed Trevor cajole several strands of yellow-coloured pasta onto a plastic fork before pulling at the zip of his own rucksack with his free hand.

'Oh...wow! It's all done then. We're all set. January the eighth, eh?'

'Yep!' Gary beamed. 'Our Ian spent all last night with me making sure we didn't cock anything up.'

Trevor did not interrupt the conversation, preferring instead to wrestle in silence with his steaming prefabricated meal. Curt felt his stomach turn as he watched whilst continuing to express his appreciation of Gary's efforts.

'Christ! Won't be long now then will it, Gaz? What...less than two months away?'

'That's right, matey. We're off in seven weeks. It'll be here in a flash!'

The gruff sound of Colin Tansley's voice boomed from the other end of the crew room. His large frame slouched itself behind a newspaper and was accompanied by an equally intimidating tone.

'I notice this jolly was all kept pretty bloody quiet from the rest of us lot. Closed shop then is it, this arrangement? No riff-raff allowed or something?'

Gary was quick to respond to the older man's gentle natured, if distinctly barbed jibe.

'You'd never keep up the pace, Col. This trip is for the young and virile. Not the old has-beens and past-its!'

The pages of the tabloid immediately lowered by a few inches to reveal a furrowed expression that feigned offence.

'You're a bloody cheeky sod, young Lockley! I'm only fifty-nine! And not quite past it just yet, thank you very much.'

Ever one with the curious eye for detail, Curt ignored the ensuing banter as he continued to scan the travel confirmation in his grasp.

'Why is it written like this? Struggles to make any sense.'

Gary gazed forlornly around the room as he lifted his feet to rest on an adjacent chair.

'That's just the way it's done now. Over the internet, you see. These holiday firms don't like to issue proper tickets nowadays until you get to the airport. Even then it's only another piece of paper to go with your boarding pass. It's all changed since you last went away Curt, my boy!'

Trevor's consistent slurping provided a mildly off-putting back-drop to Curt's growing list of queries.

'So…what's the flight company called, then?'

Gary reached across and directed Curt with a forefinger.

'God man…are you blind? It says there, look! BudgetFly. They're a new company. Dirt cheap and all.'

The next question was immediate and fully expected by most occupants of the room.

'How much are the flights going to be, then?'

'Well, what our Ian plans to do is spend the rest of this week scanning the computer for some decent accommodation. Then when I'm happy with what he's found, he'll book it for us. So, then I'll come to you with a price for the lot and just wait for my palms to be crossed with some silver.'

Trevor rolled his eyes in sympathetic frustration as Curt's next inevitable conundrum rolled from the tongue.

'Is your brother paying for everything up front, then?'

'Yeah. On the plastic. It's the easiest way. Saves him waiting for cash to roll in, doesn't it? He knows you're all good for the money and won't back out.'

Trevor Palmer interceded as hot water drizzled over his stubbled chin.

'I'm dead impressed, Gaz. Your youth doesn't hang about, does he?'

'Well, what's the point in hanging about, Trev? Everything's so simple now it's done on computer. Touch of a button. No pissing around. Plus, he's done this whole routine before, anyway. An old hand at booking flights is Ian. It would take me days to get my head round it whereas it takes him seconds. He knows all the ins and outs. Air tax and all that extra hidden crap they don't tell you about until the last minute. I can't be bothered to work it all out to be honest.'

Again, Curt pondered before unleashing another concern.

'So, including the flights and eventual accommodation, how much each do you reckon it should tally to?'

Trevor shook his head in only partially feigned dismay at Curt's intensive craving for information. However, another forkful of noodles put paid to any chance of a verbal contribution for the time being.

'I'm budgeting for about hundred quid a man. All in…job done.'

Curt raised his eyebrows in genuine surprise.

'What? A hundred pounds…for everything?'

'Yep!'

'That's cheap as bloody chips!'

'Yeah, I know! These foreign places haven't got a clue about going rates. The twats are fucking *giving* it away.'

'We'll still need passports though, won't we? I'm about to renew mine this week.'

Trevor swallowed another barely chewed portion of his dinner and mumbled something sarcastic under his breath that Curt detected but couldn't be bothered to decipher at that precise moment.

Thankfully Gary's reply was more considerate.

'Well, customs do like everyone to have one, Curt…yes. You won't be able to leave the country without it. That is still the law. That's one thing that *hasn't* changed in the last few years. Though to be honest, they hardly bother to check them now.'

Chuckles resonated around the room as Curt finally retrieved his lunchbox.

'I know. I'm a bit naïve with this sort of thing. It's been years since I went on a plane.'

Gary held a certain amount of respect for his colleague's genuine sense of interest but was becoming aware that Curt's desire for learning the minutiae of the arrangements was on the verge of causing him to look increasingly foolish.

'Relax, will you? It's all sound, mate. It's all going to be sorted out for you. All you've got to do is pack your clean pants and a toothbrush. No going back now. Eh?'

Finally, Trevor Palmer sat back in his chair, belched loudly across the table, and finally obliged his own desperate inner desire to try and make Curt Osbourne feel even smaller.

'Knowing you…you'll bring your hot water bottle, pyjamas and fucking teddy bear as well.'

Curt opted to oblige the predictably damning monologue being delivered by his counterpart from the other side of the table, even though it did raise a titter from the colleagues at the far end of the room.

'Of course I will, Trev. Actually, I can't wait for this trip to be honest.'

Curt continued to study the email confirmation as he retrieved a limp looking ham sandwich from his plastic lunchbox and nibbled it tentatively.

'So, who are the other two lads on this list then, Gaz?'

'Paul...he's married to my sister, Elaine. You've met our Elaine, haven't you?'

'Yes...I think so. Years ago, though.'

'And his brother, Geoff. By the way...Geoff's the nutter! As you'll find out for yourself! Paul's the sensible one.'

Trevor piped up again with another belch which acted as the precursor to his latest pearl of wisdom.

'He can't be all that sensible. He's married, aint he? Like this great dope sat here opposite me. Mind...you'll probably get on like a house on fire then, Curtis. Listen to the voice of experience. Your Ian's got the right idea, Gaz! Fuck 'em and then chuck 'em!'

The familiar authoritative tone of Colin Tansley found appropriate incentive to ring around the mess room once again as he responded to Trevor's latest input.

'Fucking hell, lads. Hark at Hollywood's last great playboy over there!'

Laughter duly vibrated around the walls as Trevor Palmer's self-adopted sense of comic superiority immediately crashed and burned under the weight of a far mightier adversary.

Colin continued to lap up the moment with some highly warranted additional commentary.

'Is that going to be your own personal policy in Prague then, Trev? Foot loose and fancy free and going through the women left, right and centre?'

Now rather more sheepish in his approach to the issue, Trevor suddenly found himself to be the butt of sarcasm and became distinctly guarded with his declarations.

'It might well be...who knows? We'll have to see what kind of female talent is out there, won't we?'

But the eldest member of the warehouse team was far from finished with tormenting his quivering quarry.

'Dream on, Palmer! The only woman you'll ever get is one you'll have to bloody pay for. And even then, she'll probably give you some money back out of sympathy for your tiny dick!'

41

More waves of echoing mirth rocked Trevor firmly from his comedic perch and instead of willingly escalating the debate towards his own shameless defeat he opted instead to continue with his increasingly tepid dinner without further word.

Gary's nostrils were beginning to repel the aroma wafting from Trevor's direction as the latter shovelled another heap of yellow mush onto his tongue.

'What exactly is that shit you're eating, Palmer? It smells like burning rubber.'

Trevor looked up to his colleague as liquid oozed from either corner of his over-filled mouth.

'Chow Mein chicken.' he spluttered.

'Fuck off about Chow Mein chicken! Its plastic dehydrated crap!' barked Gary.

Trevor heaped yet more of the stuff into his mouth before replying.

'Well, it tastes fine to me.'

Colin Tansley did not miss his opportunity to take to the stage for another curtain call and bow out in style.

'That's why you're such a fat bastard, Palmer! Eating muck like that. It's no wonder you can't see your own cock anymore, is it? But don't worry – your imaginary woman in Prague will help you find it!'

With most of the mess room occupants now resumed in hysterics at his expense, Trevor flicked a two-fingered gesture toward the other end of the table and immersed himself in consuming what was left in the cup nestled firmly under his chin.

'How much spending money do you reckon we'll need?' ventured Curt through a mouthful of sandwich.

Trevor's ears pricked in dismay once more as his own personal target for torment returned to the fray.

He did not hesitate to pull the trigger.

'Spending money? Fucking *spending money*? It sounds like you're going to be getting it off your fucking mum! Or your missus - which is probably more like the truth anyway, isn't it?'

'Just want to know how much cash I've got to keep by over Christmas… that's all. It's not really an issue to you Trev, is it? I mean…you've only got yourself to buy for at this time of year.'

Trevor Palmer opted not to respond to the jibe.

But then another voice decided to drive the nail a little deeper anyhow.

'Are you taking a Christmas present over to Prague for your prostitute, Trev?'

Against the might of another thunderous wave of laughter once again courtesy of Colin Tansley, Trevor attempted to shout something in return which nobody heard, leaving Gary to answer Curt's original query.

'Depends how much of a good time you want doesn't it? I'm taking about five hundred.'

Curt nearly dropped his sandwich in response.

'WHAT? ARE YOU KIDDING? FIVE HUNDRED QUID? FOR THREE DAYS? The exchange rate must be shit, then!'

'No idea, mate. And I don't really care, either.'

Having digested the initial shock, Curt returned another question.

'What is the Prague currency, anyway? It's not Czech pounds, is it?'

'Crowns, I think…or Coruna…to give the correct pronunciation.' confirmed Gary

Trevor set down his empty mug and proceeded to lick his fork clean as he attempted to conclude the tedious exchange that endured before him.

'Who cares how much we take so long as it gets us some fun? Fucking exchange rates! Christ Almighty! Lighten up for God's sake, Curtis! It'll feel like I'm taking my fucking grandad on holiday with you looking over my frigging shoulder every second of the day. We haven't even bloody got there yet. This is supposed to be a birthday piss-up not a fucking funeral wake!'

Curt ignored Trevor's ranting dismissal and pursued another aspect of the topic.

'When is your actual birthday anyway Gaz?'

'Saturday the twenty-second. My mams booked the function room at the Red Lion. She's good mates with the landlord. You're all welcome of course. Even you can come along if you want, Mister Tansley. Eight 'til late! There'll be a karaoke and buffet. Yes…and even you're invited, Mister Palmer.'

Trevor reclined in his chair, belched yet again and let his hands clasp lazily over his inflated stomach.

'Oh yeah? I'm up for some of that. If I survive Prague, that is. I fancy making a right pig of myself out there! Show them foreign blokes a thing or two about how to shag.'

'Sounds like a plan that is doomed to fail! You got your Viagra packed?' Colin intervened, giving Trevor the chance to make a surprising declaration.

'Yeah…I know. That's something we actually *agree* on, Tansley. Perhaps I'll just get pissed and abuse some local coppers instead. Now that's something I can do without any help whatsoever!'

Curt finished his sandwich and briefly studied Trevor Palmer's grinning features.

Thoughts of Caroline's comments about their potentially disruptive behaviour rang in his conscience, temporarily fuelling a pang of trepidation regarding the trip.

However, the moment quickly passed and with the sound of the siren signifying the end of the lunch break, all resumed their afternoon duties without further word on the subject.

FIVE

The Christmas holiday duly arrived and promptly exhausted itself with typical contemporary speed.

Tuesday the fourth of January dawned to a watery sunrise and an expected overnight flurry of snow. As was the case for workers nationwide, the employees of L.L. Ltd gradually returned to duty with somewhat limited enthusiasm for an unpredictable new working year.

However, for three individuals, the prospect of the impending jaunt in only three days' time had more than sufficed to generate a sense of excitement to temper the usual post-festive lull.

The banter in the warehouse was far more upbeat than prior to Christmas with even Trevor Palmer expressing some genuinely positive vibes for the upcoming trip as he spotted Curt trudging upstairs to the office and bellowed from the metal shutter doors below.

'Good holiday, Curtis?'

'Yes, thank you, Trev. You?'

'Not really. Anyway, doesn't matter. Christmas happens *this* weekend for me, mate. And I can't bloody wait!'

Curt was indeed also looking forward to the upcoming adventure, yet it had barely been at the forefront of his mind during the past fortnight. Having been fully pre-occupied with the various family arrangements and relishing the chance to properly relax, Gary's birthday trip had not been mentioned at all by either Curt or Hayley.

The birthday boy himself had obliged his pledge and had spent most of the Christmas break scouring the internet with his brother finalising the booking of some suitably appealing accommodation.

Subsequently, Gary Lockley's highly audible entrance into the warehouse was duly embroidered with a swagger and a selection of photographs of the apartments that had been chosen to house the small gaggle of friends and relatives.

His sharp rallying cry readily alerted the attentions of all concerned.

'Ayup, boys. Come and have a look at these. Ian's printed them off for us.'

Curt peered over the safety barrier before quickly jogging downstairs from the mezzanine and joining his two colleagues underneath the office.

'Some photos we downloaded of where we're staying. Looks the bee's knees, doesn't it?'

'Fuck me!' declared Trevor. 'This is a posh set of digs, aint it? Bit too upmarket for us.'

'Only the best for my lads. Came in at the right price, as well. So, the bad news is that you two owe my brother a hundred smackers each when you see him on Friday night.'

Curt was naturally the first to express his gratitude.

'Great stuff, Gaz. I actually agree with Trev for once! This place looks way too civilized for us animals!'

Gary was not finished with the resume of his endeavours.

'They do a transfer service, too. It's all arranged. A taxi will meet us when we arrive in Prague and take us directly to the apartments. Can't bloody go wrong, can it? Then we just dump our bags and hit the town.'

Curt studied the photographs as another concern quickly entered his head.

'What about getting to the airport though, Gaz? Are we all meeting up there, or what?'

'Don't panic, Curt! Paul and Geoff live the other side of the city so they're making their own way and will see us at the airport. Our Ian's mate's a cab driver so he'll do a run for mate's rates that takes us Friday and picks us up Sunday night.'

'How much for the cab?' enquired a sceptical Trevor.

'A score a man.'

Trevor's natural negativity did not take long to fester.

'Twenty quid *each*? I bet I could have gotten it cheaper than that.'

Gary was quick to defend his brother's efforts.

'Erm...no you couldn't, you ungrateful git. For four pick-ups and a return run to the airport? He's the cheapest there is. So don't start whining about pennies or you can try fucking walking it! Okay?'

Trevor nodded as a smug expression emerged across his face.

'What about clothes?' ventured Curt, somewhat cautiously.

'Yes...you will need to wear some. It's not a nudist colony.' snapped Trevor sarcastically.

'No...I mean...is it going to be cold?'

Again, Trevor Palmer could not resist the opportunity to mock the perfectly sensible approach to matters that Curt Osbourne couldn't help but convey.

'Yeah...bring your winter coat, Curtis. And your scarf. And your woolly hat. And your wheelchair blanket. Jesus Christ! It's like a fucking OAP outing already!'

Gary allowed the teasing to abate before half-heartedly confirming the weekend's weather forecast.

'Look mate. It's January. Use your loaf. They reckon it's going to snow all week over here so it's pretty much a guarantee it will be nippy out there. But, for the amount of time we'll be spending outside, it doesn't really matter. Just pack what you want to take. I'm sure your good lady will sort you out as always.'

Trevor and Gary rolled their eyes at one another before the sight of manager David Smith entering the building from the far entrance brought the excitement to a premature close and the bubbling congregation scattered to attend to the day's business.

*****

For the birthday crew, it was proving to be a meandering week at work.

The immediate New Year orders schedule was comparatively light, with the imminent weekend frivolity seemingly a lifetime away for the three members of the warehouse team concerned.

As for the Osbourne household, the routine at home continued as always with their cosy and reliable domestic schedule helping keep out the misery of the cold snap that January had rudely invited.

However, Thursday evening's family mealtime saw Curt having adopted a rather sombre mood. With barely an appetite to speak of, he sat picking at his food with unusual reluctance to eat or engage in conversation. Intermittently watching his daughters and wife across the dining table, irrefutable pangs of guilt began to envelope his conscience.

He suddenly felt ill at ease with the world and couldn't truly decipher the reason. His withdrawn demeanour had not gone unnoticed by Hayley, eventually causing her to voice her concerns.

'What's the matter, love? You're very quiet tonight.'

Returning the brief glances offered by both Hannah and Emily, Curt set his knife and fork down onto the plate, rubbed his eyes and sighed in preparation to announce the source of his troubles.

'No...I know, love. To be honest...I do feel...very...weird, tonight. In fact, I don't feel like myself at all, love. I haven't done all week, really.'

Hayley set down her own cutlery and lightly placed her left palm onto the back of Curt's right hand.

'No...I can see that. What's troubling you? Do you not feel well?'

'No. It's not that. I feel fine.'

'Is it something to do with work? Have you had a run-in with that stupid boss of yours?'

Again, Curt looked to his daughters before replying.

'No...actually...I get on fine with him. I'm about the only one who *does* if the truth be known.'

'Then what is it? Tell me. Tell us. We're all ears...aren't we girls?'

Curt smiled warmly as his daughters offered their father an expectant gaze of wonder. With their genuine interest confirmed, he suddenly felt at liberty to disclose the cause of his discomfort.

'I...well...it's just...I don't know whether I should go to Prague with the lads tomorrow. That's all.'

Facing her husband with an expression of bewilderment, Hayley shifted position in her chair and reached over to place both her hands onto Curt's.

'What are you talking about, love? Have you had a falling out with someone? Is it that Trevor Palmer idiot? You've always said he was a gobby so and so.'

'No, no, love...it's nothing like that. I just feel...uneasy...you know...leaving you three behind. I've never left you alone before. And to be honest, I'm not sure how I'll cope without you for three days.'

Quickly overwhelmed by the loving consideration of her husband, Hayley felt a hard lump of emotion form in her throat which she only just managed to conceal behind a determined yet quaking tone of reassurance.

'What are you like!? You silly thing, you. We'll be just fine! Anyway...it's only *two* days. Not three! You don't need to worry about anything, here, you daft bugger. You go and have a good time. You deserve it...don't you think?'

Partially reassured by the sentiment expressed by his wife, Curt found himself amused by the predictable back-up from young Hannah.

'Yes, Dad! Plus...if you're not here that means we don't have to sit through your favourite programmes tomorrow night. So, you've *got* to go to Prague now. We've planned a movie night with Mum!'

Curt chuckled at the light-hearted sincerity of his eldest offspring.

'Oh...so you'll really miss me, then? Yes...I can already see that my absence is going to cause some real sorrow here! And here's me fretting all week!'

Hannah and Hayley laughed as Curt shook his head in feigned indignation at an unresponsive Emily, who contentedly munched on her fishcake without offering opinion.

Again, it was Hayley who attempted to fortify the situation.

'Look, love. Stop whittling! I must say I've thought it odd that you haven't really spoken about the trip much over Christmas. What are the arrangements for tomorrow night anyway?'

Curt began to inwardly relax and resumed the holding of his cutlery.

'Well...according to what I was told this morning, a cab is coming for me about four p.m. I'm not sure who else is being picked up or in what order, but Gary's told me to be ready for then.'

Hayley presented a radiant smile which was accentuated by her earnest enthusiasm for her husband's jaunt.

'Okay, love. That's fine. We'll have time to sort out your clothes when you arrive home from work tomorrow won't we?'

'Yes. I finish at two as normal. Packing shouldn't take long. I won't need to take too much.'

Hayley resumed her own meal as the conversation developed some positive momentum through her loving inquisition.

'Have you sorted your money out?'

'I've got my English money ready, yes. Gary says we can exchange our sterling at the airport, apparently.'

'Where's your new passport?'

'Upstairs...in my underwear drawer. I think. I was really pleased how quickly it arrived. Good thing you kicked my arse to sort it out!'

'Right then. You're pretty much all sorted, aren't you? So, all you've got left to do is enjoy yourself. Think you can manage that without any help or worry?' chirped Hayley.

Curt inwardly heaped a little more guilt onto himself before responding sheepishly.

'Yeah...I think so, love. Thanks.'

'You can thank me by putting a smile on that face of yours. You're going to Prague for some *fun*, you know. Hasn't anybody told you that bit, yet?'

'I know...I know...' Curt sniggered, mildly embarrassed.

'Well then, you soft sod. You'll be in for a blinding time I reckon. They'll all look after you, I'm sure. You'll not want to come home. Now finish up your dinner before it gets cold.'

FRIDAY

SIX

Curt checked the lounge wall clock.

Nearly three p.m.

Very nearly time for him to take the first steps of a journey into the unknown.

Yet as the familiar vision beyond the front bay window slowly became coated in yet another sprinkling of snow, Curt's freshly nurtured optimism towards the trip had waned once more.

Having just watched the local news bulletin on television, he had all but convinced himself that the plane to Prague might just be grounded and the party over before it had even started.

It was a prospect that simultaneously appealed and disappointed.

Hayley entered the lounge and as usual did not hold back in vocalising her ever astute observations.

'I know what you're thinking but I wouldn't get your hopes up, love. There haven't been any cancelled flights up to now. It's about the only airport in the country that hasn't, though. So…it looks like you'll be going after all.'

Curt chuckled at his wife's knowing sarcasm and responded in kind whilst struggling to conceal his grin.

'To be honest darling…I'm actually a little bit excited now. In fact, I can't wait to get that first pint down my neck once we've checked in.'

Sidling up behind her husband, Hayley closed her arms around him and placed her lips on the back of his neck.

'Oh…good…fine…leave us, then! Go off with your mates to get hammered and desert your family. See if we care.'

Curt laughed out loud as he turned to face his wife and planted a delicate kiss on her forehead. She drew away and issued a wifely briefing.

'Right, love! Everything's ironed and neatly packed – unlike the way *you* usually do it. Your passport and money are on top of the suitcase. You're all set to go. I'm going to fetch the girls from school whilst you sit and relax. I'll be back by half past. They said they wanted to see you off, bless them.'

Curt looked Hayley deep into her blue eyes as he felt his emotions beginning to stir once again.

'Okay, love. Look…when I get back…next week…we'll all go out. You, me, and the girls. Perhaps the cinema and then pizza. Yes?'

Hayley smiled as she fumbled in her jacket pocket.

'Great! Good idea! Now, can I borrow your keys for the car? I've lost mine somewhere in the house. I'll see you in about twenty minutes. Okay? And stop worrying! You're about to have the best weekend for ages!'

Curt nodded as he handed his wife the car remote.

'Okay. Drive slowly, though! It's snowing out there!'

'Yes Dad! See you shortly!'

Curt again sniggered to himself as he moved back to the lounge window.

Watching her reverse the car off the drive and navigate a decidedly slippery route along the road, he wiped a single tear from his eye as he again confirmed the time with the wall clock.

It wouldn't be long now.

SEVEN

'It's here, Daddy! The taxi's here! It's just pulled up outside! Look!'

Hannah jumped up and down in the bay window as Curt glanced beyond her bouncing silhouette toward the view beyond the glass.

Just as his eldest daughter had pronounced, a gleaming silver, seven-seater came to a stop at the end of the driveway and proclaimed its arrival with a resounding bleat of the horn.

Hayley and Emily poked their inquisitive heads from beyond the kitchen door to confirm what they thought they had heard. Curt's heartbeat began to increase as a strange nervousness suddenly overwhelmed him.

Wiping clammy hands onto his jeans, he looked to his wife and youngest daughter as they moved to the front window to survey the cab that had just arrived.

Hayley placed a hand on his shoulder and gestured to the scene outside.

'Well, love...' she beamed with a wry smile. '...your carriage awaits. Have a lovely time without us, won't you?'

Curt crouched down to meet the pouting expressions of his little girls. However, the excitement in Hannah's features was not mirrored by that of Emily, who's unexpected disapproval was conveyed via a furrowed brow.

Her accompanying statement only served to affirm her father's suspicions.

'I don't want you to go, Daddy! I want you to stay here with us!'

Evidently verging on upset, Emily tried to remain brave as Curt swept her up in his arms and lovingly squeezed her tiny frame. He then whispered an idea in her ear, which appeared to encourage a swift change of mood.

'I'll be back before you know it, Emmy. Two days! That's all! It'll be gone before you can say your own name. Now be good for Mummy, won't you? That goes for you too, Hannah. Daddy will take everyone to the pictures next week when he gets back. Okay?'

Both daughters yelped their personal seals of approval at the promise as Hayley followed her husband from the lounge to offer a departing cuddle in the hallway. She looked him in the eyes as an unrestrained look of sadness befell her features.

'Take care, Curt. I am actually going to miss you, you know. And come back in one piece, eh? And don't get too drunk, either. You know how the beer sends you a bit daft.'

'Christ...any more restrictions? It's hardly worth going at all, now.' he chuckled in response.

The shrill interruption of the doorbell caused Curt to ponder his wife's words for a split second, before stooping to retrieve his suitcase from behind the front door.

Hayley commandeered a final check of the necessaries as Curt continued to hover with uncertainty.

'Passport?'

'Yep!'

'Money?'

'Yep!'

'Mobile phone?'

'Yep!'

'One last kiss for the journey?'

Husband and wife briefly embraced once more before their last-gasp union was disturbed yet again, this time with the loud rapping of the front door knocker.

Curt duly pulled open the door to reveal the broadly smiling figure of Gary Lockley.

'Hello, boys and girls! Ready for the off are we, Curt?'

'Yes...think so.' Curt mumbled.

Gary centred his gaze on Hayley, whose restored expression of typical buoyancy belied her own mild sense of loving trepidation.

'You alright, Hayley?'

'Yes thanks, Gary. How's the family?'

'Fine thanks.'

'How's it feeling to be reaching old age at last?'

Gary chuckled and pointed a forefinger at the playful antagonist.

'I'll never grow up me, Hayley. You know that! Eighteen 'til I die! That's me!'

The vigorous enthusiasm of the birthday boy amused her but did little to ease her natural inner concerns.

'Look after this one, won't you?'

Gary merely winked as he nodded at Curt and began to retreat down the driveway back towards the waiting taxi. His lack of a reply to her request instigated a more forceful if mild mannered repetition.

'I mean it, Gary! You're in charge. Keep an eye on him. Or else!'

Gary shouted back with feigned dismay.

'You're joking, aren't you? Curt's coming along to look after us lot! We'll see you Sunday...hopefully!'

Although avidly following Gary's path to the waiting people carrier, Curt turned around at the end of the driveway and offered his family one final reluctant glance.

Blowing his wife one last kiss goodbye and waving to his daughters as they peered through the front window, the momentary tenderness was sharply brought to a halt by murmured groans of intolerance emanating from the taxi.

Hayley managed to squeeze in her parting shot before order was brought to the arena.

'Oi! Hubby! Don't you *dare* forget my perfume!'

'How could I ever forget that?' Curt laughed.

'And text me when you get there to say you got there.'

'Okay, love. Missing you already.'

It was a tender moment between husband and wife that was not built to last.

'Oi! Curt! You getting in this bastard cab, or what?' cried Gary through the open rear door.

With a sigh of partial resignation, Curt faced the impatient occupants of the taxi and half-heartedly made his way toward it. Placing his suitcase in the boot, he closed the lid and jumped in next to Gary.

On closing the door, his attention was drawn to the other figure hunched in the cab's rear compartment. A thinner, younger looking man with a ready smirk and at least a day's growth of light brown stubble.

Gary did not hesitate to acquaint the pair.

'Thank Christ for that! I thought you were never going to make it for a minute, then. Meet my brother, Ian. I think you might have met briefly before, but I'll do the honours anyway. Curt...this is Ian. Ian...this is Curt.'

Gary's younger brother grabbed hold of Curt's outstretched palm and displayed a warm smile.

'Curt, my man. Respect to you, squire!'

'And to you, Ian. Good to meet you.'

With formal introductions over and hands shaken, it was declared time to go as Gary gave the order to depart.

'Right you are, Phil. Next stop is Trevor's house!'

Curt felt the driver find first gear as he gazed beyond the taxi window to engage with the adoring trio that were now framed within the doorway of number thirty-two.

Responding in kind, Curt maintained his attention on his wife and daughters and continued waving until the inevitable turn in the road finally obscured them from view, leaving Leyton Close firmly behind.

What followed was an uninvited and discomforting sensation for Curt Osbourne, but despite having only been travelling with his companions for less than a minute, all thoughts of his family were unconsciously relegated to the back of his mind.

With the relentless holiday banter between the brothers quickly colouring the air, Curt's uncertainty regarding the trip was swiftly eclipsed by the infectious excitement of the clowning pair sitting beside him.

'So, what do you do at work then, Curt?' enquired Ian.

Briefly detecting the smile on Gary's face, Curt obliged the query without wanting to sound overly self-important.

'Well...no doubt your brother has told you I don't do anything?'

'No, not at all! Far from it, in fact. Gaz says you're a very busy bee...licking arse and sucking cock all day in the gaffer's office. Or should that be...orifice?'

Both Lockley brothers exploded into laughter as Curt played along with the fully expected ridicule.

'Well...my official title is warehouse team facilitator.'

'What the hell is that when it's at home, then?' retorted Ian.

'Basically, I kick arses when arses need kicking.'

Ian laughed out loud again and gestured to his elder sibling.

'Oh yes...I can well imagine. I bet this lazy git's always skiving, isn't he? I bet he clocks in late...then has an hour on the bog with a newspaper. I can see him doing it now.'

'What do you do for a living, Ian?' volleyed Curt.

'Lorry driver, mate! Short haul, though. I've made sure to book Monday off as well. You know...just to allow the system to clear of any...shall we say...incriminating substances...'

Gary laughed at Ian's reference.

The mutual affection between the brothers was obvious and instantly infectious, which seemed to implore Curt to add a further compliment to the mix.

'Actually, Ian, and I know you might think I'm bullshitting, but Gary is a genuinely good worker...unlike some I could mention. A bloody all-round top bloke in fact!'

Gary opted to offer his personal contribution to the dialogue.

'Alright, Curt, Jesus Christ! You'll be asking me to fucking marry you next. Anyway... talking of idle bleeders...we're going to pick up Palmer next. You remember Trevor Palmer don't you, Ian?'

Ian rolled his eyes and shook his head.

'Yes, I friggin' do. What did you have to invite that sponging bleeder for?'

'Why...what's he ever done to you?' enquired Curt, very intrigued by the distinctly anti reaction.

'Well...for starters...last time I went out with him he spent all night trying to get me to give him some of my blow! For nothing as well, I might add! Tight as a fucking duck's backside that bloke. And he never bought a fucking drink all night, either!'

It was a pleasant change for Curt to witness Trevor Palmer being held in such derisory esteem by a third party. As such, he attempted to heap a little more into the pot of criticism whilst it was still bubbling nicely.

Gary chuckled as his brother conveyed some genuine if unsympathetic further sentiment on the issue.

'He's an argumentative bugger, too! Always moaning about something. And he's always got to be right. I had enough of him after an hour in the pub. You know what I mean, Curt, don't you?'

'Oh yeah...I know what you mean, alright. He'd pick a fight with a lamppost if it stared at him the wrong way.'

'And he'd lose!' Gary chuckled.

Curt quickly felt at ease in the company of the Lockley siblings as he turned to gaze beyond the taxi window at the darkening scenery. The wintry shower of earlier had abated temporarily, yet Curt could not help but voice his typical doubts regarding the imminent flight.

'I'll bet there'll be a delay at the airport, lads.'

'Why's that then?' Ian grimaced.

'Well...everywhere's covered in snow...look!'

Ian and Gary leaned forward to examine the seasonal vista, with the former quick to offer his positive deduction.

'This is fuck all, mate. You should have seen the snow drifts we faced at Frankfurt last Easter! Three foot deep in places! Yet they still kept the planes in the air. We'll be sound. This sprinkle of sugar won't be enough to cause any problems. It doesn't matter anyway...because we'll all be pissed as newts by the time our flight gets called.'

Gary and Ian giggled together like children as Curt continued to stare at the white-coated landscape. The cab suddenly signalled to veer left into a residential area very similar in appearance to Leyton Close.

Gary leaned forward to raise the awareness of the driver, who had so far remained wordless throughout the journey.

'Trevor lives on Norfolk Street, Phil. You know where that is, mate?'

'Yeah...reckon so.' mumbled the chauffeur as he checked his rear-view mirror.

Ian concluded his declaration of opinions with a semi-serious request as he smirked at Curt.

'And there's absolutely no hurry, Phil. The less I see of Mister Palmer this weekend the fucking better!'

The taxi weaved its way through the housing estate as Gary kept a keen eye on the street signs.

'Here you are, Phil. You nearly drove past it! Its number thirty-eight, I reckon.'

With the car eventually pulling to a stop outside the suspected address, Gary issued some rather unforeseen instructions.

'Right you are then, Curt. Go and give the fat sweaty git a wake-up call!'

Curt heard the words that were spoken but their meaning initially failed to register.

'Hey? What? Why me?'

'Cos you're nearest to his front gate. Now hurry up! We've got beer to drink!'

With a purposed grunt of half-hearted disapproval regarding the apportioned task, Curt slid open the passenger door and made his way to the privet-lined frontage of the abode.

There was no obvious indication of the actual house number, but a quick glance to his left confirmed it to be next to number thirty-six.

Curt turned to the pair of grinning brothers that were now hanging from the open taxi door.

'You sure this is it, Gaz?'

'Yes, Curt. Stop titting about and get him out of there, will you!'

Now more than a little amused by the ensuing charade, Curt pushed open the front gate and ambled up the path. He faced the wooden front door which was adorned in a blistered coat of green gloss paint. Three sharp knocks were administered, leaving him to wait as the silence from inside the house endured.

Nearly twenty seconds elapsed, leaving Curt wondering if they were at the correct address after all.

Suddenly without warning, the front door sprung open revealing Trevor Palmer; still half-dressed and seemingly half-asleep.

Rubbing his eyes with his right hand and scratching his crotch with his left, the weary occupant seemed less than impressed to identify his caller.

'Oh. It's you, Curtis. You'll have to give me a minute. I nodded off after I got out the shower. As you can see, I'm a bit behind schedule, now.'

'It's alright, Trev. I'll go and tell Gaz you'll be a little while.'

Curt returned to the taxi to disclose the reason for the delay, which only resulted in a rather unsavoury reaction from the frustrated birthday boy.

'Fell asleep? Fell *a-fucking sleep*? What a lazy... tell that slob to shift his hairy white behind into this car or we're going to fucking Prague without him. Go on, Curt. Before I really lose my rag.'

Curt resumed his former position just outside the slightly ajar front door of number thirty-eight. He did not knock again, preferring instead to listen tentatively to the increasing rustle of activity in the shadows beyond.

Time ticked slowly onward, and another light flurry of snow began to descend. Unannounced, Gary departed the taxi and popped his head over the front hedge to try and bolster the tardy progress of their final passenger.

'What's happening in there? Is he bloody coming or what?'

Curt simply shrugged his shoulders and opted to push the front door fully open to allow the party organiser to vent his continuing disapproval from the pavement.

'OI! PALMER! ARE YOU COMING OR DO I HAVE TO DRAG YOU OUT?'

A distant voice echoed back along the passageway from the kitchen area.

Three words that were conveyed in a distinctly angered tone.

'FUCKING HANG ON!' snapped Trev from the deeper recesses of the house.

Curt was quickly alerted to Gary's sudden entrance through the front gate and the fearsome expression of displeasure that he now adorned. Pushing past his friend, he positioned himself in Trevor's hallway and bellowed into the semi-dark chasm.

'OI! PALMER!'

'What?' came the distant reply.

'Hurry up! What are you pissing about at? The taxi's been waiting nearly ten minutes!'

Curt waited patiently at the front door whilst Trevor echoed his frustrations back along the hallway.

'I can't find my fucking passport, can I?'

'Hell of a time to lose it, you useless tit!' retorted Gary.

Trevor re-appeared outside the lounge once more with hands outstretched in evident desperation.

'I put it on the worktop less than an hour ago, Gaz. I swear I did. It was right next to my wallet.'

Curt glanced to the floor at the large black leather hold-all and offered a suggestion.

'Perhaps you could have put it in your luggage without thinking?'

For once, Trevor was encouraged by some of Curt's sensible advice.

'Yeah! Maybe. Have a look for me will you, Curtis? I'll go and check upstairs again.'

Several frantic seconds passed as Gary and Curt searched for the elusive document. The uneven footsteps and regular bouts of swearing that ricocheted from the top of the stairwell became increasingly intensive as they gradually emptied Trevor's luggage onto the hallway carpet.

'Oi!' Gary shouted in unbridled amusement. 'What the fuck you got condoms in here for, you sad bastard? You hoping to get lucky or something?'

The embarrassed silence that followed elapsed for a full half-minute before Trevor's grinning features finally descended the flight of steps.

'Lucky, Gareth? Lucky? Listen mate...when it comes to me and women...there's no luck involved, my son. Anyway, you pay for sex on every street corner over there. You don't have to actually pull anything. Just walk into the brothels and flash the cash. They're fucking queuing up for it...so I heard anyway.'

The sound of Curt's laughter resonated back toward the waiting taxi and its intrigued occupants. He couldn't resist the chance to jibe at Trevor's woefully basic approach to life.

'In your fucking dreams, mate. What programmes have you been watching lately? Not the holiday programme, that's for sure.'

'The only thing you'll be pulling is your own plonker in the shower!' concurred Gary, now also consumed by mirth to allay his temper.

Trevor was keen to defend his corner.

'It's fucking true, I tell you. They're all gagging for it, they are. Anyway...all the Polish blokes are over here nicking our fucking jobs...so it's only right that we go over there and fuck their women...aint it?'

Curt laughed out loud once again at Trevor's typically illogical and blunt attitude to existence.

'Yeah...except we're not going to Poland. Anyway, I bet you don't get a single bird.' Curt sniggered.

With tongue partly in cheek, Trevor joined his friends at the doorway.

'Well...we'll wait and see won't we, Curtis? Might even get you set up with a full body massage and a gob job if you're lucky.'

'Erm...no thanks!' muttered Curt, now hoping the suddenly sticky subject would be rapidly altered.

Gary was quick to oblige. He gazed down towards the open sports bag at their feet as the farcical nature of their current predicament raced back to the fore.

'Well, Trevor...me old mucker...I don't want to be a party pooper and piss on your chips...but if you don't find that missing passport...you'll be stopping here and having to make do with your blow-up doll.'

'Shit! That fucking passport! Where the fucking hell did I leave it?'

Trevor retreated inside the kitchen again for a few moments.

Another ninety seconds endured before a distant shriek of earnest triumph resonated from a far corner of the gloom.

'FOUND IT! GOT YOU! YES! YOU BASTARD BEAUTY!'

Curt and Gary exchanged amused if grateful nods at the victorious exclamation, just as Trevor re-emerged wafting his passport in the air.

'Thank Christ for that! Where was it?' enquired Curt.

'On the fucking mantelpiece. Fuck knows how it ended up there, I'm sure.'

Again, it was Gary's responsibility to try and press for a sense of urgency.

'Duh! Maybe...*you* put it there? Jesus Christ. Have I really got to wipe your lot's cracks every step of the way this weekend?'

'Well, I fell asleep, didn't I? Not my fault!' murmured Trevor as he pulled on a jacket.

Gary Lockley was no longer in a tolerant mood.

'Right, Palmer. Get that bloody bag checked now we've rummaged through it...get this fucking house locked...get in that fucking taxi...and let's fuck off to Prague!'

Trevor chuckled as he carelessly re-filled and zipped up the carry bag.

'Good idea! I'm right behind you, lads. DON'T WAIT FOR ME!'

It was a genuine feeling of positive anticipation that began to accompany Curt as he viewed the emerging silhouettes of several aeroplane tail fins on the mid-horizon.

With their expert chauffeur having weaved the remainder of the journey through the country back roads in record time, the increasing mass of Friday evening rush hour traffic had paid little detriment to their progress.

'Look at that, boys! Dead on a quarter to five!' declared the driver as he neared the airport entry barriers.

'You are a star, Phil! We never doubted you, mate!' gushed Gary as he swigged from a silver hip flask before passing it over.

'Come on, Curt! Get a nip down your neck! Warm them cockles.'

Curt glanced at the flask which had been duly positioned under his nose. The aroma of whisky was bittersweet and despite hardly touching spirits as part of his typical drinking diet, he gleefully emptied the contents in one gulp.

'Cheers, boys!' he smiled, handing the flask back to Ian, who quickly refilled it from a half-litre bottle secured between his feet.

Curt's attention once again fixed itself to the scene beyond the car window. The illuminated radio control tower acted as an enticing symbol of foreign pursuits and only served to swell his growing inner zest for the coming weekend.

The car glided its way into the drop-off zone outside the departure lounge and came to a welcome halt, with Gary heading negotiations on behalf of the passengers.

'Great stuff, Phil. Thanks, mate. Do you want the money up front or on Sunday?'

Reaching under his seat to release the boot catch and shoving open his own door, the driver swivelled to reply with the sincerity of a true friend.

'Sort me out whenever, mate. No problem. Just all have yourselves a good time, yes? And Ian...'

'Yes, Philip?'

'Be careful out there!'

'Yes, Philip.'

'And Ian...'

'Yes, Philip?'

'Leave that whiskey here with me, you piss-head! I'll look after it. I don't think they allow booze as hand luggage anymore!'

A united and mocking cheer of agreement was followed by a somewhat untidy exodus from the people carrier as the group spilled out in front of the large glass doors to the check-in hall.

Making a visual confirmation that each man was eventually with baggage in hand, Gary thanked the driver once again.

'I'll phone you when we land Sunday night, Phil. It should be around ten but its better if you wait at home rather than you hanging around for a delayed flight, aint it?'

'Good idea! I'll be somewhere on the road probably, anyway. See you all on Sunday night then, lads. Have a blinding time!'

Curt shivered in the chilly air of the winter dusk as his aptitude for the imminent celebration now grew with every passing second. One by one the group entered the departure hall as the next stage of the expedition began to unfold.

Having wilfully undertaken the role as party leader, Gary strode off in front to try and ascertain the whereabouts of the other two missing members of the group.

The lounge was not as busy as Curt had expected, with only one or two lengthy queues forming. He scanned the header boards for a familiar notice, which was not long in grabbing his attention. The green and blue logo for BudgetFly was stationed in the far corner of the hall at the end of the row of check-in desks.

Unfortunately, it was also seemingly the target for most of the occupants of the hall at that moment. Having been fully distracted by the mildly vibrant environment, Curt had temporarily lost track of his companions, until a recognizable bleating tone echoed in his ear.

'Oi, Curtis! Over here, you dope.'

Searching for the source of the unceremonious call, Curt soon spotted the smirking features of Trevor Palmer through the intermittent crowd. Beckoned over by Gary, Curt was then introduced to the final two guests of the party celebration.

'Curt...meet Paul...my brother-in-law.'

Curt shook hands with the tall imposing figure with blond spiky hair that loomed before him.

'Hi, Paul! You're the sensible one, I hear!' quipped Curt, as his arm was tugged across in the other direction by Gary.

'Yes, he is! Married and made up with my little sister. This is the idiotic bachelor, here! Geoff...meet Curt.'

The other stranger was slight of build and had a somewhat wild look in his eye, yet the immediate sentiment expressed between the newcomers was warm and apparently genuine.

'Good to meet you, Curt. Up for a few blowjobs are you, then?'

Laughter abounded which afforded Curt a chance to avoid an uncomfortable response when Gary called for temporary order to proceedings.

'Right then, listen up, you lot! First job - you all pay Ian a ton a man in Sterling, please. Second job...get some Czech monopoly money. Third job...get our cases dumped. Fourth job...get some beer down us! Keep your passports handy and your mouths under control on the way through, though. We might be in for the rubber glove treatment if customs aren't too busy and feel like a quick grope.'

After the members of the throng had swapped their English money at the nearby Bureau de Change, Ian pocketed due payment for the trip from each of them. The group then made their way to the end of the queue that originated at the departures desk some yards away.

The rapid-fire banter and ready laughter continued uninterrupted for the entire twenty-five minutes it took to confirm the booking and receive boarding passes, with Curt more than content to observe the joviality and say comparatively little in response.

Passage through security was achieved amazingly quickly and thankfully without a single hitch, with the six-strong team rubbing their hands at the sight of a welcoming and well-stocked public bar and at least an hour and a half to indulge themselves in it before take-off.

'Right! First round is on me.' barked Gary as he headed the procession through the scores of waiting passengers that were hunched on chairs with books, I-pods and mobile phones.

'Six lagers is it, boys?'

There was little in the way of protest as Ian and Geoff secured an empty table at which to base their drinking camp.

And although remaining ever so slightly guarded about what lay ahead for them all, Curt followed the others whilst nurturing an overdue personal acknowledgement that possibly, just maybe, he was about to enjoy the coming weekend far more than he could have ever imagined.

NINE

The acute sensation of inebriation was a surprisingly welcome change for Curt Osbourne as he perched on a stool being entertained by his newfound companions. The past hour had been spent listening to the group recall varying individual stories regarding one another and generally offering updates on their lives.

Curt found himself comfortable in their presence and already felt a firm part of things, which was one of the perceived hurdles that had been secretly daunting him during the past month.

Pleasingly, no one - including him - was above being subjected to tales of severe embarrassment and all took their dose of critical medicine in the affable spirit in which it was conveyed.

Gary was in his usual fine form as he and brother Ian berated each other for their various joint exploits over the years and the wonderfully infecting flow of strong beer was constant and plentiful.

Keeping a casual eye on the flight and gate numbers as he emptied his latest glass, Gary wandered across to the bar and promptly returned with six shots of aniseed schnapps.

All followed the direct order to be up-standing for the chant of friendship. Six fists began beating the tabletop to a gradually thunderous finale which inevitably drew curious glances from all corners of the now very busy lounge.

The six quaffed their final drinks before Gary reluctantly declared the first part of the festivities to be at a close.

'I'm sure they've called us, Ian.' he slurred. 'I'm bloody certain I heard our flight being announced.'

Ian swayed on the spot as he squinted at the digital data board hanging above the bar. A wavering forefinger assisted his eyes with the search.

'You're fucking right, bro! There...look! Five-oh-seven-four! Flying at nineteen thirty-five! Christ! On schedule, too! Gate twelve! Looks like Curt's worries about a world-ending blizzard were for fuck all. What time is it now?'

Paul calmed the encroaching panic with a comforting declaration.

'It's only ten past seven, boys. There's plenty of time for another pint, yet.'

Gary poured water on the unanimously enthusiastic response to such a tempting idea.

'No! We've better shift ourselves, lads. The boarding gate will be open. Come on.'

It seemed surreal to Curt to be finishing off the dregs of his fifth pint before turning to face a slowly swirling room that appeared to encircle him ever faster as he attempted to put one foot in front of the other.

Following cautiously after the others, it again occurred to him how he had managed to mentally banish all references to his normal routine in such a short space of time and indeed how relieving it felt to be temporarily liberated from his usual day to day responsibilities.

The inaudible drone of the departure lounge announcer was heard once again as the group converged in front of gate twelve with what appeared to be at least a couple of hundred other eager passengers.

The exit foyer to the runway quickly became home to a mass scrum, with the more experienced and astute travellers in the vicinity jostling for a position which would allow them a rapid exit from the terminus building.

'What seats are we in?' asked Trevor, before belching loudly into the ear of a young blonde lady standing beside him.

Ian swiftly obliged and laced his answer with blatant sarcasm.

'We aren't booked into seats. You get what you get, Palmer. Sit where the fuck you like. Perhaps I might suggest you try the cockpit...or better still...one of the wings?'

Trevor opted not to rise to the bait as he continued to belch loudly. It suddenly registered with Curt that the air around him stank heavily of alcohol and such evidence might just present the group with an obstacle.

'Look at us fucking lot. How the hell are we gonna get let on the plane in this state, Gaz?'

The birthday boy held little fear for their chances.

'Don't panic, Curtis. Everybody...just try and act sober for thirty seconds, okay?'

The petite blonde positioned next to Trevor Palmer had obviously found some amusement in the ensuing conversation as Curt caught a glimpse of her smiling at him before she decided to supply some very welcome advice.

'You can drink on the plane anyway, you know.' she beamed. 'These cheap airlines don't give a toss these days.'

Mildly flattered by the attractive young woman's actual willingness to engage with him, Curt responded in a brave yet woefully flawed attempt to impress her.

'We're all going to Prague, you know. Where are you going?'

Again, the blonde and now also her friend laughed out loud and displayed another wide smile even more enchanting than her first one. Playing along with the silliness, she encouraged further commentary on the matter.

'That's a really strange coincidence, isn't it? So are we!'

Trevor turned to glimpse briefly at the two girls before addressing Curt with a dismissive snort.

'You are a fucking thick knob at times, Curtis.'

'Why? What do you mean?'

'We're all getting on the same flight, you plank. Everybody in this room is going to Prague. Why do you think we're all standing here like fucking lemons?'

The blonde and her brunette friend giggled together as the large glass double doors were finally swung open and manned by two official-looking airport staff in high-visibility vests.

Gary felt it appropriate to convey one last whisper of warning.

'Oi! You lot have your passes ready. Don't start fumbling in your pockets. And don't speak to them if you can help it. They might smell your breath. And stand up straight. And Palmer...no fiddling with your cock! Hopefully I'll see you all on the plane.'

The heaving mass of weekend trippers suddenly lurched forward as the stewards admitted the first flurry of eager passengers. Having made it through onto the tarmac outside, it was something of a relief to Curt that trooping out into the cold evening air went someway to temporarily sobering him up.

Striding toward the aircraft, renewed reserves of adrenaline began to pump through his veins at the prospect of the imminent flight.

In the short distance, the large tail of the stationary jet plane boasted the impressive blue and green airline insignia. It was a vision that encouraged Curt to feel his weekend vacation was now truly commencing in earnest.

Following the blonde lady and her friend to the base of the plane's steps, he realised that Gary and the rest of the group had somehow jumped ahead and had already made their way on board.

Yet it mattered little at that moment. For Curt Osbourne, the absolute novelty of the entire experience was now totally intoxicating.

With every second that passed he relaxed more and more as he climbed the steps, whilst ensuring with a lecherous smirk that the blonde's shapely backside remained at eye level. A polite nod to the female crew attendant at the aeroplane door was quickly supported by the recommended facade of sobriety until he was safely aboard the cabin.

Once inside, the effervescent tremble of enjoyment attuned with Curt's somewhat numbed hearing as the deep hum of the plane's parking engines was immediately left behind.

Looking down and along the centre aisle, he saw a vision of frantic activity as people clamoured for seats.

Indeed, it was a scene that resembled little more than barely organised chaos.

And to Curt it felt invigorating as he shuffled along, immersing himself in the very vocal merriment of the other passengers.

'OI! CURTIS! HERE! THERE'S A SEAT BACK HERE. WHERE ARE YOU GOING, YOU GOON?'

Curt thought he heard the definitive sound of Trevor Palmer's voice, but despite scanning the array of vacant and filled seats in front of him, he could not locate anyone familiar to the Lockley party. In his state of pleasant semi-drunkenness, the amusing thought briefly occurred that he might just have boarded the wrong plane by mistake.

'Back here, you twat.' blurted another recognisable tone. This time the call from Gary's brother Ian echoed over Curt's shoulder.

It soon dawned on Curt that in his confused enthusiasm he had walked straight past his companions and was now standing aimlessly in the middle of the cabin causing something of an obstruction.

Once his brain had assimilated its bearings, he re-directed himself back along the aisle carrying a wide grin.

'Sorry, lads. Thought I'd been deserted for a minute, then!' he stuttered before reaching his friends and finally slumping in the empty space next to Gary.

'No...how this works is...we desert *you* when we get there, Curtis.' quipped Trevor.

Geoff poked his head over the back of his chair to assess the expression of weary contentment that had slowly etched itself across Curt's features.

'Jesus Christ, Gaz...' Geoff murmured. 'Look at the state of him! And we haven't even left fucking England, yet!'

The sound of laughter accompanied the electronic voice of the captain authorising his staff to perform their pre-flight checks, as the Lockley party vocally generated some momentum for a second wave of alcoholic intake.

For Curt Osbourne, the anticipation was now totally addictive.

Arrival in Prague could not come soon enough.

TEN

Travelling at two hundred miles per hour in darkness along a runway was not an everyday experience. Indeed, for a certain proportion of the passengers on board it was also a relentlessly stressful test of endurance.

However, the intermittent shouts of drunken joy emanating from one particular corner of the cabin were proving something of a positive distraction for most as the plane gradually departed terra firma, leaving the other occupants of flight five-oh-seven-four in little doubt of the mood such a thrill ride had induced.

Within what seemed less than ten minutes the aircraft had found its cruising altitude and the seatbelts were well and truly off.

'WHERE'S THE BOOZE TROLLEY THEN, GIRLIES?'

Ian's booming enquiry to the airline crew echoed along the aisle toward the cockpit and seemed to spur the four stewardesses on duty into action.

Half-sized cans of beer and quarter bottles of champagne were cracked open as Gary and his merry men avidly commenced episode two of their weekend drinking binge.

'How long's the flight, darling?' slurred Trevor as a red-headed and long-legged flight attendant presented him with his change and an immaculate smile.

'Just under two hours, sir. If you need me...just call.' she replied, before moving onward to the seats in front.

'Tell you what, Curtis.' claimed Trevor in a barely concealed whisper.

'What's that, Trev?'

'Couldn't half give her one!'

Curt did not respond to the comment other than displaying a sympathetic grin and instead applied his full attention to the can of lager being handed across by Gary, who requested a toast.

'Cheers boys! Here's to us! And here's to one hell of a weekend!'

*****

The jovial shenanigans among Gary Lockley and company endured throughout the flight, with a significant percentage of the plane's occupants seemingly very amused by the good-natured fun being cultivated at the rear of the cabin.

The blond and her brunette friend were however somewhat weary of the predictably boisterous males just a few yards away, although it made the typical monotony of their journey infinitely more bearable.

Especially when Gary decided to encourage his friends to stand up and offer a harmonious salute their local mascot of sporting excellence.

'Come on, lads! Forest for promotion this season! Premiership here we come! Relegation for Derby! Fucking sheep-shaggers! Let's have a fucking sing-song, then!'

The volume suddenly lurched upward, giving cause for the cabin crew to increase their vigilance in observation just in case matters went beyond limits.

However, the airline staff were seemingly content to allow the Lockley group their chance to perform. The effort was well intended and humorous, if not to everyone's personal preference.

'AND IT'S NOTT-ING-HAM FOR-EST...NOTT-ING-HAM FOR-EST FC...THEY'RE BY FAR THE GREAT-EST TEAM...THE WORLD HAS EVER SEEN...'

The improvised selection of terrace chants was quickly followed by a rather less tasteful rendition regarding their favourite city.

'OH NOTT-ING-HAM...IS FULL OF FUN...OH NOTT-ING-HAM IS FULL OF FUN...IT'S FULL OF TITS, FANNY AND FOREST...OH NOTT-ING-HAM IS FULL OF FUN...OH NOTT-ING-HAM...'

Finally requested by the cabin crew to cease the collection of football related tributes, Gary and the boys reclaimed their seats to the sound of rapturous applause from the watching audience and the six-strong choir duly bowed their appreciation before collapsing onto their backsides in a fit of hysterics.

For Curt, the luxury of such a diverting yet simplistic indulgence was his to feast upon. Now sitting quietly in his seat and receiving a regular supply of encouraging glances from the blond across the aisle, he felt invincible and untouchable.

Then the fantasy of the moment was temporarily halted as nature's call intervened and signalled him with some necessity.

As he once again hauled himself from his chair and joined the queue for the toilet, the gravity centre of the plane noticeably shifted slightly as the red-headed, long-legged stewardess advised those in the queue to hurry things along.

'What's the rush?' asked Curt.

The attendant fluttered her eyelashes and pursed her lips to perfection.

'Prague is just over ten minutes away, sir. We're commencing our descent very soon.'

Trevor Palmer decided to contribute a timely quip as Curt became next in line for the water closet.

'Hope you don't need a fucking dump, Curtis. You'll have to snap it off when we start diving! We're nearly there, you know!'

As a giggling Curt finally entered the toilet, locked the door and commenced expulsion, mirth took its full grip once more and didn't relent for the duration as he gradually felt the plane list harshly, causing him to hold on to a conveniently placed handrail for support.

Employing the flushing mechanism and realising that the aircraft was now immersed in full descent procedure, his thoughts turned briefly to his family as he staggered back along the aisle and re-claimed his seat.

Whilst belting himself into place, the images of his two daughters unexpectedly appeared at the forefront of his mind.

Then his lovely wife, Hayley, who in that instance seemed on a different planet somewhere, in a different time, somehow.

Curt again sniggered to himself in amusement as he settled himself for the final touchdown and mumbled under his breath.

'Jesus Christ, Hayley...if you could see me now! Pissed up and we've not even landed yet...'

ELEVEN

'You guys have a good time won't you. Make sure you behave yourselves!'

With his features carrying an expression of sexual vacancy, Curt waved goodbye as he watched the blonde and her brunette companion retrieve their bags from the luggage carousel and made to leave the airport.

They were indeed the fortunate pair, as more and more new arrivals poured into the lounge and huddled around the baggage belt in tangible impatience for their weekend in a foreign city.

Gary put an arm around Curt and mocked him as the two young ladies departed the hall.

'Don't worry, mate. She wasn't that nice looking anyway. Well...I didn't reckon so, anyway. Big nose! They'll be plenty more fish in the sea for you.'

Smiling at the knowing overview from his friend, Curt centred his attention on the conveyor containing various suitcases not dissimilar to his own.

Trevor sidled up and conveyed a positive opinion for a change.

'I tell you what, boys. This airport's bloody smart. Its fucking massive! Looks pretty modern, too!'

Ian created further laughter as he took the undeniable chance to belittle Trevor once again.

'If you like the airport that much, Palmer...why don't you stop here for the weekend? We'll collect you on Sunday when we check out. Promise!'

Trevor wanted to respond with an equally barbed repost but wasn't afforded the opportunity.

'Oh yeah...' murmured Ian. 'I forgot...you've got to stick around with us because of all those birds you're lining up to shag.'

More merriment ensued as the large gathering of travellers convened around the carousel gradually began to collect their pieces of luggage and slowly disperse.

The minutes passed as boredom slowly began to set in. It was in fact nearly half an hour before all the members in Gary Lockley's party had been reunited with their suitcases and holdalls.

All that is, apart from Trevor Palmer, who had wandered off and found a seat a few yards away from the luggage belt.

Dazed and weary from the waiting around and the intake of drink, he began to let his gaze fall to other more interesting aspects of the vicinity. It was indeed an impressive complex, with the bright lights and large dark glass panes presenting a futuristic feel to the airport's design and layout.

More time passed, with the only eventual remaining item on the baggage belt being an unclaimed pushchair. Trevor sat and stared in growing disbelief. The realisation that his bag might possibly have been misplaced began to irritate him as he glanced annoyingly at the continuous, now un-laden carousel.

'Well...what a fucking good start this is to the weekend.' he muttered under his breath. 'No fucking case. No fucking clothes to wear No fucking shower kit...'

His anger was now beginning to visibly froth just as another damning factor to proceedings became apparent.

The rest of his companions were nowhere to be seen.

Trevor quickly realised he was alone in the arrivals lounge.

Completely alone.

'Typical!' he mumbled again before retrieving his mobile phone from his jacket pocket. 'The fucking wankers have done a runner on me.'

With an intention of trying to contact Gary, the plan soon crashed and burned as his phone display indicated there was no network signal available inside the airport building.

'Fuck me! Fucking useless! Can anything else go wrong in this fucking foreign shit-tip?' Trevor's volume had now increased to shouting, inadvertently alerting the attention of a passing member of the airport staff who instantly became aware that something was amiss.

'Excuse me, sir? Can I be of assistance?'

The wiry, pale-faced gentleman's accent was definitively local, yet the English he spoke was nigh on perfect. Trevor looked up in obvious annoyance and explained his dilemma in typically simple terms.

'Yes, you *can* help! You fucking load of idiots have lost my bag. I put it on the plane in England and you fucking dopes have gone and lost it.'

The attendant was on the verge of replying when another voice interrupted the exchange.

'OI! PALMER! ARE YOU COMING OR WHAT?'

From the exit door nearly fifty yards across the hallway, Ian Lockley stood grinning from ear to ear as his victim's impassioned repeat of the announcement echoed around the hall.

'THESE TWATS HAVE LOST MY FUCKING BAG, HAVEN'T THEY?! YOU LOT GO ON WITHOUT ME. I'LL PROBABLY HAVE TO GET THE NEXT FLIGHT HOME.'

Ian remained in position at the exit; as did his broad smirk.

'IS THIS WHAT YOU'RE LOOKING FOR BY ANY CHANCE?'

On recognising the black leather hold-all that Ian mischievously up-lifted from the floor behind him, Trevor stood to his feet as a combination of intense vexation and inner relief washed over him.

He turned to explain the development to the waiting member of the airport staff who now appeared justifiably bemused.

'It's okay, pal! Forget it. I thought my bag had been lost. But it seems my so-called friend was having a laugh at my expense. Cheers, anyway.'

The ground steward offered a stern glare as he spoke.

'Oh... a misunderstanding. I see. So, our staff did not lose your luggage as you claimed?'

'No...it's over there...look. My friends have got my bag.'

The polite assistant looked Trevor up and down before a vaguely satisfied expression befell his face.

'No problem, sir. You are from England...yes?'

Trevor was evidently disinterested in encouraging the conversation and made little attempt to convey any strain of civility.

'Yeah? So what?'

'Nothing, sir. Just that I hope you and your party enjoy your visit to Prague. Goodbye.'

Nodding in vague embarrassment, Trevor ambled across to Ian, snatched his bag and followed him out towards the exit where the rest of the highly amused throng were awaiting him.

'Very funny! You bunch of arseholes. I thought my weekend bender was over before it had even started!'

Gary offered a consoling arm around his colleague's shoulder.

'Trevor, my lad...you're gonna have to watch your back every step of the way now...this lot don't miss a trick! Come on, boys...let's find these taxis. We're wasting valuable drinking time standing around here.'

Having made their way from the arrivals terminal and out to the frontage of the airport, Gary led the group across to the taxi rank whilst checking the now rather torn and tattered reservation slip withdrawn from his back pocket.

He intermittently studied the information whilst hoping to attract someone's attention among the array of apparently disinterested drivers who were convened in a group around the front car in the rank queue.

'Which cabs are ours then, Gaz?' enquired Geoff, as the rest of the six-strong party stood gazing vacantly into space for inspiration from their leader.

'Fuck knows.' replied Gary. 'Any clues, bro?'

Promptly answering the fraternal call for assistance, Ian stepped forward and began to study the piece of paper in Gary's hand. Whilst the scrutiny took place, Curt allowed his wavering attention to wander back and forth across the scene as he observed the steady flow of departing passengers paying their cab fares and wheeling luggage back toward the check-in hall.

The airport was decidedly hectic, and as such there seemed to be no one available to offer any clue as to the next stage of proceedings.

In the shadows adjacent to the glass double doors of the main terminus entrance, Curt spotted a pair of what he perceived to be police officers, who were both standing with arms folded and chatting quietly to one another.

The woefully misguided thought suddenly struck Curt that they were perhaps in the ideal position to assist the group's cause.

'Hey, Gaz...why not ask them two coppers over there?'

Gary diverted his concentration from his friends and toward the policemen positioned in the half light of the terminus foyer.

His response to the suggestion encouraged a rather less than positive overview.

'You must be fucking joking. Are you mental or something? Six pissed up Englishmen just arrived? We'd be sitting ducks. Easy pickings! We'd be banged up for the weekend, mate. In fact, by the look of that ugly pair, you'd be lucky to make your flight home, too.'

As if to affirm Gary's cautionary statement, Curt then noticed the outline of the imposing looking handguns that both officers were openly carrying in their torso holsters.

Trevor's grinning expression of dismay further convinced Curt of his potentially erroneous if well-meaning proposal.

'Yes, Gaz...perhaps you're right. It was just an idea. That's all.'

With the minutes passing and the party members slowly becoming agitated about the apparent absence of their pre-arranged transport, Gary made a decision to counter his friends' obvious frustration.

'What about heading back inside for the bar? I can make a phone call to the travel agent from there to find out where our transfer has vanished to.'

'Bloody good idea! Six large beers sounds like a superb plan! What do you say, boys?' vouched Ian as he staggered among the group.

However, just as the appealing contingency was about to be employed, it was suddenly rendered wholly unnecessary.

Two white estate cars of dubious make and model suddenly filed at speed from the dual carriageway and cruised into the pick-up lane just beyond the terminus, coming to an abrupt halt in front of Gary and his confused companions.

All attentions were rapidly focused on the unmarked vehicles as both drivers quickly exited their seats and walked purposely toward the waiting gang.

With a sense of cautious hope beginning to encroach among the party, Gary was mildly impressed to hear that at least one of the approaching men could speak English, as the smaller and stouter of the two bald headed drivers promptly muttered a greeting from underneath a thick black moustache.

'Good evenings, gentlemen! Lockley party? From the U.K.? For De Tatiava D'Apartmentos?'

The man's accent was evidently from a foreign clime, but its true origin remained something of a mystery.

With a wave of relieved gratitude now washing over him, Gary quickly confirmed the driver's enquiry by displaying the written details of his holiday confirmation.

Within seconds the arrangements were double-checked and confirmed, with Gary now distinctly illuminated as he turned to his waiting friends.

'This is it lads. These are our cars! Well...what are we waiting for? Let's go!'

Unfortunately, Trevor remained less than happy with the unexpected delay in the schedule and expressed his disapproval in typically brash style.

'About fucking time, and all! Fucking foreign drivers! Bet he's not so sloppy in throwing the tip on top of the fare!'

'It's all pre-paid with the accommodation, grumpy. Now get in!' barked Gary.

With everyone's luggage secured in the rear of the cabs the chauffeurs were soon back behind their respective steering wheels and grinding through the gears.

Curt shared his taxi with Trevor and Ian. Tentatively peering through the rear passenger windows at the increasingly distant vision of the airport, his temporarily inert sense of adventure returned to fuel his anticipation of what lay ahead.

England seemed in another universe at that moment. Leyton Close and the family he had left behind felt even further afield. Curt had almost foregone the fact that he was now in a completely alien environment, and he found himself to be acknowledging the most innocuous of things through the taxi windows.

The fleeting glimpses of movement under the uncertain glow of the road lamps.

The sway of the trees as they flirted with the amber rays from above.

The strange, almost haunting silhouettes perched behind the wheels of other cars and lorries that they passed by.

The black night sky with its apparently complete absence of stars.

In actual fact the motorways looked more or less the same as they did back in England.

Similarly, both drivers were manoeuvring their cars like crazed speed merchants whilst barely uttering a word for the entire duration of the journey from the airport to the accommodation.

Neither of Curt's companions readily volunteered conversation either, with both Trevor and Ian maintaining a keen eye on the identical taxi racing away in front just to ensure that their own driver didn't get them lost at this critical stage of proceedings.

The trip lasted less than twenty minutes yet felt significantly less so as they finally departed the motorway and threaded their way through the streets of the city centre outskirts.

Both cabs eventually pulled up nose to tail outside a large stone clad building with a modernised facade, which was delicately imbued from the ground by violet-shaded floodlights.

'Fuck me!' declared Trevor on alighting from the rear of his carriage. 'This is fucking big, aint it? Where are we? Buckingham Palace?'

Curt avidly followed Trevor's gaze skyward, to the high tiled roof of the building and beyond into the endless night above. Indeed, the apartment complex was visually very impressive, with its name inscribed in individually carved stone panels three quarters of the way up the patterned frontage.

Trevor continued to study the large lettering bathed in blue-purple light.

'What's this gaff called again, Gaz?'

Gary was momentarily distracted from dealing with the drivers and the luggage as he turned to elaborate on his friend's source of curiosity.

'It says...DE...TAT-I-A-VA...D'A-PART-MENT-OS!'

'Well, we can all see that! What the fuck does it mean, then?'

Gary turned to his brother and shrugged his shoulders.

'I don't fucking know, do I? Who cares, anyway?'

The squatter, bald driver with the moustache gestured for the group to gather round as he retrieved a small brown envelope from his car's glove box and proceeded to wave it around in front of them.

Trevor and Ian nudged one another as they mocked the man's evidently loose grasp of their language.

'Please...gentlemen...you are listening up...yes? These here are your swiping cards for room entry. You are splitting into two groups sharing two rooms. Three in each room. Room numbers...eleven and twelve. There are two swiping cards provided for each door. There are also some printed cards provided which you should carry around with you. They contain the apartmentos name and address...because we know what you English are like for getting lost, yeah?'

The driver began to snigger under his moustache as did his taller counterpart.

An act which instantly served to displease Gary's brother.

'What you laughing at egg head? What do you mean...*us* English? What exactly are we like then, *us* English? Tell us, please we are all ears!'

Gary had to restrain Ian from encouraging any chance of confrontation as the evidently oblivious driver continued.

82

'Pleasing, sirs...what I mean to say is...you English...from UK...this *strange* place...yes? You...very...forgetful...yes?'

Curt opted to clear up the confusion and quickly allay any possibly fraying tempers.

'Yes, yes...of course, lads! That's why we must carry the cards! For getting around in taxis and buses and stuff. So that we know where we're staying. Good idea.'

The small driver rolled his eyes, gave a thumbs-up and a thickly hair-lined smile.

'Yes, sir...you are understanding! You clever man! You tell your friends! Yes? Good!'

'Okay, okay...what about pick up time on Sunday?' enquired Gary.

The driver nodded and then turned to his wiry colleague. They briefly exchanged words in a totally indecipherable dialect before the shorter one focused back to the group with the intent of obliging Gary's question.

'On Sunday...you must be coming to agent's main office...across town. We all go to airport from there.'

Ian jumped the gun with his aggressive approach.

'Fuck that! Why can't you come here and get us? We've paid for all this, you know.'

'Because, sir...that is rulings of our contract.' grinned the driver, knowingly.

Trevor was the next in line to venture a query.

'So where is your office? How do we know where to find you?'

The driver did not offer a smile this time.

Instead, he reached out and turned over one of the information cards in Gary's grasp.

'On here! The apartmentos is on this side! And our office is on here on this side! The street is on here! There...you see! Across footbridge...just there. Then...left at surgery. Green cross on wall. You be coming with luggage cases at say...mmm...midday. You sign back swiping cards. Then you go for dinners...drinks...walkings...then you be coming back to agent office for six in evening. Then we going to airport for eight-thirty flight home. Okay? By the way...Prague is one hour in front of English time. Change your watches now before...you...forget...'

With the group seemingly satisfied as to what had in fact been fairly clearly explained, Trevor made one final request of the departing drivers.

'OI! AMIGOS! WHERE'S THE NIGHTLIFE AROUND HERE? WE'RE ALL SPITTING FUCKING FEATHERS!'

The taller driver immediately pointed back over Trevor's shoulder as his smaller colleague declared the directions.

'You wanting drinks, now? Okay...turning back along that way. Along the River. Getting to Charles Bridge. Then turning right. Not turning left! NOT left. You then getting into Wenceslas square. About...one mile...or perhaps...two miles. Then you finding your drinks.'

Trevor cast his weary gaze some way toward the roughly designated area in the murky distance and nodded without word before retrieving his bag from the floor and following the rest of the group up the flight of steps to the front entrance of the complex.

Curt entered behind the rest, keeping an eye on the two taxi cabs as they sped out of the parking bay and rapidly merged with the inner-city traffic.

The group's footsteps echoed loudly through the internal stairwell. Trudging wearily up two flights of stairs eventually brought the six to a grey marble floored landing with very ornate fixtures and fittings.

Outside their appropriated apartments, Gary swiped his card through the brass access panel next to the door handle and a small green light duly indicated the door to be unlocked.

'Right, here's the other cards. Me, Ian and Geoff are sharing this room. You three lightweights can have the other.'

Curt took the plastic swipe cards from Gary and promptly repeated the action on the adjacent door panel which was inscribed with a gold-painted figure twelve.

On entering their plush lodgings, Curt, Trevor and Paul were immediately taken aback by the very stylish interior.

'Fuck me, Curtis! This is better than my own gaff. It is a fucking palace after all!' barked Trevor as he lazily dropped his bag in the doorway.

'Yeah...very, very nice! And they've even put the central heating on for us!' smiled Curt as he carefully placed his hand on a radiator. Dropping his own suitcase onto a bed he cast his eye carefully over the swish decor.

With a response to nature's call briskly attended to, Paul emerged from the bathroom to the sound of flushing, having de-illuminated the en-suite facilities after fiddling with the confusingly positioned light switch.

'Christ, I needed that piss! I tell you what...it will be a pleasure to take a dump in there, my friends. A veritable delight, in fact!'

Laughter abounded as all three claimed their beds and quickly unpacked.

Curt pulled his mobile phone from his pocket and checked for a signal. It was a comparatively weak trace yet possibly usable and so he proceeded to send Hayley confirmation of his arrival as agreed.

Making sure he was alone and undetected, he began to compose his text message as thoughts of his absent wife and daughters flooded his mind with pangs of guilt.

He read through the words, hoping that the signal would be strong enough to carry them to their destination.

HERE SAFE AND SOUND.

JUST CHECKED IN TO APTS – VERY NICE INDEED.

HOPE U ALL R OK.

GOING OUT FOR A FEW BEERS NOW.

LUV U ALL + MISS U ALL

DADDY XXX

With the message seemingly despatched, Curt was jolted from his momentary sentimental immersion by a resounding voice.

'You can put that fucking phone down before you start, Curtis.' sneered Trevor as he hung his remaining items in an enormous dark oak wardrobe. 'The last thing you need to be doing right now is communicating with the missus.'

'I know...I know. Chill out! Just telling her we're here. That's all!'

'Well, that's the first and last time! This is a boys only party! And another piece of advice that might just prove useful to you...'

'What's that then?'

'What goes on tour...*stays* on tour...right, Paul?'

Geoff's brother lifted his head from the bottom of his bag and nodded in sympathetic agreement.

'Yes...I do believe that is the general rule, chaps. Discretion is everything when on the road!'

Curt glanced between his two companions whilst switching off his phone and placing it into a bedside drawer with his passport.

'Alright, alright! I'm not that stupid! Anyway, what are you looking for, Paul?'

'Oh...nothing, Curt...nothing important. I just felt sure I'd put a couple of novels in here when I packed...that's all. I suppose I must have forgotten them.'

Trevor looked at each of his roommates in turn and shook his head in moderately controlled disbelief.

'What a fucking pair of wet weekends I've been lumbered with. What with you and your fucking library books and him pining for his bloody wife already. Let me remind you both. We're on a bender. Come on! Let's celebrate our two days of freedom! Leave routine behind!'

Within fifteen minutes, the three occupants of room twelve had ensured to pocket their wallets and door cards before exiting back outside onto the landing.

Curt pulled the door closed with a mild strain of doubt cursing his piece of mind.

'Do you reckon the room is properly locked now? I mean...we don't want any unwelcome visitors raiding our stuff whilst we're out, do we?'

Trevor was quick to appease his friend's undue fears.

'I can tell you're sobering up, Curtis. Bleeding panicking about nothing again, aren't you! Look...there's fuck all worth nicking in there anyway apart from pants and socks! And our passports aren't any good to anyone, are they? Come on you clown. Let's give the others a nudge.'

Trevor knocked loudly on the adjacent door, which promptly swung open to unleash Geoff and a uniquely pungent aroma.

'Christ alive! What the fuck are you lot smoking?' yelped Trevor as he entered the doorway to find Ian and Gary perched on their own beds of choice and each holding a smouldering spliff between their fingers and thumbs.

Gary fixed his highly amused gaze on the dumbfounded entrants.

'Just a little preparatory exercise before we embark on the visit to town, Trevor. A little loosener, before we...well...you know...go and indulge ourselves.'

Curt couldn't believe his eyes and expressed his amazement whilst pointing at the opened plastic bag of weed strewn across the coffee table.

'You mean...you got that little lot through security at two airports? Bit of a risk, wasn't it? You could have gotten us all in clink.'

Ian laughed and reclined back onto his headboard.

'No worries, boys! There's plenty to go around...for a small price, of course.'

'Not for me, thanks all the same.' remarked Curt swiftly. 'I'd rather stay in some kind of control if you don't mind.'

Trevor threw his counterpart a frustrated glare whilst kneeling before the coffee table and placing his nose near to the bag of grass.

It was an act that received short shrift from the provider.

'Oi! Fucking hands off it, Palmer. Unless you've got some readies on you?'

'What? You just said we could dab in!'

'Yes...but not for free, you tight cunt!'

Looking more than a little disconsolate at the remark, Trevor challenged Ian's prerogative on the matter.

'You mean to say you would actually charge your mates money?'

'Well...now I think about it...no...I suppose not. Not now you put it like that. I couldn't really charge my friends, could I? But you...I can charge *you*...definitely! Call it...risk money, for sake of argument. I'm sure if you're desperate enough to sample some then there won't be any real problem...am I right?'

The amusement that resonated around the room left Trevor feeling he had little choice in the matter.

'Yeah, yeah...okay.' he sighed in submission. 'How much?'

Ian inhaled a particularly deep draw before responding.

'Oh...I think a couple of rounds of drinks should suffice. Currency need not ever change hands...after all...this is a birthday party, isn't it?'

Trevor rolled himself a cigarette-sized joint and promptly lit up with the book of matches placed conveniently inside the bag, whilst the others slowly got themselves ready to embark on their long-awaited tour of the town's nightlife.

Within ten minutes, all six in the group were ready for the off, with Ian securing the stash of grass underneath an armchair cushion.

Curt's fears regarding discovery of the weed being uncovered were soon obliterated by a wave of renewed excitement about the next few hours.

As the gang made their way idly from the apartments and downstairs into the vacant lobby, a tangible sense of euphoria began to spread between them.

Ian led the way out through the large front doors of the complex and down the exterior stone steps whilst making a solid declaration as he draped an arm around his elder brother.

'I tell you what, Gaz...this is a cracking start to my weekend! Good flight. Good digs. Good smoke. Now let's get us some good foreign fanny.'

As the throng emitted a barely united shout of agreement, Curt followed somewhat hesitantly, with reservation now only slightly hampering his conscience.

The most prominent and prevailing concern for all was the prospect of encountering the alluring sights and smells of their new environment.

The untold mysteries and unexpected delights of Prague awaited discovery, as six curious visitors ventured ever deeper into the unknown.

THIRTEEN

'I can't see many friggin' pubs along here, Gaz!'

Gary trudged a few yards ahead of the pack, closely followed by Curt, whose personal fascination for the unfamiliar surroundings was swelled even more by the unpredictability of darkness.

The Vltava River flanking the main carriageway was akin to a sheet of glass. There seemed to be no disturbance to the smooth surface, as though the waters had become trapped in time somewhere in the past.

It quickly dawned on Curt that there also seemed to be a dearth of people in the immediate vicinity. The unworldly architecture of the grey-looking buildings that lined the route was slightly intimidating. The differing patterns in the ornate stonework almost cast shadows within themselves and gave cause for second and third glances toward the confusing dance performed under the glow from the streetlamps.

Curt stared upward in attempting to ascertain the vague rooflines, but it was a near impossible task as the towering constructions appeared to stretch away forever, almost masking the jet sky with their clad peaks and twisting spires.

Ahead in the mid-distance, twinkling yellow lanterns stretched intermittently across the river. Although a very popular attraction for daytime tourists, Charles Bridge looked to be a formidable and mysterious path into the ancient territory that lay beyond the other side of the still, murky fathoms.

However, the fact that the bridge was within a few hundred meters indicated that the inns and hostelries would also hopefully soon be in close attendance.

It was a welcoming thought, as the previous drink for Curt and his merry band of travellers had been tasted well over two hours ago and thirsts were definitely generating once more.

'I hope them drivers weren't having us on, Gaz! My feet are killing me in these new shoes!' moaned Trevor as the entrance to the bridge drew ever nearer.

Gary shook his head, more than a little perturbed by the constant whining from behind.

'Having us on? What do you mean, Trev? Having us on about what, exactly?'

'About where the fucking pubs are. My throat feels like sandpaper.'

A few shouts of half-hearted agreement groaned from the group as they finally arrived at the end of the bridge and promptly veered right as instructed.

Suddenly, Prague's rumoured nocturnal activity came alive before Curt's very eyes.

As the six slowly merged with the buoyant melee, his ever-keen eye darted quickly between the silhouetted groups of revellers.

Scores of well-dressed couples walked arm in arm along the partially illuminated cobbled streets as the lure of the square enclosed the Lockley party into its merry maw.

Groups of men and women of all ages were gathered in discussion at outside bars as laughter peppered their secretive unions.

There was a distinct vibrancy in the air that only seconds earlier by the riverbank had been strangely absent. And despite the relatively cold temperatures, the al fresco diners and drinkers sitting outside the varying eateries and bars were fully indulged in their efforts to absorb the authenticity that the local culture had to offer.

For Curt, this not only looked like the place he had envisaged in his head whilst back home, but it also instantly felt like the easy-going scenario he had expected to find when he arrived a couple of hours earlier.

Respectable, well-mannered, and attractive people were occupying every space within the square. Tourists speaking in unusual tongues were evidently from all corners of the globe and had travelled many miles to sample the attractions of the purported crown jewel of Eastern Europe.

The place rang with a considerate civility and an inherent respect for the history that Prague proudly demonstrated.

And then, as if working to some resident mental cue, rang out the very identifiable tone of Trevor Palmer to immediately quash Curt's private mental absorption of his foreign wonderland.

'NOTT-ING-HAM...NOTT-ING-HAM...NOTT-INGHAM...NOTT-ING-HAM...NOTT-ING-HAM...NOTT-ING-HAM...'

Ignoring the confused gazes of the many surrounding patrons, Trevor continued to clap his raised hands to a childish, primitive beat as he then excitedly gestured to some apparent point of interest across the square.

The others found themselves to be slightly embarrassed by their companion's unwarranted display of national pride and began to give him a gradually wider berth.

'Wrap that row up, Palmer. You're making a right twat of yourself.' snapped Gary.

'What's rattled his cage?' enquired Ian, struggling to source the cause of Trevor's jubilation.

With a grin stretching from ear to ear and an accompanying if ill-coordinated jig on the spot, Trevor proceeded to identify the subject of his indisputable joy.

'Look over there, boys! The Union Jack! Got to be an English boozer, ain't it! Come on! My round!'

With little more persuasion required, the other five followed Trevor's bouncing stride toward the familiarly decorated public house.

'You can get the first *two* rounds in actually, Palmer!' commanded Ian firmly from the rear of the group.'

'Eh? Why's that then?'

'One for the sake of friendship...and the other one for that joint I cadged you earlier...remember?'

Trevor's disappointed expression soon evolved into a beaming smile.

'Right oh! Come on then! And you call *me* a tight arse! And you call *yourself* a mate!'

Ian winked at his brother before providing the expected reply.

'Erm...no, Palmer! Definitely not a mate!'

SATURDAY

Six bars later and an indeterminable alcoholic intake had left Curt's inebriation levels at their fully restored peak. He stared vacantly through the blurring and overcrowded room in the search for his companions.

As the resonance of raucous chatter battered his ear drums, a myriad of smiling faces and jostling bodies heaved and pouted their way across his viewpoint, yet not one of the passers-by seemed even slightly familiar to memory.

Standing very unsteadily to his feet, Curt instantly received a light tap on the shoulder as he endeavoured to commence an uncertain quest to locate the gents' toilets.

'Hey...Curt...'

The voice was slurred yet vaguely identifiable.

Curt turned slowly and glanced down at the table he had just vacated.

'Oh...it's you, Paul. Where...where is everybody?'

'Well...there's a story... if ever there was one...' stammered Paul, evidently very drunk himself and struggling to compose a coherent sentence. 'I'm not...not entirely... sure...exactly.'

'Well...where are we?'

'We...are here...Curt...we...we...are waiting!'

'Waiting for who?'

'For Trev...'

Curt's attention travelled around the room once more. Wearily scanning the many assorted characters and their converging conversations, his brain failed to match anyone that could compare with the aforementioned Mister Palmer.

'Why are we waiting for Trevor, then? Where's he got to?'

Paul's focus settled over Curt's left shoulder and was accentuated with a lazily directed forefinger.

'There look...getting more beer...for us...'

Curt turned again to finally register with the plump figure through the crowd. Handing some money to the bartender as he slouched over the counter, Trevor then faced the centre of the room with three large glasses of beer and three glasses of what appeared to be shots, all of which were precariously balanced on a small wooden tray.

'Oh no...I don't think I could drink any more...I'm shagged out...' murmured Curt as his stomach began to lurch at the prospect.

Incredibly, Trevor weaved his way through the melee completely unscathed and finally resumed his place at the table without spilling a drop. He began to apportion the beverages before noticing Curt's failing disposition and suddenly mournful demeanour.

'What's up, Curtis?'

'Don't feel too well, Trev. Need some food, I think.'

'Yeah...good idea. Drink these up, boys! Then we'll go for some fried chicken. I noticed a place near the bridge when we first got here. Just do me fine, that will.'

Curt slumped heavily back into his chair and tentatively retrieved one of the shot glasses from the tray.

'What the fuck is this, Trev?' he asked, whilst tentatively sniffing the fumes emanating from the small vessel in his grasp.

'Oh...just a local recipe. Some regional schnapps, I guess. Wop it back and stop whittling, Curtis. You don't have to admire it! Just sink it! There's a good lad.'

Following the orders, Curt downed the sample of sour tasting liquor before slamming the glass back to the tabletop.

'Right...now I really do feel sick!' he mumbled, whilst staring dejectedly down at his feet. Trevor felt prompted to agree.

'No problem, Curtis. Just neck that last beer and then we'll make our way out for some supper, okay?'

Reluctantly standing to his feet once again, Curt promptly lifted the frothing flagon of exotic lager to his lips and gulped the contents in a matter of seconds. Crashing back onto his seat once more to a round of sympathetic applause from his companions, he repeated his earlier query.

'Hey...where's the other three gone?'

'Who do you mean?' teased Trevor as he downed his own shot.

'You know...thingy...Gaz...and his brother...whatsizname...and this fella's brother...erm...whose-it...'

Paul leaned across the table to present the information Curt required in a discreet whisper.

'Let's just say they've...well...gone off to attend to their needs...'

Curt did not register with the nature of the riddle.

'Hey? What do you mean? What...needs?'

Trevor took up the mantle of translator with a rather less subtle strategy.

'They've gone to find some women! You know! Brothels! Sex? Get laid! Are you clear, now? Fuck me.'

Curt thought about the answer Trevor had conveyed before bursting into misplaced fits of hysteria.

'But that's...that's very naughty...isn't it? What...what would their wives say about such a carry-on?'

Paul found himself to be highly amused by the ensuing conversation and volunteered another contribution.

'That's the point, Curt! They're all free and single, aren't they? They can do as they like.'

Curt stared vacantly into space whilst attempting to summon some logic to the situation.

'But...well...why can't I go out and look for some sex, then?'

Trevor now found himself coming to a conclusion.

'Come on, Curtis...let's get you out of here. Definitely time for some food, I think. Give us a hand to get this piss-head to his feet will you, Paul?'

*****

The harshly acidic if largely diluted taste of vomit was only slightly tempered by the fortuitous minor level of sensory response that Curt could summon at that moment in the alleyway.

Hunched over at the waist with the top of his head resting firmly against the brickwork, he watched the cascading residue of his evening splash onto the drainage grate positioned conveniently between his feet.

With a gut convulsing according to nature's whim, Curt attempted to lift his head and verbally engage with the waiting figures at the end of the arched twitchell.

'Oh Jesus, boys! This is bad! This feels really...bad...I hate being sick...fucking hate it.'

Trevor and Paul could not help but laugh as they watched their companion retch another helping of his liquified innards onto the floor.

'You're a disgrace, Curtis.' mocked Trevor. 'But I'm damned proud of you, lad! Never thought you had it in you. You've just proved you are a proper bloke after all. Now...do you want some food or not?'

With a dismissive wave of his hand, Curt forced himself upright and attempted to ascertain his surroundings.

'No...no food! No food...definitely not! Where am I?' he whimpered.

'Prague. In all its glory.' giggled Trevor.

'Yeah...I know *that* you knob-head. But *where* am I?'

'About half an hour from your bed!' chuckled Paul.

'What time is it, then?'

Trevor checked his watch and walked toward the crumpled, groaning figure in the alleyway.

'It's just about four o' clock, mate.'

Curt squinted through the semi-darkness at his unwilling assistant with an expression of drunken bewilderment.

'What...four o'clock...in the afternoon?'

'No, you tit. Does it look like it's afternoon? We're getting a couple of hotdogs to walk back with. Most of the places are shut now. You can stagger along behind...but not too far behind, eh? If we lose you around here, you're fucked.'

Curt nodded, wiped his mouth on his sleeve and began to follow the paths of his two friends as they navigated their way from the back streets and through into the near deserted square.

The central astronomical clock re-affirmed the time with a ritual display of its expert craftsmanship. It was an intriguing sight; one that enthralled Curt enough to make a proclamation to his two counterparts who were now some way out in front.

'Look lads!' he yelped.

Trevor and Paul stopped their stride and turned to face Curt as he pointed up toward the famous ornamental landmark.

'WHAT?' they shouted back in unison.

'It's a pretty thing, isn't it? It's telling me the time...look!'

The beautiful sights and sounds of the town clock were the last things that registered with Curt before his feet turned leaden and he finally blacked out, leaving his partners in crime with little choice but to carry him dead weight the entire two mile walk back to the apartment complex.

'This idiot's heavier than he looks, Trev.'

'Fucking tell me about it! I bet he's going to feel like shit all day tomorrow. I bloody hope so, anyway.'

'I think we all will. My head's really throbbing now.' sighed Paul, as he grabbed Curt under the armpits and heaved him upright. 'I'll lead, you follow.'

*****

Having eventually made their way back to the apartment and then spending ten minutes or more fumbling for a door card to gain entry, the three occupants of room twelve slumped gratefully onto their beds and wilfully succumbed to instantly encroaching fatigue.

A couple of minutes passed without a word between the dormant trio.

Curt then mumbled something completely inaudible before commencing a bout of loud snoring.

'Trev...' whispered Paul across the darkness of the bedroom.

'What is it?'

'Do you think the others are back in their room yet?'

'Not if they've any sense. But at this precise moment I can't say I give a fuck either way.'

A few more seconds of silence endured before Paul broached another concern.

'Trev...'

'What now?'

'Been a good gig up to now, hasn't it!'

'Yeah...great...' sighed Trevor.

'I reckon we've supped about two gallon each since teatime yesterday...plus all the shots...'

'Yes...maybe...now try and sleep some of it off, will you?'

More silence; then another query.

'Trev...'

'What, for fuck's sake?'

'You know you said you hope Curt feels ill in the morning?'

'Yes?'

'Well...it is the morning...'

Trevor summoned a last breath in reply.

'Paul! Fucking go to sleep! See you tomorrow.'

More silence; a fit of giggles; then one final statement.

'Trev...'

'WHAT?'

'...it *is* tomorrow.'

FIFTEEN

Curt stirred under the bedclothes as sunshine ruthlessly pierced his firmly closed eyelids.

The disorientating symptoms of intoxication had thankfully passed him by in the previous hours. Now he was firmly in the grip of stage two.

Instead of feeling ill, he now simply felt like an episode of death itself.

Yet he was evidently not the first to awaken.

The sound of water flushing through the toilet cistern in the adjacent room engaged his mind to the fact that visiting that very same destination would be an imminent necessity.

Daring to allow a minimum amount of daylight to penetrate his fragile conscience, he slightly opened each eye and attempted to ascertain his current condition. The checklist wasn't positive.

Yes; the skull pounded in time to every heartbeat.

Yes; the stomach felt as though it had been rinsed inside out.

Yes; his bladder was full to bursting.

And yes; the inside of his mouth felt like a privet hedge.

To attain even a minimal level of sympathy from his companions, he changed position in bed and groaned audibly.

'Oh my God...I just want to kill myself!'

The sound of Trevor Palmer's laughter could be duly heard from the next room. Shuffling to study the source of the pained cry, Trevor leaned through the bedroom door and chuckled once again.

'What a fucking state YOU were in last night. An absolute...top to bottom... fucking...mess. I think you're my new hero, Curtis!'

Curt opened his eyes a little more to identify the slightly rounded form casting a shadow across the room. The baggy white undershorts were evidence enough to take a reliable guess at the visitor's identity.

But Curt was in no mood for an argument at that moment.

'Trev...take me to the toilet...please...'

'Fuck off! Get *yourself* to the bog. Me and Paul carried you all the way back here last night as it is. You take liberties, Curtis. But I have to say I was thoroughly impressed. You were battered beyond belief. I never thought you were capable. And just to put icing on the cake you spewed up everywhere.'

Another figure appeared in the doorway next to Trevor.

'Morning, sleepy head.' mocked Paul. How's the aftermath?'

Curt offered a feeble two-fingered reply which only served to create more amusement at his pitiful condition.

'Ready to get back to the pub, Curt? They open at eleven!' giggled Paul.

The very notion of more alcohol incurred an involuntary twist of Curt's bowel, forcing him to sit up and throw off the covers in preparation for any impending gastric reaction.

'Don't do it, guys! I don't know whether I need a shit or a haircut at this moment. Can I swap bodies with someone, please?'

The observing duo laughed loudly again at the desolate sight of their friend. Curt stood to his feet and felt the back of his head thud as though he was being repeatedly smacked with a croquet mallet.

'Where is that fucking toilet?' he grimaced, whilst brushing past his grinning pals.

'I take it you won't be resuming the bender in too much of a hurry, then?' asked Trevor, sniggering at the sight of Curt's frustrated attempts at trying to locate the bathroom door handle.

'I'll be alright...just need to sort myself out. What time is it, anyway?'

'Nearly a quarter to ten.' confirmed Paul.

'What? You're joking! It's still way early!' mumbled Curt through the open bathroom doorway as he squatted gingerly onto the toilet seat and began to evacuate.

'Time waits for no man!' sniggered Paul.' We've only got two days here, you know. There's plenty more pubs to hit, yet. And shut that fucking door behind you. You fucking stink!'

Curt's pained whining echoed around the apartment for the next five minutes or so. He then stood under the shower for nearly half an hour until his general senses became partially functional once again.

Brushing his teeth was a relatively pleasant process which quickly allowed his taste buds to flourish once more. A fresh set of clothes was the next stage of the recovery plan, leaving Curt comparatively lively considering his state just under an hour earlier.

A dash of aftershave completed the physical rejuvenation before he joined Trevor and Paul in the lounge area.

'Have you guys heard from the others?'

'Not a thing.' replied Trevor, fiddling with the television remote control.

'You're wasting your time watching that. It will all be in Czech.' claimed Paul.

'I know...just thought I'd take a quick look at the sort of shit these foreign types like to gawp at during the day. I wonder if they get the same rubbish we have to watch at home?'

Curt twisted his stiffened neck and glanced through the main window of the apartment to survey the scene below. The river had attained a more definitive flow, yet there still seemed to be very few residents in sight.

Then a thought struck him which definitely appealed.

'I tell you what, lads. I could murder a fry-up. Let's get the others up and get out for some breakfast?'

Trevor's eyes lit up at the mention of food.

'Great idea, Curtis. Greasy spoon time. Just what the doctor ordered! We missed out on grub last night thanks to you. Hang on, though...are you sure your arse-hole can handle bacon and eggs at this moment?'

Curt offered a wry smile and ventured into the bedroom to fetch his wallet and shoes.

Within seconds the occupants of room twelve had gotten ready to embark on the next phase of their weekend.

'Has someone got the swipe cards?' asked Paul.

'Yes...somewhere...yes...my inside pocket.' affirmed Curt as he pulled open the door with his other hand.

Paul offered a reminder of the search of only a few hours ago.

'Took us a while to find them last night. But they're safer with you than with us. We put em back where we found em. Not that you would remember.'

No sooner had the three moved out onto the landing, they were confronted by the prostrate figure of Ian, who had presumably managed to get himself locked out and evidently decided that sleeping on the landing was a preferable option to waking everybody else up.

'Jesus Christ...' mumbled Trevor. 'Look at the fucking sight of him! Must have shagged himself into a frazzle.'

The sound of laughter encouraged the door of room eleven to suddenly fly open, revealing the smirking faces of Gary and Geoff. Their gaze immediately fell to their recumbent companion, who had not flinched a single muscle despite the increasing volume of voices around him.

'Fuck me...' shouted Gary. '...God knows what time he arrived back here. Just look at it! If he was a racehorse they'd have shot him!'

Trevor kneeled to observe their slumbering, slobbering counterpart, and carefully attempted to lift him from the cold tiled floor.

'Give us a hand guys. I think our Ian will be a lot more comfortable in bed for bit. We can't leave him out here.'

Having helped to secure his brother under the nearest convenient duvet, Gary turned to his friends; three of whom carried particularly curious expressions.

'What the fuck's up with you lot?' he demanded.

'I suppose your youth lost his door card last night, did he?' grinned Paul.

'No...not...exactly. Me and Geoff came back here well before him...that's all. Never thought about whether he could get in or not, to be honest. Mind you...judging by the tart he was with last night I think coming back here was the last thing on his mind. I never thought he'd make it back at all, actually.'

Trevor could not resist broaching the obvious question.

'We just wondered...did you erm...do alright last night, then? Shagging-wise...I mean?'

Gary tried hard not to reveal too much regarding the trio's personal nocturnal pursuits.

'Yeah...very well, actually! Well worth the money! You surely don't want all the gory details do you, Trev? Though knowing you you'd probably get off on it! Anyway...enough said on the matter. I think we'd better leave my bro here and go and find some brekkers. I'm famished! Don't suppose anyone spotted a cafe on our travels last night?'

Curt observed the fatigued form of Gary's brother slumped face down on the bed. His natural concerns would not be allayed and in turn forced a question that was received with a certain derision.

'You sure Ian will be okay on his own, Gaz? He doesn't look very well to me.'

Gary placed a hand on Curt's ever-burdened shoulder and attempted to satisfy his friend's doubts.

'If you had been doing what he was doing last night, Curt, you wouldn't look very well either! Now come on. Stop fretting about him. He's big enough and ugly enough to look after himself. Let's go and eat!'

Out on the landing beyond room eleven, the other four gazed vacantly at one another before Gary sensed his companions' apparent indecision.

'What's up with you lot?'

'Well...' claimed Trevor. '...we're not too sure where to go and eat are we? There was a fried chicken place up near the bridge.'

103

Gary sighed and pulled his apartment door shut.

'Okay, okay...down to me again to sort you all out, is it? You lot are fucking useless. Right oh...follow me, then. I'll find us a frigging cafe! God it's like looking after fucking boy scouts.'

Squinting under assault from the daylight, Curt noted that the air was surprisingly mild for early January as he descended the stone steps of the apartment complex. Following closely behind the other four, his gaze immediately settled across the river and to the scene on the far bank.

Generally described in the tourist brochures as the Old Town, the absence of any obvious civilian activity on the other side of the water struck Curt as being rather odd. Hundreds of dwellings seemingly perched on top of one another with their identical terracotta tiled rooves. A distinctly different vista to the side of the river on which the five partygoers currently strode.

Yet the streets were so quiet. It was almost as though he and his friends could have rightly claimed the area to be their own for the duration of their stay so far. Although the nightlife they had experienced presented a very different picture.

The previous evening had proven to be very enjoyable for all and despite being first time visitors to the country, no one in the group had professed any semblance of social discomfort since arriving just a few hours earlier; aside of course the inevitable hangovers.

Indeed, for certain members of the Lockley group, the natural strangeness of the region had been something to become fully indulged in, as opposed to being immersed in an environment that perhaps should induce any wariness.

Curt glanced upward as he unzipped his jacket. The skies above were almost pure white with the low-lying layer of thick cloud that attempted to smother the extremes of the nearby buildings. The sunshine that greeted them ten minutes earlier had now fully dissipated.

The fine architecture that flanked the group's path appeared far less daunting by day, giving Curt the opportunity to fully embrace the artistic splendour of his temporary residence. However, his attention settled instinctively back to the river; no longer appearing as the motionless sleeping serpent he had perceived some hours earlier.

Two swans glided atop the water's moderately flowing surface and seemed to stare directly at the five Englishmen striding purposely alongside the main road towards the centre of town.

'How's the headache, Curtis?' prompted Trevor from the front of the group, leering back at his colleague.

'Pretty good, thanks. Bit of fresh air and all that. In fact, I'm about ready for starting another boozing session actually.'

Gary turned to look at Curt and smiled in earnest as he addressed the others.

'Now...I could be wrong, boys...but I reckon old Curt back here is actually enjoying his time off the leash. Am I right, Curt? Or am I right? Come on...admit it. You're in your element. You've just forgotten how much you like being single and pissed. I knew you'd soon get back in the swing of things!'

Curt could not help but laugh along with the gentle mockery.

'Well...it's certainly been a welcome break from family life. And that's all I'm saying. I'm not going to incriminate myself any further by getting drawn into talking about the wife.'

Trevor added a little more fuel to the lapping fire for the gang's amusement.

'Oh yeah? What do you reckon lads? He's only drowning his sorrows because I gave him a bollocking last night for trying to phone his missus. That's why he's sorted his act out pretty sharpish.'

The entire group gazed at Curt in feigned disapproval.

'Oi...Curt!' pointed Geoff with an extended forefinger. 'No more of that silly romantic stuff. Or there will be trouble from us. Are you listening? I know you and Paul are the only ones here with marital status, but that's no reason to dampen the atmosphere with your soppiness, is it?'

Amid the continuing mirth, Gary opted to change the subject to something far more pressing.

'I tell you what, boys. There will be some fucking trouble if we don't find a cafe along here somewhere. My stomach thinks my throat's been cut.'

'Do they do greasy stuff over here, then?' enquired Paul.

'They'd fucking better do!' snapped Trevor. It's an Englishman's right to order an English breakfast...wherever he happens to be in the world. Right, lads?'

Gary smiled before responding with his usual barbed sense of humour.

'Dead right, Trev. Even though you haven't worked up an appetite in quite the same way *we* did last night. And by the looks of that overhanging gut of yours you should probably consider a salad bar instead!'

With the subject of sex rearing its potentially discomforting head once more, Trevor was more than relieved to switch attention away from himself and readily identify what looked to be a restaurant in the short distance.

'What about over there, boys? Looks decent enough to me. And there's a few free spaces inside by the look if it.'

In full if mumbled agreement, the eager throng quickly veered across the road towards the establishment in question.

Large, dark-tinted arch windows concealed the exact detail of the interior, but it soon became apparent that *Festonio's* looked to fit the party's immediate requirements.

A moment of deliberation seemed inevitable as Trevor, Geoff and Paul temporarily stopped their march at the advertising board to scrutinise the cuisine on offer.

'Can't understand what half this stuff is on here! Does that word mean 'fry-up' then?' asked Trevor, innocently.

Geoff chuckled at his companion's genuine ignorance.

'Er...no...don't think so, Trev. This is written in Czech. That is a fish dish. Sea Bass...I believe. Don't think you'll find any sausage and chips in here, mate.'

'Fuck this hanging about...' snapped Paul. '...let's just get in there and order something.'

Gary led the way up the steps to the double entrance doors of the rather grandiose looking restaurant. The doors were manned by a young and handsome waiter dressed in a pristine white shirt and black bow tie, who greeted the incoming patrons and duly showed them to a nearby table.

Curt removed his jacket and gazed around the spacious dining room. The gold and green decor was warm and inviting, although the surrounding vacant tables prompted a moment of concern from Trevor as he hung his coat onto the back of his chair.

'Oi...garcon! Where the fuck is everybody?' he barked across to the waiter, before slumping clumsily into his seat.

'Yeah...bit quiet, isn't it?' affirmed Gary as he positioned himself at the table.

The waiter quickly returned with a smile and some menus, and also an answer to Trevor's query as he presented them.

'Yes...very quiet today. It is a little early though, sir. Dinner is generally not served until three.'

'*Three*? Fuck that! I'd never last that long. Well at least you speak English. That's all that matters to us, pal!'

Gary briefly glanced at Trevor's grinning features before analysing the selection of dishes available.

However, he could only indulge himself in a code of civility for little more than thirty seconds before broaching the issue currently on everybody's mind. He beckoned the waiter nearer as he conveyed the request on behalf of the group.

'We don't really want dinner. Do you do a Full English?'

The waiter looked at Gary carrying an expression of pure bemusement.

'Sir? I'm not sure...full...English?'

'Breakfast, pal! Fried breakfast?' Trevor intervened. 'DO YOU DO IT...OR FUCKING DON'T YOU?'

The puzzled waiter disappeared for a few seconds to register the request with the kitchen, before returning to finally acknowledge the evidently unfamiliar demand.

'Full...English...yes...yes...the eggs...the bacon? The bread? This is good for you, yes?'

'At fucking last!' moaned Trevor, slumping onto his elbows with a resounding clatter.

Gary swiftly confirmed the order with a rather more polite manner.

'Yes! Please! Five of those! And hurry!' he chuckled.

With the food ordered and supposedly on its way, pots of tea and coffee were eagerly poured as Gary began to let his thoughts dwell on the day ahead.

'Right then...who's for getting this grub down us and getting back to the apartments to shower up?'

Trevor's genetic curiosity led him into a familiarly uncomfortable trap.

'Why? What's your plan, Gaz?'

'More women, of course. Are you with us today, fat boy? Work yourself a good sweat up with a dirty whore?'

The giggles that rumbled around the table served to embarrass both Trevor and then even Curt, willing the latter to offer an alternative itinerary.

'I quite fancy going across the bridge, to be honest. Is anyone else up for some urban adventure?'

'Good idea!' Paul agreed. 'The castle and cathedral are over on that side, aren't they? Got to be worth a look by all accounts.'

Gary split a bread roll with his knife as he listened to the secondary plan.

'Well...I can tell you now...me and our kid aren't planning on doing too much exploring. I need to roust him up from his pit and get him ready for action. We've got some more shagging to do! You with us again, Geoff...or are you hanging out with the culture vultures over there?'

Geoff smirked as he answered.

'Not much of a choice to make is there, Gaz? Looking at boring historical buildings or plenty of fit young ladies? Gee...let me think...very difficult...'

Trevor was secretly thankful of being rescued from the subject of visiting the local brothels, and rapidly offered a suggestion for the group to convene later in the afternoon.

'Hey guys...I'm sure Chelsea versus Liverpool is on the box later. They've got football on TV over here, haven't they? We could all meet up for the match and a few beers at teatime, couldn't we?'

Gary nodded as he noticed the kitchen door swing open on the far side of the dining room.

'Sounds fine to me, Trev. Should have had my fill of tarts by then, So...is everyone up for watching the footy later?'

The united grunt of approval coincided with the re-appearance of the young waiter, who carried all five plates of food simultaneously to the impatient group.

There was no vocal response as the table hand smoothly set down each serving and conveyed his earnest thanks.

'Anything else I can get for you, gentlemen?'

'Yeah...a fucking full English breakfast...like we ordered!' said Trevor sarcastically as he studied the dubious items that had been carefully arranged on his plate.

Gary also struggled to force his attention from the mysterious ingredients before answering the call.

'Erm...have you got any brown sauce, pal?'

Now the young waiter was very obviously confused.

'Sorry, sir? Brown...sauce?'

'Forget it!' snapped Gary. 'It doesn't matter!'

The waiter smiled, seemingly under the presumption that his customers were happy.

However, the strains of wondrous disapproval soon arose among the table once the attentive member of staff had retreated to the kitchen.

Inevitably, Trevor was the first of the five to voice his dismay.

'Gaz...this...is not...in any way...shape or form...a fry-up.'

Gary tentatively picked up a fork and began to prod the items of food in front of him.

'Well...let's see what we've got here then...' he murmured without conviction.

Trevor was rather more forthcoming with the verdict.

'There's no sausages or bacon for a start. And why the fuck have I got lettuce? On a fucking breakfast? Who are these twats? Call themselves cooks?'

'You're right. This isn't bacon...its sliced ham!' blasted Geoff.

'And what the fuck have these eggs been cooked in? Bleeding snot?' queried Gary.

Curt attempted to quell the rising discontentment with a positive contribution to the food analysis.

'Well...we are on the continent, you know. It's a bit more refined, I suppose. This isn't some greasy spoon back in Notts!'

Trevor argued in further defence of the party as he spiked something small and green onto his fork and gestured with it towards Curt's face.

'Listen smart-arse...Benidorm's on the continent and you can get better fry-ups there than you can in bloody England! Since when did anyone ever eat a fucking gherkin with their morning cuppa, Curtis? Tell me that!'

Curt's amused gaze fell to his own plate as he picked up some cutlery.

'Well...it smells okay! And it all looks fresh enough. Get it down you, for Christ's sake. If only to shut you all up for five minutes. Take plenty of bread and butter with it. You won't even notice.'

With Curt seemingly bringing the debate to an end, the rest of his companions opted to follow the advice and eat what had been put in front of them.

Ten minutes of virtual silence elapsed aside the clanking of knives, forks and coffee cups, ultimately resulting in five, totally clean plates.

Curt gazed around the table in quiet satisfaction.

'There you are, lads. All gone! All that whining for nothing. Told you you'd like it!'

Gary was not about to be patronised and reacted in turn.

110

'Yes...thank you, *Dad*! I've only eaten that fucking green peppery shit 'cos I'm starving. Do I get a pat on the back then?'

Trevor laughed out loud and sat back into his chair.

'It'll do...I suppose...for a start...but I still wouldn't class it as breakfast. Nowhere...bleeding...near!'

Gary shook his head and rose to his feet.

'Look...I'm out of here. Let's get this bill paid up and fuck off. I need to raise my stupid brother from his bed and get us cleaned up. Time's pressing on. It's nearly Midday, already.'

With the group duly settling what was owed and even offering the young waiter a generous tip and fragmented goodbye as he held open the exit door for them, it was time to split up.

Gary issued the basic schedule for the day as his four friends convened before him outside the restaurant.

'Right then...me and Geoff are off to fetch Ian. We'll meet back up with you guys at four-thirty under that big clock in the square. Is everybody okay with that? Then we'll watch the game with a few beers in hand. You can try ringing me later if you want but I haven't had much signal since we got here.'

With enthusiastic nods of agreement from all, Gary and Geoff headed back to the apartments leaving Curt, Trevor and Paul to follow the opposite route further along the river toward the very distinctive vision of Charles Bridge.

'That was some shitty food!' moaned Trevor as the trio ambled slowly along the main road.

'We've all had worse back at home, mate. At least it was edible.' claimed Paul.

Trevor announced his immediate ambition as he strode off in front.

'Yeah? Well, my first port of call is a burger joint when I see one.'

Curt smirked in exasperation at his greedy companion's woefully misguided hopes.

'You'll be bloody lucky over here.'

'Oh yeah? What's that fucker there, then? Scotch mist?'

'Where are you looking?' puzzled Paul.

As Trevor pointed excitedly across the steadily streaming waters to an uncertain destination on the opposite bank, it soon became obvious as to the source of his growing euphoria.

Right on cue, the three focused their attention on the large signage.

A brightly coloured cartoon image of a cheeseburger on a red backdrop, a which could be seen resting on a tall metal stem some way above the lower-level rooftops.

'Come on, lads. Greasy spoon time!' sniggered Trevor, as his stride gained an extra bounce on toward the bridge entrance.

Strolling happily behind, Curt absorbed the sights and sounds around him as the thought suddenly struck that he hadn't remembered to check his mobile phone for a possible reply from Hayley.

However, any fleeting thoughts about his family were quickly erased by the prospect of a quarter pounder and fries.

At that moment, Charles Bridge was subconsciously deemed by all three as the symbolic pathway to culinary heaven.

SEVENTEEN

'Fuck me, Curtis! Take a look at this. Your lifelong dream's just come true, mate. God, I wish I had a camera on me. Curt...where are you? Get the fuck over here. Now!'

As the trio took their first few steps onto the cobbled entrance to Charles Bridge, Trevor Palmer's laughter resonated loudly among the many other fellow tourists that were frequenting the attraction.

'What's tickled you?' Paul asked, mildly confused by the highly audible giggles of his companion.

'Over there look! Near that lamp post! A fucking black sailor! Curt's ultimate fantasy! Fuck me...where's Gary Lockley when you need him!'

Curt's attention fell to the tall slender gentleman of supposedly Afro-Caribbean origin, whose incredulously dark brown complexion contrasted starkly with the pristine maritime costume he was attired in.

'Go and give him a kiss! Ask if he does tongues!' Trevor mused as he joyfully bobbed up and down on the spot.

'What the hell is he doing dressed like that?' mused Curt in growing amusement.

'I believe he is selling boat trips!' concluded Paul. 'River cruises to be precise. Fancy a ride on the water for fifty Crowns, lads?'

'I bet Curt fancies a ride! All twelve inches...eh Curtis?'

Trevor's unbridled merriment would not relent as the group neared the boat cruise booking station. The man in the sailor outfit spotted their approach and beckoned them over with a large smile and gleaming eyes.

'You gentlemen take trip today? Today nice day. Relax you very much.' he grinned, displaying a perfect set of teeth and a definitive French accent.

'What did he offer you, Curtis? A blow job?' Trevor guffawed in the background.

Curt observed the highly illuminated features of his tubby friend and shook his head in dismay as he attempted to walk past the subject of Trevor's evident fascination whilst hiding his smile.

'You are fucking sick, Palmer. You know that don't you? Sick to the core!'

As if by magic, Paul quickly produced a digital camera from his coat pocket and trained it on the ensuing scenario, which duly served to increase Trevor's enthusiasm for the moment in front of the lens.

'Let's get a photo for the rest of the guys. Come on Curtis. Please! Play along with the fun. There's a good lad.'

Curt continued to edge away in mild embarrassment, yet the tempting pang of obligation was very strong.

He stopped his stride and turned back toward the man in costume before proceeding to place an arm around him.

'This won't take a minute, mate. Just to keep my friend over there happy. For some strange reason he wants a picture of you and me together? God help me if my little girls could see this. They'd disown me on the spot.'

The Frenchman dressed as Popeye smiled broadly once again before tightly mirroring Curt's physical gesture and duly offering a thumbs-up towards Paul's finely poised camera.

'Right...go on...Paul...take your fucking photo and hurry up! This is becoming very squeamish very quickly.'

A few seconds of unexpected and extreme self-consciousness befell Curt before he was finally able to bid farewell to the smirking if slightly bemused man in the sailor outfit, who politely thanked him for the photograph with a handshake and another display of his near perfect dental arrangement.

A pat on the back from an evidently delighted Trevor as they walked away was due reward for supplying the temporary laughs.

'Well done, Curtis! Fucking brilliant, mate! You aren't a boring bastard after all. That will make a cracking photo for the works' notice board.'

Curt eyed his giggling companion as a rushing sense of panic suddenly increased his heart rate.

'You bloody dare, Palmer. Just you bloody dare!'

The trio meandered contentedly further along the bridge, happily intertwining with the vast mixture of nationalities and languages. Curt felt very relaxed as the highly pleasant strains of a nearby string quartet floated gently on the air.

As Trevor hung his head over the bridge wall and stared down at the slowly stirring river, Paul and Curt took their chance and stopped to admire the delightful musical performance, even garnering a smile from the very attractive female lead violinist as she glanced periodically at the music sheet before her.

'Don't see them much these days do you, Curt?'

114

'What's that, Paul?'

'Harps. They make a lovely sound. Don't see much of them now, though. Deemed to be old hat. Incredible instrument though, I reckon.'

The pair recommenced their stroll in and around the multicultural melee and eventually caught up with Trevor, who was still hunched over the rim of the bridge wall in his attempt to scrutinise the mysterious waters below.

Different creeds and dialects indulged in a plethora of indecipherable conversations, with Trevor feeling relatively at ease in presenting his primary observation to his oncoming fellow travellers.

As he resumed an upright position a familiar grin grew across his face.

'Tell you what, boys. There aren't half some fit women on this bridge. All of them foreign and all! I haven't seen a single ugly bird, yet. Unbelievable! Why can't the Nottingham fanny be as classy as this?'

Aside from offering knowing smiles, neither Paul nor Curt replied to their lecherous companion as they engaged with one of the intermittent statuettes of various notable dignitaries that perched proudly atop dark stone plinths.

'Why is this called Charles Bridge, then?' queried Trevor, as they reached the midway point of the crossing.

'Not quite sure.' returned Paul. I'm pretty sure that it will be easy enough to find out, though. We'll have to go to an information point for some leaflets.'

Trevor stared straight ahead as he marched ever onward towards their priority destination.

'Yeah...okay, lads...but after we've been for burgers, eh?'

'Now *that*...is what I would call...*breakfast!*' declared Trevor as he reclined back in his seat and patted his now fully replenished stomach. 'Can't fucking beat a plate full of cholesterol after a night on the ale. Might come here for supper as well!'

Curt and Paul finished their own food, paid the bill and wearily trudged out of the restaurant to allow Paul a cigarette. Trevor followed on behind whilst taking a brief hiatus in his exit to study the menu just inside the door.

'Curt...does that bloke think about anything else but grub?' Paul enquired, as he lit up and inhaled deeply.

'Erm...now you mention it, Paul...food is usually the foremost consideration for our friend Mister Palmer.'

Both chuckled as they observed Trevor eventually weave his way beyond the restaurant door and sidle up beside them eagerly rubbing his palms together.

'Right, then! That's the belly sorted. Now what?'

'How's about...another beer?' quipped Paul as he continued to draw on his smoke.

'Now you mention it I am pretty thirsty again.' nodded Curt, eagerly.

'Follow me then, boys. My round.' instructed Trevor as he traipsed onward along the block-paved causeway, leading them in the direction of a quaint selection of eateries and drinking holes.

As they ambled along behind, Curt made a point of studying the hordes of people around them.

Initially without due concern, he noticed through the crowd that one figure in the mid-distance appeared to be gradually honing closer toward them.

Indeed, as they wandered toward the shopping arcade, it became evident that the group were being followed.

Having been previously informed of the poverty levels in Eastern Europe, Curt recalled the casual dictum that certain members of the community who seemed overtly sociable were only so for one purpose. Theft.

As the three continued to walk, the pursuer drew up ever nearer with a direct yet furtive shuffle. Curt found himself alone in his alertness to the imminent intrusion and glared at the figure now striding almost beside them in the gutter.

116

Judging by the man's visual appearance, he did not instantly portray himself to be the stereotypical victim of hardship. He could have been about fifty years of age. Attired in a dark grey suit jacket paired with ill-matching black trousers, he proudly adorned a head of neatly combed thick black hair which looked to be dyed.

He appeared to be recently clean shaven and relatively bright of eye, yet his dubious presence pricked at Curt's instincts.

Curt naturally assumed him to be a beggar, yet the typical traits of any vagabonds he had ever encountered were oddly absent.

As his attention became totally absorbed in the potential ambition of the adjacent stranger, Curt quickly realised that his curiosity had been mutually registered.

Once the unspoken invitation to converse had been acknowledged, the man then hopped onto the pavement without warning and approached Paul rather brusquely from behind by grabbing his hand and shaking it.

'Hello...hello...how are you all today? Good, yes? Yes good.' the man barked in coarse gravelly tones, naturally taking Paul by surprise and unfortunately attracting the attention of Trevor who had obliviously separated from them a few paces in front.

The man's accent could have originated from anywhere in the world, but his grasp of English was acceptable if basic.

His breath carried the stench of hard liquor and on closer inspection his physical features conveyed inner strife and indeed a certain anger, confirmed by a deeply furrowed brow and a very strong grip.

Similarly, Paul was not feeling particularly enamoured either by the rear-end assault of their unwanted chaperone, nor the abrupt manner of his greeting.

'Erm...what the *fuck* do you think you're up to? Can you let go of my arm, mate? What do you want?'

Paul halted his stride and stood his ground with shoulders firmly back and looked down at the man, whose uneven smile revealed a broken set of yellow teeth.

'You have any change, sir? You have change for a poor victim, sir?'

Paul glanced nervously at both Trevor and Curt before offering a rapid and blunt reply.

'No, mate. I'm poor, too. I've just spent it all. Sorry!'

The stranger seemingly did not wish to register with the polite refusal, giving cause for Paul to forcibly remove his hand from the man's considerable grasp.

Now the atmosphere suddenly altered to one of unease as the scruff re-worded his desperate introduction.

'Ahh! You all Englishman, yes? England very nice place...Wembley, yes...the Queen...yes? Very special! You have change for poor man today, yes?'

'No! No change! Not today!' Paul reinforced, as the trio attempted to recommence their route along the pavement.

Curt noted Trevor's predictable expression of angered intolerance and acted quickly to intercept the inevitable confrontation.

'Quick, lads. In this bar here. That'll shake him off.'

Nobody else in the vicinity seemed to notice the tramp, who, on seeing his current targets flee for cover instantly turned his attention in the opposite direction whilst the three dived through the doors of the nearest public house.

Once inside, Paul and Curt looked at one another as their reactive smiles grew broader by the second.

'Fucking scroungers!' bleated Trevor, as he followed in behind and escorted his companions to a free table. 'He's lucky he didn't try it on with me! He'd be fucking picking himself up off the floor. Fucking robbing wanker!'

The trio sat themselves down as Paul attracted the attentions of the petite young waitress and placed the order.

'Three very large beers, please.'

Curt's unsteadied nerves began to settle once again as he glanced around the pleasantly decorated bar room, of which every available flat surface appeared to house some form of potted plant life.

'It's like a bloody jungle in here, boys.' he quipped.

'Well...so long as it's got rid of that dirty twat.' nodded Trevor. 'Good thinking to get in here, Curtis. Saved the day, mate.'

The waitress promptly returned and parked three tall glasses of lager on the table. A momentary peace resumed as each sampled their drink.

'How's yours going down, Paul?'

'Not bad, Trev. I think my hangover's about sorted to be honest.'

Curt took another deep swig from his glass and confirmed the instantly soothing effect.

As his attention cast itself around the room, he briefly gazed through the large bay window which was trimmed with the shoots of a shrub bearing green leaves the size of dinner plates.

With a realisation looming, he thought it only appropriate to signal a warning under his breath.

'Shit! Watch out, lads…'

Trevor and Paul engaged with Curt's fixed stare, with the former enquiring about the sudden outburst.

'What's up, mate?'

Curt nodded toward the entrance of the pub.

'Our friend…the one we've just got rid of…he's hanging around outside. He keeps looking in here as well.'

Trevor diverted his gaze through the front window and offered a stern proclamation.

'If he takes one foot near me, he's fucking mincemeat.'

Curt placed a hand of reassurance on his companion's shoulder.

'I understand how you feel, Trev. But you can't go around thumping people. I think the police might just have something to say about that?'

'What fucking police?' snapped Trevor. 'We haven't seen a fucking copper anywhere since leaving the airport. I know something…if there were any police knocking about…that dirty fucking scrounger wouldn't be!'

Paul hoped in all sincerity to avoid an unenviable problem.

'Well…fingers crossed he'll get bored and move along pretty soon.'

No sooner had those hopeful words left Paul's lips, than the vagrant pushed open the door of the pub and quietly entered.

He glanced around the room, which fortunately was occupied by several other groups of tourists.

From their corner snug, Curt, Trevor and Paul warily observed the unwelcome figure as he moved between the tables, forcibly shaking hands with varying confused patrons and asking for money.

Meandering considerately around the entire floor without any promise of financial reward, he swiftly changed direction and faced back to the entrance, giving the clear suggestion that departure was now his plan.

'Go on…fuck off out of it!' murmured Trevor, with a grimace of mild hatred.

Just as the three collectively breathed an expectant sigh of relief, the man suddenly appeared to react with appropriate timing to Trevor's commentary and spun on the spot to focus directly on their table.

'Brilliant, Palmer. Well done. Why don't you just buy him a pint and ask him to sit with us?' nudged Curt.

The desolate stranger duly made his way slowly across the room once again and displayed his now familiar tainted grin and nicotine-riddled expression.

'Ahh...Englishmen, again! Yes! Wembley! Good! The Queen....yes? England very special place. You have change for poor man, today?'

None of the three uttered a response as the hobo positioned himself next to Trevor's chair.

The renewed proximity of the beggar was tangibly discomforting for all three.

Now pressing his hips firmly into Trevor's left shoulder, the beggar lifted an arm and rested his hand on Trevor's head before expanding on his proposition for charity.

'Okay, Englishman...you not want to give me money for nothing? Of course...perhaps then...I earn the money from you...yes?'

The trio did not supply any response and simply stared at the swaying loafer.

Without warning, the stranger's fingers began to trace a delicate march along Trevor's scalp, then the back of his neck before stopping at his left ear. He then began to ruffle Trevor's hair, before pretending to straighten his shirt collar.

'Maybe...I will do a kind favour for you Englishman...yes? You like favours...yes?'

Curt and Paul watched the stomach-churning episode in mutual disbelief as the tramp's palm continued to stroke the back of their friend's head.

Under such provocation, a stern reaction was unavoidable.

Trevor decided to adopt a more resilient method of repellent as he immediately rose to his feet and shoved the nuisance in his chest, causing him to flail backward and collide with a nearby empty table and chairs.

An act which instantly aroused the attentions of those in the vicinity – as did the tirade that followed.

'Now listen up, cunt-face...' barked Trevor, standing above the tramp and forcibly placing his forefinger into the end of the man's nose. '...I am English...yes. I've got no fucking money...no! I don't know the fucking Queen, either...but I do know this...touch me again and you'll be waking up in fucking hospital. Do you understand me, sunshine? Or do you want me to teach you an English lesson outside?'

Without further word the stranger picked himself up off the floor and was gone from the premises, leaving Trevor to slump angrily back into his seat, regain some composure and quickly finish his drink.

He scowled with partially feigned menace at his two companions, who were now consumed by hysterics at what had just transpired.

Curt could not resist the wondrous opportunity to even the scores.

'I tell you what, Trev...'

'What's that, Curtis?'

'...if you put that picture of me and the sailor on the works' notice board...you can be damned sure the whole plant will get to know about this. Palmer and the penniless poofter. Frigging perfect!'

Trevor squirmed against the sound of laughter booming from his colleagues across the table, before offering a potent suggestion to bring the matter to a close.

'Curtis...'

'Yes, mate?'

'Shut up and get the fucking beers in.'

*****

The afternoon passed without further uncomfortable incident or indeed further unwanted intrusion from inquisitive locals. Venturing out from their alcoholic refuge, it was jointly decided that the three should explore the scenic castle grounds.

Making a slow stride along the winding pathway that wrapped itself around the plinth of rock and interspersed civilian residencies, Curt was becoming slowly enamoured with the increasingly impressive views of the city that spanned away beneath them.

He stopped and observed the enormous patchwork arrangement of orange-coloured roofs below, breathing in the history and significance of Prague's insistently beautiful landscape.

All around, fellow visitors snapped their cameras and posed for pictures as the admirable sights abounded as far as the eye could see.

Stone towers and brickwork spires that proudly boasted hundreds of years since their inception stretched up and away from the activity at their roots, as the altitude of the castle setting increased with every enticing step.

Mentally lost for several minutes within the pictorial splendour that history had painted, Curt had almost forgotten about his companions, who were eventually to be found perched on a low bench at the forecourt of the mighty cathedral.

'I'm fucking knackered!' moaned Trevor as Curt approached the pair.

Yet the latter was far more interested in admiring the never-ending peaks of the building now imposing him to near insignificance.

'Impressive...isn't it?' claimed Paul.

Curt could only nod in open-mouthed reverence.

'It's bloody amazing, mate. You don't find things like this in England. York Minster perhaps...Westminster...but that's about the lot.'

Paul rose to his feet to join Curt as both scanned the skyline high above.

'Fancy a trip to the top of the spire?' mused Paul.

'You must be off your fucking rocker!' interrupted Trevor, whose expression of discomfort was evidently sourced at his feet. 'If I don't get these fucking shoes off, I'm going to scream.'

Curt and Paul exchanged humoured glances before the former declared the next part of the schedule to be confirmed.

'Come on you lazy git. This is too good *not* to see. Let's go.'

Trevor's approach to the idea adopted a rather more positive slant once it had been established that admission to the monument's interior was free.

Inside the echoing chambers of the cathedral, Curt found himself to be in awe of the ornate and inspiring architecture. As the friends wandered in and around the pews, buttresses and prestigiously maintained alter, Paul eventually pin-pointed the way to success.

'There we are lads. It's the entrance to the stairwell. Come on. You too, Trev! No slacking!'

No words were exchanged as the trio trudged into the alcove and commenced their ascent to a familiar backdrop of complaint.

'Oh, my bloody feet! What the fuck have I done to deserve this?'

Curt thought it best to offer Trevor some sound advice as he glanced behind at his wincing companion.

'Trev...I wouldn't start swearing too much in here mate...this is a house of God, you know. I hope they've not got a swear box...it'll cost you a fortune.'

*****

122

Almost an hour since entering, the three emerged from the cathedral grounds a little wiser and a little more educated. However, the full appreciation of their brief historical expedition was not necessarily unanimous.

'Two hundred and eighty-seven fucking steps? I can't believe you made me go through that. I must need my head looking at. Is it time for the football yet? I'm gagging for a pint.'

Paul placed a sympathetic arm around Trevor as they began the slow descent back along the castle's pedestrian access road.

'Tell you what, Trev...being as you've been so accommodating in our little plan...me and Curt have decided to go along with whatever you want to do, now. You name it...and we're both right behind you. Right, Curt?'

'Right, Paul!'

'So, Trev...come on, then. Anything you want.'

A smile slowly spread across Trevor's face as he gazed around at the nearby smattering of shops and cafes. Giving each Paul and Curt in turn a wink, he then rubbed his stomach before broaching his first query.

'What time is it, Paul?'

Curt robbed the honour by swiftly glancing at his wristwatch.

'Erm...nearly half-two. Why?'

'Well...I was just thinking. I wouldn't mind sampling some of that spicy beef goulash that's being advertised over there...that's all...'

Paul and Curt followed Trevor's nodding head and identified a small yet appealing wooden fronted restaurant which was neatly flanked by a jewellers and craft outlet.

'You mean...you're hungry *again*?' mocked Curt.

'Well...it is well after dinnertime, Curtis...and all that walking has soon seen off my burger...so...well...yes...I'm famished again...alright? Not a problem, is it?'

Without further ado, the trio ambled across the narrow road and prepared themselves for yet another short-awaited dietary indulgence.

'Just one thing, Trev...' warned Paul as they entered.

'What's that?'

'Keep an eye out for your boyfriend, eh?'

NINETEEN

'Clever idea, that.'

'What's that then, Trev?' Paul replied as they left the restaurant and ventured back toward the bridge.

'You know...putting the goulash inside a pot of bread like they do. So, it acts like a bowl...but you can eat it, too!'

Somewhat mystified by Trevor's genial observation, Curt glanced at Paul before supplying a sarcastic summary.

'Rocket science, Trev. How do they think of these things? Sheer genius!'

'Bloody nice though! It went down a treat! Think I've eaten a bit too much, though.' concluded Paul.

The weather had turned distinctly warmer since the journey in the opposite direction some three hours earlier. Incredulously mild for early January, Curt found himself removing his jacket and slinging it over his shoulder.

As the three wandered idly back over the river toward town, Trevor stopped his stride and beckoned for the other two to listen to his latest discovery.

'Fuck me...I can't believe what I've just seen.'

'What's up?' mused Paul.

'Them two little fuckers there...that's what's up.'

Curt allowed his gaze to settle on a couple of young children in the mid-distance, neither of which looked to be into teenage years. Sporting olive skin and shiny black hair, the unkempt looking boy and girl seemed very interested in the varying activity around them, yet whatever had appealed to Trevor's eye remained elusive to the other two for the moment.

'I don't get it, Trev. What are you saying? What is it they are supposed to be doing?'

'Just watch, Curtis. Just act casual and watch them. They haven't noticed us, yet. But I've seen their game, alright. Little bleeders.'

Now completely confused, both Paul and Curt covertly studied the energetic youngsters who continued to move quickly between the closely-knit groups of tourists.

Almost a full minute had elapsed before it became obvious to them what their friend had witnessed earlier.

The boy and girl separated.

The former retained his position next to a group of middle-aged men and women who were engaged in conversation near to the bridge wall. Meanwhile, the girl marched some twenty paces away from the scene before turning on her heel and heading directly back toward her friend.

In the flash of an eye, the boy's hand had delved into a shopping bag protruding from the oblivious gaggle of tourists and deftly retrieved a purse, which he covertly handed to the girl as she walked quickly by.

Fleeing from the oblivious victim, the pair then assumed their pre-arranged rendezvous some way further along the bridge and hurriedly rummaged through the contents of the purse, duly extracting some cash before coolly casting it over the bridge wall and into the river below.

'Caught in the act. Just kids as well...little bastards!' growled Trevor as he watched the children avidly count their latest haul.

Paul enquired as to the purpose of his companion's obvious disapproval.

'Yeah...it's difficult to believe like you say, Trev. But who cares? Pickpockets are everywhere, aren't they? It's a way of life for them. They're brought up on thieving. It's all they know.'

Trevor turned to Paul and snarled his disgust before an idea suddenly emerged.

'It's fucking wrong, though, Curtis. It annoys me. I know...let's set the little bastards up! Curtis...you face the river with your wallet hanging out of your back pocket and I'll get ready to jump on the cunts when they strike. You up for it, or what?'

Curt could not believe his ears.

'Are you off your bloody trolley, Trev? And what exactly are you planning to do with the two kids once you've got hold of them? Beat them to a pulp?'

Trevor shrugged his shoulders and began to giggle.

'Well...I hadn't really thought that far. But at least it will teach them a lesson? Scare 'em a bit!'

'Oh yeah?' asked Paul. 'And likely get you put away for ten years! Let's just forget about the pickpockets, eh lads? The same problem exists in Nottingham Market Square each and every lunchtime...but no one bats an eyelid back home, do they?'

The trio stood still and watched as the two wily juveniles in question approached and walked calmly past, evidently satisfied with their day's work.

Curt attempted to appease his friend's nagging sense of injustice.

'Come on Trev. Time to move on, mate. What shall we do now, lads?'

'Not bothered, really. Has anyone else got belly ache? I reckon that beef stew was off.' declared Paul.

Curt begged to differ before Trevor broached a request of his own.

'Yes! It's just come back to me. There is something else I'd like to do.'

'What's that?' puzzled Curt.

Trevor pointed along the bridge in the direction of the main road.

'Let's all go on a tram ride. Come on!'

Without further ado, the trio picked up the pace and were soon back across the river and heading for the nearest tram stop. The queue was lengthy yet the chance to stand and rest again was most welcome, especially for Trevor.

'I tell you what...I'm glad I packed my other shoes...cos I aint wearing these fucking things when we go out tonight.'

Curt's natural reservations regarding the plan to board the next tram were soon raised as the three lined up with the two dozen or so civilians and tourists.

'Are we supposed to have tickets to get on these things, or what?'

Trevor smiled knowingly.

'Fuck knows! It's half the fun finding out though, aint it?'

The next tram duly appeared around the corner with a signature ring of its very audible bell and pulled to a gradual stop adjacent to the waiting travellers.

'Jesus Christ!' observed Paul. 'It's jam-packed already. They'll not be room for everybody in there, surely?'

Despite Paul's mildly hopeful claim, the queue in front dispersed relatively rapidly and it was soon the turn of the trio to step aboard.

As Trevor stood before the open sliding door with one foot on the step, he began to giggle.

'I'm not exactly sure what we have to do, lads. But come on. One for all and all for one!'

Once all were crammed uncomfortably inside the carriage, the doors quickly shut behind them, with the situation quickly inciting Trevor into a bout of mild hysteria.

'I don't know what you find so funny, Palmer. Where are we going, anyway?' queried Curt.

'Fuck knows!' laughed Trevor, naturally attracting the curious attentions of many fellow passengers.

'So how do we pay for the journey?' enquired Paul.

'Fuck knows!' repeated Trevor, his mirth now becoming more audible and raucous by the second.

'So how do we know when to get off?' panicked Curt.

'Fuck knows!' came the reply once more, with Trevor now uncontrollably amused by the predicament.

However, Curt was struggling to see any humorous aspect to the scenario and in typical mode expressed his concerns.

'I don't understand this, Trev. We could get fined for travelling without a ticket. You have no idea what you're doing, have you? This could end up costing us big time.'

Trevor continued to chuckle, his rounded unshaven features adopting a gradually deeper shade of scarlet as his mirth abounded.

The tram wound its way rapidly around the outskirts of town offering the trio precious little indication of their actual whereabouts or destination.

Curt briefly glanced through the steaming windows at the strange scenery that flashed past, before turning back to observe his giggling friend across the crowded aisle.

'You're a twat, Palmer! Stop laughing for Christ's sake. People will think you're a nutcase!'

The increasing dearth of oxygen in the carriage and repeated clanking momentum of the chassis began to make Paul feel more than a little queasy as his stomach conveyed one or two symptoms of potential unrest.

The tram's seemingly excessive top speed didn't appear to relent as it stopped briefly at various stations along the mystery route before accelerating along the track once more.

Paul looked at his two companions whilst his gut suddenly twitched once again in rebellion against the ride. The carriage slammed its brakes on once more to allow passengers access and egress before racing to its top pace for the sixth or seventh time in as many minutes.

As he swayed and sweated amid the tightly packed throng of travellers, Paul commenced conveyance of his worry as an ailing disorientation ensued.

'Boys...' he whined.

'What's up, mate?' enquired a genuinely concerned Curt.

'I think I overdid the beef goulash. I'm telling you...I'm gonna spew here and now if I don't get off this fucking bus!'

There was little time afforded for any constructive response to the damning claim.

No sooner had Paul announced his warning, than his stomach fully surrendered to the effect of the rickety momentum and unleashed its recently ingested contents all over the floor.

As the residue of his swirling insides splattered the shoes and lower legs of several fellow and evidently disgusted tourists, Curt placed a hand of sympathy onto Paul's back as he hunched helplessly over at the waist.

And as those in closest proximity looked on in horror at what had just transpired, the laughter echoed unrestrained around the tram's interior.

Holding his own stomach as he became submerged in twisted hysteria, Trevor pointed to Paul with little concern for his friend's acute pain and unyielding embarrassment.

'Stop fucking laughing, Palmer. This isn't funny.' pleaded Curt, notably carrying a wry smile himself.

With the tram thankfully coming to another convenient halt the sliding doors opened, offering the trio a most welcome opportunity to evacuate the scene.

As they tumbled from the carriage and down onto the platform, Trevor and a very reluctant Curt could not help but see the funny side of Paul's supremely shameful experience.

'That...was pure comedy gold!' guffawed Trevor as he leaned against a lamp post for assistance. 'Absolutely fucking brilliant! That's made my weekend already!'

Curt's own minor enjoyment of the spectacle was promptly cut short as he noticed that the tram had failed to move on.

It was then an even more worrying sight to observe two men in dark coloured uniforms making their way through the crowds along the carriage aisle and toward the exit doors.

It fell into Curt's hands to advise his fellow men as to the imminent likelihood as Paul slowly straightened himself whilst taking deep breaths.

'SHIT LADS! RUN FOR IT! WE'VE BEEN RUMBLED!'

No sooner had the warning been emitted, the two tram inspectors pointed through the window toward the suspects loitering outside on the pavement.

'FUCKING HELL! YOU'RE RIGHT! THEY'VE SEEN US! MOVE IT!' barked Trevor.

In all, the pursuit lasted no more than twenty seconds.

With the men in uniform quickly evaded, the hapless threesome bounded along a side street as increasing laughter returned to accompany their every stride.

They lightly jogged until the coast was apparently clear before securing their position in a red brick alcove, with Paul again lurching over and repeating his vomiting act as a final bow to conclude proceedings.

Looking down at his wheezing friend, Trevor giggled before issuing one last nugget of wisdom.

'I'll tell you one thing, lads. I can see why that goulash was so cheap. Why didn't you say you felt ill before we got on the bloody tram?'

Paul adopted an expression of distinctly miserable unease as he stood upright to address the question.

'I was alright until it started moving! Then...bam! Turned my stomach upside down, it did.'

Curt looked at his grinning colleague with a shake of the head.

'There's only one bloke I know that could ever find the sight of somebody vomiting so funny.'

Still consumed by the moment, Trevor opted to divert the subject.

'Well...like you said, Curtis...I am sick, aren't I? Now then...it's got to be about time to watch some football, surely?'

TWENTY

'So, whereabouts are you, then?'

Still smiling at recent events concerning the tram, Trevor and Curt walked slowly behind Paul and listened as he talked into his mobile phone in an attempt to locate and hopefully regroup with the others.

'Yeah...the big clock...we're there now...yeah...okay...across the square...yeah...'

Curt checked his watch.

It was nearly four p.m. Time had passed incredibly quickly.

It didn't seem like five minutes since they had eaten breakfast.

He was almost sorrowful that their only full day in Prague had already come and gone so soon. The place had become something akin to a temporary yet very comforting environment to all six in the party, with Curt in particular feeling supremely carefree.

Paul stopped his stride and caused the other two to follow suit as he ascertained the whereabouts of the Lockley brothers and Geoff, who was supposedly providing the instruction.

'Right...so...on through the square...but not actually in it...right...'

Trevor nudged Curt and began to snigger once more as he gestured toward Paul. The image of their friend being ill on public transport was one that, whilst not providing the most savoury of episodes, was nonetheless one aspect of the trip that would accompany them for several days to come.

The subject of their cruel amusement beckoned the pair to follow with a wave of his free hand.

'Yeah...I can see it I think, Geoff...yeah...the brick archway...through that...follow the pathway into the back street...turn left...and you're in a pub on the corner. Right...what's it called?'

Paul recommenced his stride as he continued to converse with his phone.

'The name? The name of the fucking pub, of course!'

Trevor and Curt obligingly followed suit and gazed around the immediate locale with relative disinterest as Paul's tone became laced with growing intolerance.

'What do you mean you don't fucking know! You'll have to stand outside then, or we'll never find you! There must be bleeding five hundred pubs in this area alone! Every building I'm looking at is a bar!'

Curt was surprised to hear Paul's voice carry a strain of annoyance and he shrugged at Trevor.

'Right...okay... we're walking through the archway now. Come outside and wave at us, for Christ's sake! See you in a minute.'

Paul disconnected the call and inserted his phone into his coat pocket.

'Fuck me! Geoff's such a brain-dead dickhead at times. No wonder he can't keep a woman interested.' he concluded.

The trio began to move forward once more as Trevor broached a query.

'How long have they been in the pub, then?'

'Geoff said they went straight there after fetching Ian from the apartments this morning! He sounded a bit pissed to say the least! I don't think they bothered with the massage parlour today by the sound of it.'

'Do we know where this pub is, then?' asked Curt.

'No idea, mate! We'll miss the fucking kick-off at this rate. The pub's got a big widescreen TV, apparently! Not that it's much use to us at the moment?'

It fell to Curt to announce the successful visual contact with Geoff, who appeared from the confines of a rather shabby looking building with a dark painted wooden frontage.

'There we are lads! He's over there! I'll get the first beers in!'

*****

Eventual reunification of the birthday party was successful, with the six thoroughly enjoying the re-immersion into their favourite weekend pastime of watching football with booze in hand.

It didn't take long to rediscover the group groove. The banter flowed as readily as the beer. At full time the friends re-convened away from the television set to sit themselves around a large wooden circular table in the corner of the room.

'Chelsea were fucking robbed! Never offside in a million years.' slurred Ian as he finished his latest pint before clumsily slamming the empty glass onto the tabletop.

'Since when did anyone give a flying fuck about Chelsea, anyway?' challenged his brother.

'True. Very true! My round, is it?' Ian mumbled, before venturing off to the bar.

'So...' asked Gary with a smirk. '...you know what *we've* been doing all day. Where did you three end up, then?

Trevor unveiled the full chronicle of their relatively sensible activities which only served to encourage the inevitable sarcasm and disapproval of the elder Lockley brother.

'I'm getting worried about you lot!' declared Gary as he drained his glass. 'Fucking cathedrals and castles? What a bunch of lightweights! What are we doing later, then...going to the museum and art gallery?'

'To be honest...I don't mind just doing another crawl.' claimed Paul. 'How does that sound to you lot?'

'No problem with me.' proclaimed Geoff, with Curt and Trevor nodding in mildly inebriated agreement.

'We could come back here if you want.' suggested Curt, as he noticed a poster advertising the pub's entertainment for that very night. 'There's a singer on, look! Might be a good laugh?'

Gary observed the luminous green coloured poster by the door and confirmed the arrangements with everybody.

'Curt has got a great idea, there. Right then...that's sorted. We'll finish these drinks...then get back to the apartments for a shit, shave and shower. Back out again for about half seven...a few beers around the square...and then back here for the singer. If he's crap, then we can move on somewhere else.'

Ian seemed to be very enthused by the prospect as he belched across the table and set down a tray of replenished glasses.

'Crack on, Gaz! Everybody up for that then, are they? I know it's a bit spit and sawdust in here but its cosy, enough. And the landlord's a laugh!'

Ian raised the volume of his voice and directed his call to the other side of the pub.

'ALRIGHT, CHARLIE?'

At the sound of his nickname echoing across the room, an elderly grey-haired man in a pristine white shirt moved from behind the bar and gave a thumbs-up in response. He offered an earnest smile before responding in a gruff Italian accent.

'Alright Ian, my mate? Can I get you and your friends anything?'

'No, mate. We're all good! Just fetched 'em in! We're coming back here tonight though, Charlie. That okay with you? See what this singer's like!'

The landlord shuffled further toward the smiling group of Englishmen.

'You guys are welcome back any time! Any time! The singer is very good. Yes. He's from Austria. But sounds like American! Very good! Sings very popular songs! Very popular! This room being very busy tonight!'

'That'll do for us, Charlie!' shouted Trevor as he slugged back another mouthful of lager. 'What's the name of this place anyway?'

The landlord smiled and raised his eyebrows.

'*L'Osvaldo's*!'

'Los what 'ohs?' shrieked Gary.

'Osvaldo! After my father! This was *his* inn before it became mine!'

'So, where the fuck does Charlie come into it then?' queried Trevor.

'Well...my first name is Guiseppe. But I prefer Charlie. Charlie was an English descendent of my family.'

Gary stood up and ordered his band of merry men to drink up.

'Right oh...come on you lot. That's enough of the boring history lesson. Let's get these drinks down us and get ourselves sorted. The night is yet young and we are wasting valuable time! We'll most likely see you later then...Charlie!'

One by one each of the six quaffed their full glass in record time.

The landlord made sure to escort the group through the main door of the pub and sent them away with a smile and a promise.

'Tonight, you have best night of your stay here in Prague! Tonight will be very special! A night you won't forget!'

Just over an hour later, all six in the Lockley party had congregated back at the apartment complex and were in varying states of preparation for the evening's festivities.

In room eleven, Gary and Ian had fallen asleep on their beds after inhaling the product of two significantly sized spliffs in addition to the afternoon's considerable intake of alcohol. The sweet and smoky residue of their exotic indulgence hung around the ceiling like a seductive garland and laced the air with a pungent aroma.

Meanwhile, Geoff had showered and changed before taking the opportunity to commence a private immersion into the potential entertainment available on cable television.

Next door in room twelve, Paul, Trevor and Curt were suitably cleansed and already attired in their drinking wear.

'What the fuck have you got on?' grimaced Trevor from his armchair, as Curt exited his bedroom.

'What's up with it? It's just a hoody. That's all. They're actually supposed to be quite trendy, you know.'

'Yeah...very modern...if you're about thirteen-years old! Fuck me, Curtis. No frigging idea, have you?'

Paul sniggered as he emerged from the bathroom and switched off the light.

'Christ almighty! I'd give that toilet a wide berth if I were you, boys! I daren't try and have another shit! I reckon my back doors will either explode or just fall off their hinges completely!'

Curt chuckled as he considered Paul's warning.

'Thanks for the information, mate. Bit too vivid to be fair...but it's much appreciated.'

Trevor swivelled position in his chair to face the deemed culprit.

'Jesus Christ! You didn't need to warn us, Paul! That stench could kill a gang of rats at twenty paces. The windows are bowing! You dirty bastard!'

Paul laughed out loud as he checked the contents of his wallet and then confirmed the time on his phone.

'We about ready to hit the town again then, lads?'

Trevor, as ever, did not miss the chance to take a dig at Curt.

'Well, I'm definitely ready...and it looks like you are...but Curtis over there needs to get changed by the looks of that rag he's got on.'

Curt displayed a well-worn grin of tolerance at the mercy of Trevor Palmer's unbridled tongue before a thought entered his head.

'Yes...nearly there...be back with you in two ticks, lads.'

Returning to his bedroom, Curt delved into his bedside drawer and retrieved his mobile phone. Switching it on, he was relieved to eventually hear the text tone sounding as an indicator that he may well have had a message from Hayley.

Much to his pleasure, flicking to the in-box did indeed unveil a text from the family which served to remind Curt how much he had missed them in the past twenty-four hours, after all.

GOT UR TEXT YESTERDAY.

HOPE UR ALL HAVING GOOD TIME.

WE R ALL MISSING U.

C U SUNDAY NIGHT

CAN'T WAIT

HAYLEY

XXX

Curt smiled inwardly at the thought of seeing his wife and daughters once again. Their communication was most warming and went some way to appeasing his inner yearning to see them.

Although one particular individual was rather less approving of the loving exchange as he hung in the doorway.

'Oi! Curtis! I fucking well knew it. What have you been told about talking to the missus on our weekend away? It's banned!'

'I've just received a text, Trev. That's all. I'm not phoning her or anything.'

'Right then! Enough said. Put the phone down and come on. We're off next door to rouse up that shower of layabouts!'

Out in the echoing corridor, Curt secured room twelve whilst Trevor and Paul knocked loudly on the adjacent door.

Another issue encouraged another query from Curt as he tested the door handle.

'Have you got the swipe cards for our room, Trev?'

'Yeaaassss!' Trevor sighed with impatience. 'And the maps and info cards. Stop flapping, man! Here – take one just in case.'

Curt thanked Trevor and slipped the card into his wallet.

Geoff pulled open the door to room eleven and immediately resumed his position on the lounger.

He was also more than willing to indulge his companions to share the visual treat he was in the middle of enjoying.

'Hey you lot. Look at this. A bit of tit and fanny on the telly...and its only half-six at night!'

With Trevor, Curt and Paul gathering excitedly around the back of Geoff's armchair, the four observed the events unfold on the tiny TV.

A brunette in black lingerie reclined seductively on a four-poster bed, whilst a ticker-stream of telephone numbers flickered across the bottom of the screen.

'So, what's supposed to be happening, then? Apart from the obvious?' murmured Trevor. 'Have you got to ring her up or something?'

'Yeah!' Geoff giggled. 'You phone that number and tell her to get her kit off! She must obey your orders. She had to do exactly what you want her to. Fucking brilliant idea, isn't it? What a fucking sound programme! Whoever invented this should be knighted.'

'First thing I'd get her doing is cooking me a decent fucking breakfast. And then wash the pots afterwards!' chuckled Trevor as he leaned over Geoff's shoulder.

Curt looked at the deliriously perverse expression residing across Trevor's face just as a familiarly cutting voice resonated from the rear of the room.

'You gonna ring her up then, Palmer? Cos that's the only female you'll get talking to this weekend and that's a fact.' quipped Gary, swaying unsteadily through his bedroom doorway.

'Thought you two were kipping.' snapped Trevor in response.

'Yeah...I was...didn't realise I'd dropped off. It's getting on for seven, you know. You lot ready and raring for the off, are you?'

'More than ever!' declared Geoff. 'So, get that little brother of yours up and let's get at 'em! And by the way, lads...try and stick together tonight, eh? We are supposed to be one group...not two...'

Gary yawned and scratched his crotch.

'Yeah...alright, Mum. I'll get our kid up and we'll be with you.'

*****

Having briefly trialled the rather lacklustre television schedule for half an hour or more, Curt observed the time to be seven-twenty-five as the six finally left the apartment block and trotted down the stone steps to the lower forecourt.

The January air remained pleasantly mild and unseasonably still.

Curt again observed the black sky above as they walked. It appeared to emit a subtle hint of mystery and menace, whilst below the roadside the dark, snaking body of the river once more offered the illusion of being completely static and unfathomably deep.

As the group strode rapidly toward town, tiny silhouettes flickered under the orange glow of distant streetlamps. The yellow lanterns spanning Charles Bridge flanked the route across the water, but the bridge was not on the agenda that evening.

Now vaguely familiar with the central attractions of the city, the group's anticipation of the hours ahead of them was vigorously fuelled with every step.

Prague by night was a very tempting mistress; never willingly surrendering its secrets and ever alluring to the senses of the vulnerable.

And for Curt in particular, his increasing attraction to such uncertainty had reached unprecedented levels.

Indeed, most of all among his companions, Curt now found the magnetism of his temporary surroundings to be overwhelmingly irresistible.

TWENTY-TWO

'Now *she*...is someone I would really appreciate getting to know a little better!'

Gary followed his brother's leering gaze through the myriad of flitting figures that inhabited the overcrowded bar room.

'Whereabouts are you looking?' he asked, searching among the many patrons for the lady in question.

Finally, Ian revealed the source of his evidently fond fascination with a whispered sense of desire.

'There look...end of the bar...blonde hair...blue top...legs up to her fucking armpits...'

The tall, athletic looking female was indeed a physical vision to be admired.

Curt also let his gaze wander lazily upon her imposing and impressive figure. Attractive in her facial features also, she was obviously the centre of attention for many others aside from the Lockley party, who had conveniently housed themselves by the bay window of the public bar whilst the drinks were collected.

'Where's that fat twat with the beers?' demanded Ian. 'He's been gone for hours.'

Curt pointed across the room as the slovenly image of Trevor Palmer carrying a tray of six lagers shuffled his way back toward his fellow revellers.

However, at that moment, he was definitely not in party mood and the cause of his sudden despondency soon became clear.

'What a fucking rip-off! I've needed to take out a mortgage to pay for this little lot.'

'Why?' chuckled Gary. 'How much were they?'

Trevor set down the tray of drinks and slumped angrily onto his stool.

'I reckon about nearly seven quid a fucking pint! *Seven quid* for a bastard pint! The beer's been dirt cheap everywhere else! I can't fucking believe it!'

'Stop whining, Palmer!' laughed Ian as he apportioned the glasses of lager around the table. 'It's only money. It's not like you were going to spend it on shagging, is it? And you forgot my pork scratchings.'

Trevor could not maintain his air of indignity and quickly smiled in recognition of Ian's earnest bluntness.

However, the pain of such an unexpected financial expense was compounded slightly by Gary's conclusive statement.

'Right boys! When we've drank these, we'll move on, eh? Palmer might be stupid enough to spend fifty quid on six drinks but I'm fucking not!'

Curt laughed to himself as he cast his eye around the room.

The evening was now in full swing and the current ratio of women to men seemed to be at least two to one. There were many striking looking females to satisfy the curiosity and for once he felt liberated in absorbing the willing parade of attributes on view.

Then arose a wholly unanticipated if fleeting moment.

A petite young woman with jet black hair cut into a bob style honed into his frame of vision. Squeezed into a black, skin-tight dress with a plunging neckline, she passed through the melee and certainly offered Curt more than casual interest in the way she engaged with his stare for a few seconds and flashed a beguiling smile.

Then, as if by magic, she was gone once again through the swelling throng of the club.

*****

Three bars later and the Lockley party had successfully replenished their alcohol levels from earlier. Trevor had been mercilessly ridiculed for the extortionate cost of his first round, especially considering the comparison with the subsequent outlay of the others.

As they pushed open the door to *L'Osvaldos* and streamed inside, the vibrant atmosphere had already built to somewhere near electric. Scores of conversations echoed around the low walls of the room as a juke box pounded a thudding rock music back-drop.

Ian led the group forcefully through the stifling number of attendees toward the bar and audibly announced his arrival above the ever-increasing rumble of voices.

'HEY...CHARLIE...WE'RE BACK! JUST LIKE I PROMISED! ANY CHANCE OF SOME SERVICE, MATE?'

The elderly landlord raised a hand of recognition and beckoned Ian closer to him with a wave. The pair exchanged a brief dialogue which concluded with Ian smiling from ear to ear and presenting a gentle pat on the back to the proprietor.

With his friends suitably confused by the apparently secret arrangement, they were naturally very eager to learn what had been discussed on his return.

'What's cracking off, bro?' shouted Gary.

Ian raised his hands and gestured over the heads of the group.

'Right, you lot! Get your hairy arses over by that far wall. Over there, look. That's our base camp for the night according to Charlie.'

All six looked across to the empty seats in question.

In the corner snug depicted, a single tall table remained vacant due to a handwritten sign perched on its surface which read *RESERVED*.

Still puzzled by the plan, Trevor ventured another query in order to satisfy the group's evident curiosity.

'I don't get it.'

'Look! It's quite simple. Charlie's saved us a VIP area! Right next to where the singer will be playing. Can't go wrong, can we? And it's all for you lot!'

'Brilliant!' cried Geoff. 'But the bar's fucking miles away if we sit over there. You have to fight your way through this lot for a drink every half an hour'

Ian shook his head, smirked, and expanded on the evening's itinerary.

'Oh no you won't, mate. You don't have to move a muscle. I've slipped Charlie a few notes to keep his staff happy. They are going to make regular deliveries of top quality, top strength lager, every thirty minutes. So, I repeat, get your fucking hairy arses at that table because the first round is being poured even as we speak.'

More than contented with the arrangement, the group altered its direction by one hundred and eighty degrees and the six made their way to the seats in question.

No sooner had their behinds settled on the stools, than the first order of drinks duly arrived courtesy of a very attractive middle-aged waitress with a permanent and endearing smile.

Ian honoured her welcome presence with a semi-polite introduction.

'This cracking bit of fluff is called Suzy. She will be our serving wench for the evening. Now...is everybody happy? Any complaints?'

Attention from around the room briefly locked onto the newcomers as a united and very loud cheer resonated from the Lockley table. A sentiment of appreciation which was confirmed as they held their flagons of beer aloft and drank deeply.

Of course, it was Curt who had rankled most with his recent observations and felt compelled to raise the subject.

'Ian...how come you managed to sort all this out, then? How come you know Charlie so well?'

Ian leaned forward to allow his voice to carry across the vibrant vocal competition to hear himself think.

'I don't know him at all. But when we came in here this dinnertime, I got talking to him about the football in England. He's from Italy so he's real big on footy. Anyway, I splashed some advance cash his way and he's our best mate for the night. Fucking easy, ain't it, Curt? Got to make it easy for my brother, haven't I? Especially as it's his fortieth soon.'

Trevor valiantly attacked the contents of his glass and decided to make a personal contribution in expressing his gratitude.

'Just try and enjoy yourself will you, Curtis? This time tomorrow we'll be traipsing back to the fucking airport and back to reality. Make the most of tonight. I want to see you go for glory with some dirty tart.'

Curt smirked nervously at the ridiculous premise and instinctively thought about Hayley and the girls as he sipped his beer.

Back home tomorrow.

Despite the fact he was really enjoying his time away from his family the forthcoming trip back home instantly fuelled him with excitement.

As his thoughts settled contentedly on his wife and daughters the moment was disturbed by the sound of raucous clapping that slowly spread throughout the room.

The cause of the applause soon became clear, as a young fair-haired man made his way steadily through the dense audience toward the makeshift stage where a microphone and guitar awaited him.

Positioning himself between two large amplifiers, he looped the guitar strap over his shoulder and unclipped the mic from its stand. Switching it on, he commenced his opening patter for the eager audience.

His voice carried a dialect which was not immediately familiar, but the origin was not long in being disclosed.

'Good evening, ladies and gentlemen. I am Andre from Austria and I hope to have you singing louder than me by the end of the night! Okay...if you're ready to rock, I'm ready to roll! Let's play!!!'

Cheers erupted as the opening chords of his electric guitar pounded out the first fevered riff. The entire building immediately began to vibrate to the intoxicating beat.

The Lockley party joined with the sizable throng in singing along and the next delivery of lager promptly arrived before them on the table.

Brimming with a sudden burst of adrenalin, Curt looked around the room as he conservatively mimed along to the tune.

With the evening barely under way, he was now at ease and ready to embrace the next few hours.

Charlie was quite correct with his statement earlier that afternoon.

This was indeed already promising to be one memorable night in Prague.

TWENTY-THREE

Andre the singer clasped the neck of his guitar with both hands and attempted to shout above the cries and hollers for more. Laughing heartily as he scanned the smiling faces and their eager responses to the gig so far, he nodded and quickly relented.

'OKAY...OKAY...YES! I do perhaps one more hour for you being as you are my favourite audience ever in history! If you like rock, then you'll know this one...'

A quarter to eleven on a Saturday night.

L'Osvaldo's was now reaching full capacity point.

The infectious live music had swelled the numbers inside to double during the past hour and more eager customers continued to pour through the door drawn by the rapturous atmosphere.

Curt had now shifted position from the table and had decided to sit on a raised shelf that ran the entire length of the room, affording him a greater vantage over the pub's pulsing activity.

His considerably inebriated gaze wandered slowly across the many heads of the bustling patrons as another popular track commenced its first chorus with full choir accompaniment of around two hundred and fifty.

Curt chuckled at the crowd of enthusiastic singers as he began to try and mentally locate everybody in his personal group.

Gary and Ian were easy to spot.

They had occupied the dance floor in front of stage and were strutting their stuff alongside at least twenty or thirty other highly lubricated ravers.

Most of which, unsurprisingly, were of the young and female variety.

Standing to the side of the stage next to the now redundant jukebox, Geoff and Paul were deeply ensconced in conference about something well beyond Curt's earshot.

From his position against the wall, he offered the pair a distant wave which was eventually acknowledged and reciprocated before the brothers delved back into their secretive discussion.

All were accounted for.

All except for one, very notable absentee.

Curt vainly searched the throbbing room for Trevor.

More than a couple of minutes elapsed but his colleague remained firmly elusive from view. Jumping down from his adopted perch, Curt weaved a path through the heaving melee and joined Geoff and Paul by the jukebox to enquire about their supposedly missing counterpart.

Competing with the volume of the music, Curt practically had to shout to be heard.

'Hey, you two...how's it going? Where's Palmer gone?'

Both Geoff and Paul looked vacantly at Curt before mutual grins etched across their faces. They opted to enlighten him as to the subject of their covert debate with Paul pointing over Curt's shoulder.

'Trev is at the bar, Curt. Can't you see him slouching all over it? Right at the end...nearest the toilet door.'

Curt soon identified the lost member of the party and was given instant cause for a follow-up enquiry.

'Fuck me! Who's that cracking looking bird he's chatting to?'

From a distance, Trevor's brown-haired and voluptuous companion appeared to be incredibly interested in what he was talking to her about. And it was also evident by their body language that she was more than keen to allow their as-yet-brief acquaintance chance to flourish.

Curt could not help but express his astonishment as he watched the surprising display unfurl.

'Am I seeing things? He's got his arm around her waist, lads! Christ almighty! He has pulled after all. Wonders never cease. Do the Lockley boys know about this? Where are they?' yelped Curt with considerably amused excitement sending his voice to a moderately higher octave.

Geoff pulled Curt a little closer to avoid further raising his voice unnecessarily and conveyed another angle to the apparent proceedings.

'Oh yes...Gaz and Ian know all about it, alright.'

Curt was slightly bemused by the revelation, encouraging an expansion from Paul on the evolving scenario.

'You see the bloke dancing by the speaker. He's near to Gaz and Ian. Thin, long blonde hair...black t-shirt. Black jeans? Looks like a heavy metal band reject...'

Curt scrutinised the over-spilling dance floor and soon identified the figure that had been described.

'Yeah? I see him. What about him?' mused Curt.

'Well...' explained Geoff. '...*he* was with Palmer's bird about an hour ago. They were together when they arrived. You try and work it out, mate. Cos we're still struggling.'

Curt's innocence in such worldly matters usually betrayed him and yet again he found it difficult to come to terms with the situation.

However, this particular riddle offered few clues as he pressed again for some kind of theory on unfolding events.

'You mean...that girl...the one chatting up Trev...the heavy metal band reject is her boyfriend?'

'We don't know, do we!?' shrugged Geoff.

'But Palmer's all over her!' concurred Paul.

'Yeah...he sure is...' chuckled Curt. '...and Trev doesn't have a clue that he's probably heading for a knuckle sandwich?'

Geoff shook his head.

'We don't *know*, do we? He might be...he might not!'

'But...don't you think he should be put in the picture...and pretty sharpish?'

Paul was quick to douse Curt's very credible and timely advice.

'What? And spoil the fun? You must be joking, Curt. This is going to be hilarious, mate. Free entertainment right on your doorstep. The fuse is lit. Stand well back and enjoy the view!'

Curt Osbourne was by no means the number one member in Trevor Palmer's fan club, but the ensuing situation was looking decidedly uncomfortable for all involved.

The potential for altercation encouraged Curt to make a further stand in the name of common sense as the music continued to swell the dancing troupes to invade most areas of the room. He continued to shout above the din.

'Come on, guys! You can't just let Trevor carry on oblivious. I know he's a bit of a twat, but this isn't fair. I'm going to tell him. Put him out of his misery before something serious happens.'

Geoff placed a firm hand on Curt's shoulder and conveyed another vital nugget of information into his ear.

'It's not quite as simple as that, Curt me old mate.'

The evident concern in Curt's demeanour was touching, yet slightly misguided at this point. His confusion was also now matching his compassion.

'What do you mean? Not as simple? Trev's hitting on some bloke's bird, for fuck's sake. He's gonna get pummelled. I can't pretend I don't know, can I? He needs yanking out of it. And quick!'

Paul stepped closer and supplied yet another important piece of information to the rapidly expanding conundrum.

'The thing is, Curt...he and Trev have already had words! Pretty friendly ones, though. That guy with Gary and Ian practically told Trevor

145

to take his missus to the bar and ply her with booze. And I'm not making this up, either. We all heard it. So, you see...everything's seems cool at the moment. Very weird, yes. But all is pretty cool, nevertheless.'

Curt rankled with the bewildering situation as his brain strived to register the possible implications.

A partial conclusion presented itself.

'So...Trev's being set up for a threesome, then?'

Paul laughed out loud and clapped his hands together.

'Well done, Sherlock. Very clever of you. Took your fucking time, though!'

Curt felt mildly embarrassed at his evident naivety in such untypical social matters.

'Oh...right...so...I suppose...I'd better leave well alone then?'

'Yes...you bloody well had!' smirked Paul. 'Cos if you ruin all Trev's hard work now...it will be *you* getting a bang on the nose! From *Trev*! Now...do you get it?'

Curt nodded meekly and decided to signal the waitress to replenish the beers at their table. As the trio re-joined Gary and Ian for a welcome sit down, they scanned the immediate vicinity for the male stranger with the long blonde hair.

'Where's your new mate gone, Gaz?' asked Paul.

Gary looked at the three in mild bemusement as he lifted a full glass of lager from the table.

'What mate? Who you mean?'

Geoff was next to try and extract some information.

'You know...the one Palmer's gonna end up clashing heads with in bed later. The bloke whose bird he's been slobbering over for the past hour.'

Both Lockley brothers burst into fits of laughter as Ian supplied a fitting analysis to the bemusing recent encounters.

'I tell you what, lads. That situation is fucking freaky. I've done some shit in my time...but this! Her fella's acting like he's our best mate whilst his woman is over there with her hand practically down Palmer's pants. Don't know what the fucking crack is! I don't think I *want* to know, either!'

*****

146

With Andre the singer taking a brief hiatus in his performance, the noise descended to a more sensible level as the jukebox offered a more low-key backdrop.

Quaffing the dregs of another glass of beer, Curt noticed Trevor and his newly acquired attractive companion begin to move their way slowly through the tightly massed crowd toward the group's reserved table.

The Lockley brothers simply sniggered and nudged one another as Trevor approached, with Paul quickly adopting the role of chief communicator.

'How's things then, Trev? There's a couple of beers here for you, mate. You're a bit behind with your supping. Having a good night, I see?'

Trevor slumped heavily onto a bar stool as the woman instantly nestled herself seductively between his knees and draped an arm around his shoulder. He grasped a drink from the table and swallowed half of it before belching loudly.

'My night...is...abso-fucking-lutely brilliant...so far, Paul! How are you guys going on?' slurred Trevor, before placing his forehead on the woman's shoulder and allowing his free hand to openly rest on her buttocks.

'I'd say nowhere near as good as yours...for obvious reasons.' commented Gary, desperately trying to conceal his amusement.

The female stranger joined in with the immediate laughter, fully aware that all eyes in the group were on her ample charms.

Then Curt noticed the approach of her supposed boyfriend who, also with drink in hand, placed himself at the table without any hesitation and spoke in near perfect English through a wide, gleaming smile.

'Hello, guys!' he nodded eagerly.

In dubious disbelief, those in the vicinity nodded before stuttering various civil responses. The man with the long blond hair flashed another winning grin and introduced himself.

'My name is Fabio.'

He then reached over and softly placed a hand on the girl's cheek.

'And this...is Maria!'

Again, the unexpected nature of his actions and undiluted bravado caused a slight pause in the conversation before Paul revealed the names of those in closest proximity.

Having observed Trevor's fingers now wandering freely in and out of his lady companion's top, Gary eventually took the ultimate honour and asked the question that lay on the tip of everybody's tongue.

'We're pleased to meet you both. Is...erm...Maria...is erm…she...your wife...by any chance?'

The man laughed out loud causing his neatly trimmed goatee beard to widen and long fair mane to sway back and forth.

'My wife? Maria? Oh no! No! No! No!'

'Oh...' surmised Ian from across the table. His curiosity now inflamed, he probed again. '...is she...perhaps...your...girlfriend, then?'

Once more the diminutive stranger became consumed by a fit of what appeared to be genuine hysteria before astounding his newfound companions with the stark reality.

'Maria...is my *sister*!'

Curt almost spat his mouthful of beer across the table as he observed Gary and Ian hold their midriffs in barely bridled amusement. The battle to continue the exchange in a cordial manner seemed to last forever, with Paul again attempting to disperse the cloud of acute discomfort that had suddenly descended upon the group.

However, his honourable intentions were belied by the sheer clumsiness of his next statement as he observed Trevor's dribbling mouth nuzzling into the girl's neck.

'Oh good...so...you don't mind...Trev...erm...you know...making a play for her, then?'

The man appeared somewhat puzzled by the phrasing but wasn't given the chance to answer as Trevor's entire right hand disappeared under the girl's bra.

'Bit late for shutting the stable door anyway, now.' chuckled Ian from behind the rim of his glass. 'This horse looks like he's well and truly bolted...'

The stranger confounded the occupants of the table yet again with another confession of exasperating honesty as he pointed to Trevor.

'Oh yes! When we arrived in here Maria very much liked the look of him. I don't discourage her, you see. He seems to be a good man. Very reliable! No trouble. That is what we like, isn't it, Maria. Is it not?'

Maria engaged stares with her fair-haired accomplice and nodded coyly as Trevor continued to rummage clumsily around her cleavage.

Ian stood to his feet and eyed both the woman and man in turn as his suspicions suddenly became aroused. However, he could not resist the chance for a verbal joust.

'Well...I for one don't know what the fuck's going on here...but I can tell you both now that Trevor Palmer is anything but reliable. In fact, I'd say he's nothing but a fat, useless waste of space.'

The laughter that erupted around the table went some way to diffusing the increasingly dubious responses to the episode.

Even the target for Ian's gentle ridicule was giggling, although Trevor was quick to denounce Ian's claims as he let his tongue play around the girl's ear lobe whilst whispering to it.

'Don't listen to him, Maria. He's always calling me names. He loves me, really. He's only jealous!'

And with his stout proclamation, Trevor stood to his feet and promptly escorted the girl back to the bar, leaving his friends in a state of open-mouthed vacancy.

Curt was striving to assess the implication of what was playing out before him. He observed the booze laden features of his companions and watched Trevor's unsteady path back toward the bar.

The blonde-haired stranger calling himself Fabio finished his drink and took out a cigarette, completely un-swayed by the actions of those around him.

However, it became quickly obvious to Curt that the Lockley brothers no longer carried the impression of being overly comfortable with the issue.

An assumption that was about to be confirmed.

Ian leaned toward Gary and issued a tentative warning.

'I don't like this, bro. Trev's well out of it. Keep an eye on the twat, will you? And keep an eye on his so-called girlfriend and her so-called brother. Something's not right here. I smell a big stinking rat.'

SUNDAY

With the now customary accompaniment of vigorous cheering announcing his presence, Andre the singer resumed his position in front of the microphone, adjusted his guitar strap and commenced to strum the chords of his next song intro.

'Thank you everybody for applauding my second set. Which will be starting with this…'

The room suddenly began to pump to the beat once again and the semi-vacant dance floor instantly refilled.

Trevor had remained chatting to the brunette at the bar as her male companion hung around the Lockley party like a limpet. The situation had now ensued for nearly three hours, with the true motives of the two strangers still firmly under wraps, although opinion was slowly building among the Lockley party.

The man danced with Gary and Ian and joined in with the football chants that intermittently broke out around the room.

It was noticeable that although he pretended to sing along to the numbers, he blatantly had little clue as to the actual lyrics.

Everywhere Ian or Gary went, whether to the table, to the bar or to the gents, their newfound acquaintance would be close by.

His uninvited presence earlier in the evening was initially confusing and amusing.

However, it had now developed into becoming overbearing, annoying and downright surreal.

The man acted as though he had been a friend to the Lockleys for years, yet aside from his overly enthusiastic participation on the dance floor, he would not engage in conversation with any of the group regarding the true nature of his business.

The Lockley boys were certainly not accustomed to having their evenings gate-crashed and it didn't take long for the increasing wariness of earlier to manifest itself as outright frustration.

Of course, the intake of alcohol had also naturally contributed to sensitivity levels as the evening ticked by.

'Fuck this!' shouted Ian across the din to his brother. 'These two are fucking mental! This knob-head's getting right on my fucking wick! And Palmer seems to have lost the fucking plot as well! He's pissed as a newt!'

Within seconds the entire Lockley group had reverted to the dance floor, except Curt, who opted instead to overview the continuation of events from his customised wall seat.

Trevor had now opted to join his friends once again and danced intimately with the girl as her blonde-haired male shadow bobbed up and down in the background.

Curt observed the man and woman carefully as they interacted with the hordes of dancers.

However, despite the gathering distrust, it was still the case that nothing untoward seemed to be in evidence as the procession of popular rock songs kept the entire pub on its feet.

As the comparatively most sober member in the party, Curt was still basically able to keep himself partially aware of what was occurring.

With their arms intertwined, Trevor and his lady friend now seemed physically inseparable. They whispered in each other's ears, and each smiled in mutual response as the young performer on stage again addressed his legion of newly discovered fans.

'And now...ladies and gentlemen...it is well after midnight...and my final song of the set...is dedicated to every single one of you...for being the best audience ever...'

The closing track encouraged all to join its slow build-up and familiar rousing finale as the room exploded into a crescendo of appreciation for the singer.

The dance floor displayed its gratitude with earnest shouts for another encore, but alas Andre from Austria declared two and a half hours to be more than plenty and switched off the microphone in pleasured relief.

Curt observed the changing activity around the room, which slowly saw the venue begin to discharge its patrons through the exit door and into the street beyond.

Trevor and his female friend remained at the bar whilst Gary and the rest congregated back at the table to finish their drinks.

Charlie approached the group and thanked each of them with a handshake and a kiss.

'You all have a good night, boys?'

Ian offered the landlord a hug and having already presented him with the final kitty for the evenings drinks, deftly slipped more money into his shirt pocket.

'You are a fucking superstar, Charlie! A fucking superstar, you are!'

'Next time you in Prague...you come visit me...yes? You all come back to L'Osvaldo's very soon!'

The earnest gratitude and goodbyes were in healthy abundance as Gary maintained a careful eye on proceedings by the door.

The man with the long blonde hair was now chatting to both Trevor and the woman.

The discussion seemed civil enough to begin with.

However, it was obvious there was now something amiss.

Judging by his body language and facial expression, Trevor was in the midst of a disagreement and Gary was not about to let matters grow beyond retraction.

'Ian...now...come on! Follow me! This might be trouble.'

The Lockley brothers flanked the trio near the exit as Curt, Geoff and Paul followed closely behind. Curt's felt his heart pounding through his chest as the anticipation for altercation flowed through his body.

Confrontation had not been on the agenda, but Ian Lockley was irrefutably drunk and subsequently now angry at the apparent arrogance and rudeness of the two strangers.

He forcefully interrupted the trio's argument much to the evident chagrin of the mysterious couple.

'Is there a problem here, Trev?'

The obvious aggression in Trevor's features was fortified by his rasping if slurred tone and an accusatory forefinger.

'This bloke here...says I can't take Maria to another pub! Says I've got to go where he wants to go. Says he's sticking around! Won't leave us alone! Reckons he's a bit of a hard nut as well!'

Ian gestured to Gary, who ushered the others outside to avoid a plethora of witnesses to the imminent fracas.

Luckily, most occupants of the inn had swiftly dispersed.

With all eight concerned with the matter at hand now reconvened outside the building, the two strangers persisted in remaining with the Lockley group.

Ian issued an order for Geoff to lead them all out of sight.

'Where do you want us to go?'

'Fucking anywhere but around *here*...just walk to somewhere it's a bit secluded. A bit off the beaten track. I don't think we're going to shake these twats off too easily. Talking nicely to them doesn't seem to work.'

In single file, the group marched away from the frontage of L'Osvaldos and toward a series of cobbled archways.

The rain had begun to fall quite heavily and as he walked, Curt noticed the stones underfoot had become slippery and polished due to the persistent soaking.

Ian purposely walked next to Trevor in an attempt to calm him down and put him in the picture as to the web into which he had nearly been ensnared.

'Look, Trev...mate...I know you're well pissed but listen. They just want your money. She doesn't want you. They aren't your friends. They've been plying you for cash all night. They're just waiting for the chance to pounce.'

Trevor Palmer carried the sullen look of a man being denied something that he supposed was rightfully his.

His response hardly suggested obedience as he turned on Ian in the middle of the street.

'What do you fucking know about it, eh? Fuck all! That's what! Just leave Maria and me alone, will you? I don't need any help from any of you!'

Under cover of shadow, Gary joined his brother's side in attempting to convince Trevor of the disappointing and unsavoury facts.

'If we let you go with them now...anything could happen. If we weren't here with you now, they would probably be planning to rob you around the next bend. Or worse. You could end up anywhere!'

Despite the best intentions of the Lockley boys, Trevor was remaining reluctant to agree.

'Nah...she wouldn't do that...not Maria...she's special...'

Ian now began to lose all sympathy with Trevor and the issue.

'Right...fucking listen up Palmer...one question...I'm not fucking around with this bullshit all night. Do you want rid of them, or shall we leave you to it?'

Trevor stopped his laboured stride as an expression of hopelessness befell his face. He looked briefly through the semi-darkness at Curt, whose own features had glazed over in sincere concern for his colleague's state of mind and the potential predicament they were attempting to retrieve him from.

He gazed in turn to stare at the evidently impatient man and woman who stood a few yards away in the rain.

The strangers that had plagued him and his friends for most of the evening.

Thankfully, despite the drink that had severely infiltrated Trevor's train of thought, he finally saw the deceit in their eyes.

Facing his true allies once again, he didn't need to affirm his wishes with words.

He slowly nodded to Ian, who quickly initiated the next part of the plan.

'Right...Geoff...take Trevor's arm and get him the fuck away from here. We'll deal with these two arseholes.'

On seeing their quarry disappear into the darkness forever, the man and woman began to protest in a completely different language to that which they had spoken all evening.

They then attempted to follow the group that was escorting their lost prize.

It was a move that triggered the inevitable response from the Lockley brothers.

Gary stepped across to obstruct their path, which instantly led to the female offering an impolite shove through his midriff.

The man with the long blonde hair then became forceful, brushing his way past Gary, almost knocking him over into the swilling gutter.

It was Ian's thumb and forefinger which brought a rapid and decisive halt to the brief attempt at pursuit.

Clamped firmly around the male stranger's windpipe, the action easily disabled him, and he was drawn back into the amber-hued murk and slammed heavily against a moss-covered wall.

Ian drew his face closer to the evidently angered foe, as the woman stood by defenceless, now watching without protest as Ian dispersed the problem with a hissed warning with his brother standing guard as cover.

'Now then...Fabio...me old mate...we have a saying back in good old England. It says...sling your fucking hook...before I rip your fucking balls off and eat them in front of you.'

The stranger squirmed limply in Ian's grasp, which duly tightened to quell any further attempt at rebellion.

He then muttered something indecipherable in a foreign tongue and received a slap around the face for doing so, as Ian completed his sermon.

'Go and find another daft prick to suck the life out of...cos you aint doing it to any of my friends. Is that clear...Fabio...my old mate? Good! Now do one! And take your fucking slapper with you! Before I *really* lose my temper!'

Vanquished, the would-be thieves obligingly merged back into the shadows from whence they came.

As Gary accompanied his brother to reunite with the others, both ended up convulsed by a relieved amusement at the thought of what had just transpired.

Curt was the first to express his gratitude on seeing the Lockley brothers approaching. The unrequested obstacle to the evening had been removed relatively quickly, with Ian offering the gang a briefing as to the remedy just administered.

'You won't be seeing them again, lads. I've just taught them about a couple of Nottingham rules and regulations. Come on. Don't let it spoil the night. It's nightclub time! Over there, look! Let's try and enjoy ourselves again! Just a lull in proceedings...that's all!'

With the group now firmly united once more, Trevor murmured his gradual appreciation of Ian's involvement. Curt listened to the distorted words of thanks as pink and green neon reflected randomly among the puddles on the pavement.

There was no queue outside the venue and the six-strong party were surprisingly admitted without an entrance charge.

It was no small relief to Curt that the strangers had been dealt with. He entered the club and hung his damp hoody on the back of a stool.

With a certain peace of mind restored among the group, the drinks were ordered promptly.

It was presumed by all that the fun and frolics could resume once again.

And that the recent flirtation with risk was now a closed chapter.

TWENTY-FIVE

The six sank their drinks as they stood quietly at the bar. Curt's mind and body quickly re-adjusted to the now much preferable and familiar mode of considerably happy drunkenness. As he glanced around him in the partially lit interior of the nightclub lounge, he felt part of an invincible collection of beings.

Super-heroes from the U.K.; almost.

Untouchable; untamed; unmatched.

They had come to Prague as curious visitors.

And would soon depart as self-appointed conquerors.

This land was now theirs to behold and rightfully claim.

And even though Saturday evening had crawled relatively unnoticed into the early reaches of Sunday morning, the group still felt zestful, undiscovered and fresh.

'Where's all this fucking foreign fanny I've been hearing so much about, then?' demanded Trevor, as he sidled up beside Curt and pointed at the numerous vacant red leather seats dotted around the edge of the room.

Curt chuckled at his colleague's slurring commentary.

'Don't you think you've seen enough female company for one night?'

'He's right though, Curt. It's like a fucking graveyard in here!' affirmed Geoff.

Gary felt it his duty to enquire as to the location of the other patrons and clumsily leaned over the counter to ask the attendant.

'Ayup, my mate...where is everyone tonight? Have they gone home already?'

The young barman smiled and gestured with a thumb which he inverted towards the ground.

'What's that supposed to mean?' chipped Ian, as he mirrored his brother's slouched posture to hear the barman answer in pidgin English.

'You wanting to dance...yes? Downstairs, gentlemen...in the basement discotheque!'

Ian turned to the rest of the group and announced the plan.

'Come you lot! Off we go! The women are all hiding downstairs, apparently!'

There was little in the way of protest from the others, with Curt opting to move his hoody on to a hook by the entrance as he followed last of all.

'Don't let me forget my top when we leave, lads.'

Descending a narrow metal staircase at the back of the room led them to a closed door, which was evidently well soundproofed due to the inviting din that discharged once it was swung open.

Curt tailed Ian toward the smaller bar in the corner of the disco and asked about the worrying altercation of earlier.

'What did you do to get rid of them two weirdos, then?' Curt asked, genuinely intrigued.

Ian turned to him with a stern expression.

His eyes did not wander from Curt's as he partially disclosed the truth.

'A little move I learned in the army that never, ever fails. Let 'em think they're going to die, and they'll do anything you ask. Now...cheer up, Curt! It's ancient history. Here's a tequila slammer to salute the future. Neck that...stop being a wimp...and get mingling.'

Curt obliged the friendly commandment and eagerly emptied his shot glass in one gulp. The pounding room was almost in darkness aside a persistent set of coloured strobe lights that flickered incessantly to the infecting pump of the dance track.

One by one, the group gradually went their separate ways to varying corners of the dance floor. Curt himself rapidly finished his pint and suddenly feeling fancy-free he began to immerse into the music. Without any hesitation he commenced a very loose attempt at his long dormant yet most-favoured dance moves.

The booze intake was now at a point where Curt barely noticed the other occupants of the club. His head was blissfully light and his limbs seemingly beyond his own control as he shimmied and slid his way around the floor to the rhythm of the deck-mixers.

Flitting efficiently between shadow and light, Curt was briefly re-acquainted with Paul, whose own badly co-ordinated endeavours to impress the female revellers in proximity caused immense amusement for them both.

Curt spun around again, noticing between the strobes the very low corrugated arch ceiling; a fact that only encouraged his inclination to keel over at any given second.

Many of those around him seemed quite young in comparison.

Indeed, as he squinted through the nebula of purple and green dry ice, nobody looked to be much over the age of twenty-years-old.

Another blast of fake smoke introduced a new track with a much faster bass beat.

His body rotated loosely in irregular time to the tune as his conscience floated contentedly away into infinity.

All around him similar figures threw their own individual shapes and formed similar poses as the abiding spell of the place gradually consumed one and all.

Curt Osbourne was swiftly enveloped by a very real and renewed sensation of liberty.

This was a good feeling, indeed.

This was a welcome surge of adrenalin that he felt he had probably needed for a long time.

And he embraced its inducing flush as the music became even more up-tempo and the atmosphere ever more intoxicating.

Curt felt un-typically wild and supremely confident.

He began to actively wallow in the attentions of those sitting around the edge of the dance floor on their virtually invisible benches, as once again he himself cast a keen eye on the surrounding observers.

Groups of young smokers and drinkers; all sampling the same high-fixing mood that washed over, around and through him at that very moment.

Every single second brought him closer to a rampant state of euphoria.

This was surely the weekend away that he had craved.

Nothing could surpass his irresistible empowerment in that moment.

And then, he saw her.

Her deep, wide-eyed, and indulging glare, engaging directly with his through the haze of smoke and shadows.

Her alluring half-smile suggesting everything; and yet revealed nothing.

Curt recognised her.

It was the same girl he had seen at the beginning of the evening in another forgotten place from the very recent past.

That black, clinging dress.

The plunging neckline; the tantalising glimpse of bare chest.

The jet-black hair; cut into a tight bob style.

There she was; staring right into Curt through the ever-shifting swathes of buffering young energy.

And after absorbing her for a few heavenly seconds, Curt then turned away, his mind's reflexes suddenly responding accordingly.

Perhaps, in partial embarrassment.

161

Yet certainly in instinctive excitement.

His eyes focused anywhere but where she was against the wall.

He looked down to the darkened floor, and then upward to the flashing ceiling.

Through the alluring, coloured mists; into the blinding lights.

Reacting to every flicker cast by every dancer.

He resisted temptation for second after tormenting second.

But was he tormenting her or tormenting himself? He was not sure.

He dared not become enticed any further by this beautiful and mysterious creature.

Yet his inner will was striving to prove victorious.

Succumbing to primitive desire, he quickly beckoned himself to face her once again.

And now totally immersed in inherent male weakness, Curt did indeed turn again; and did indeed look; and did indeed prepare to embrace her vision.

His heart thumped wildly as his legs struggled to retain a semblance of fluidity.

Building himself up to the sublime moment of mutual and glorious acknowledgement, the anticipation was beyond anything he had ever known.

And as he slowly altered position to fall under her incredulous scrutiny once more, the shameful truth crashed down all around him.

Despite stern hope and wasted seconds of wishing, the girl had vanished.

Gone from her seat.

Gone from the moment.

Gone from the recesses of his wildest imagination.

Gone.

As Curt instantly wrestled with stupid, immature, futile remorse, he suddenly sensed hands on his hips.

She had approached him from behind and moved enticingly close.

Now fuelled by the full knowledge that she had decided to make the move on him, Curt's last strands of inner restraint dissolved completely.

Quickly engaging her in the sparkling, sultry atmosphere of that throbbing basement, he lost himself in the devouring attentions of the gorgeous stranger. She continued to smile, yet said nothing, simply letting her body talk for her as they began to move naturally as one.

Demanding him with her dark crystal glare, Curt felt bold enough to lower his hands to her buttocks and pull her gently into his now raging groin. Her lithe, slim figure fitted his to perfection.

She resisted nothing he dared to chance.

Pressing her warm pelvis into his; her pert bosom into his torso; they writhed to the music as though they might be the only dancers left on Earth.

Still the beat persisted; still she accepted his every physical wish and whim.

Curt's palms lightly cupped her breasts. He could feel her lean, taut flesh under the thin material of her sumptuous, barely existent dress.

Surely no more than twenty-five years of age, the woman continued to hypnotise him with her jet pools of eyes as her fingers wandered down and rested on his bulging crotch; and yet still she did not flinch or retract.

On realising the extent of his arousal, the girl's smile simply broadened.

A good few inches shorter than Curt, she buried her tiny form ever closer and let herself become lost as she gazed up into him.

Still not a single word had been exchanged, as their bodies melted seamlessly into one.

Curt was master of all he surveyed at that moment.

He was now the self-appointed King of Prague.

There was no competition; no other man could match him.

There was merely himself; alone with this goddess that had entranced him so.

And then she drew away, as yet another even more imploring dance beat thudded through the room.

More smoke; more flashes; more dancers; more shadows.

And then she gestured to him with a slightly curled forefinger tipped in dark nail varnish.

Her command for him to follow was his to obey.

And obey her he instinctively did as he helplessly joined her at the bar.

The girl offered him a drink from a small glass, which Curt eagerly sampled by finishing in one.

Then she moved away once again.

Avidly pursuing her across the room through the swaying mass of bodies, he watched as she retrieved her tiny handbag and jacket from the sofa in the corner.

Then he suspected she may have conversed with somebody else in the vicinity, but the vision was awkward and confusing.

Suspicions were quickly confirmed. He watched as she stood talking to another figure in the blurred mid-distance.

Or was Curt imagining this exchange?

A tall and slender man.

Older than Curt and proudly sporting a mop of curly hair; with a rucksack slung over his shoulder.

And as Curt attempted to register the unfolding scene, the man briefly glanced toward him before nodding and duly vanishing from sight.

As Curt pondered the brief episode, the girl approached him, still smirking seductively.

Now becoming relentlessly dizzy with expectation and the detrimental effect of far too much alcohol, Curt allowed her to take his hand and escort him through the exit to the stairwell, where instead of heading back up to the lounge bar, they descended yet another flight of stairs which had been concealed through another door.

Floating on his agonising yet tempting presumptions, Curt timidly followed his stunning companion step by step as the music gradually dimmed and the ineffectual light became gradually further eclipsed by darkness.

His vision was now definitely becoming blurred; his train of thought and bodily coordination slowly venturing beyond his control.

Then through another door they walked.

From the darkness of inside; to the darkness of outside.

To fresh air, and into the realm of supreme adventure that the night was surely about to bring forth.

He did not sense the rain.

He did not sense the danger.

Alone in that secluded alcove at the rear of the nightclub, Curt found himself so yearning for her to turn back into him, so he might explore her form even further.

He admired her silky silhouette as she remained facing in the opposite direction, stroking her own body's slender outline as though to purposefully tease him.

Then slowly but surely, the moment came.

She spun around on her heel as her unreadable expression suggested something undefined; an indeterminable wish.

Curt could withstand the distance between them no longer and readily submitted to his physical cravings. And despite the increasingly confusing messages within his brain, he resolutely opted to take the initiative.

He had decided.

Now was his time.

There and then, she would belong to him.

And during that very split second of wondrous, fantastical, unstable premise, the Devil himself struck out to abruptly retract the chance of pending glory.

An unseen monster that had been lurking in the shadows.

An ambush; no less.

The claiming of drugged prey; innocent and oblivious to the silent jeopardy that had surrounded him.

Curt Osbourne, on the very threshold of his wildest experience, was unwittingly now a sitting target for stealthy opponents.

A heavy blow to the back of the head sent his lean tall frame reeling defencelessly to the floor.

And as he lay sprawled on the concrete, his right cheekbone taking the recoil of his fall, he was deemed completely vulnerable and at the mercy of the undetected assailant.

And with the unpredictable hands of fate now assessing his immediate future, Curt's friends upstairs in the nightclub had not even begun to question his absence and potential whereabouts.

Indeed, nobody in the building was aware of what had transpired during the last twenty seconds.

Presuming that each companion would likely be coming to no harm, those same five friends upstairs continued with their evening in blissful, drunken ignorance.

And in similar, blissful, drunken, drugged ignorance, Curt Osbourne was about to enter a chapter of his life that would serve to haunt him for the remainder of his days.

TWENTY-SIX

'God I'm so pissed!' declared Geoff as he sprawled over the urinal trench with one hand against the wall by his head and the other hand tending to business.

Next to Geoff was Ian, who shuffled along the trench before issuing a giggling reply.

'Fucking great though, ain't it? This is what we came out here for, man! Come on...it's my round. I think...'

Both emerged from the toilet block simultaneously and struggled to locate the remainder of their group through the haze-filled room. The occupants of the nightclub had begun to reduce slightly, but the place remained adequately vibrant and interesting.

'What time is it?' enquired Trevor as he joined them at the bar.

Geoff squinted at his wristwatch.

'Christ! It's ten to three, mate. What you having to drink?'

Trevor's gaze wandered around the murky interior of the room as he studiously considered the question.

'Erm...just another pint, I think. Cheers. Hey...anyone seen Curtis for a while? I can't even recall talking to him since we came down here.'

On observing their respective brothers securing another round, it didn't take much prompting for Gary and Paul to appear from the smoke-filled depths of the dance floor to claim their beverage.

Ian took their orders and put his arm around Gary.

'So, big bro...have you had a good weekend so far, or what?'

Gary playfully kissed his younger sibling on the side of the head.

'Brilliant, little brother. Fucking brilliant! I think we're all glad we came...aren't we, lads? Prague's magic! Fucking magic! Can't fault it!'

In a joint display of agreement, glasses were raised aloft in a salute to the imminent fortieth birthday boy.

Yet surprisingly it was Trevor who reinforced the issue regarding the notable absence of the sixth member of their party.

'Where the fuck's Curtis? You seen him on your travels, Gaz?'

Quaffing deeply, Gary shook his head whilst barely controlling a mouthful of ale.

'Not for a while. Mind you...he was immersing himself in some fit bird just after we got in here. Bet the lucky bastard got off with her.'

Trevor did not miss the opportunity to make a jibe, albeit with a pang of sincerity.

'Well, I don't think so. Curtis doesn't do things like that. He's probably asleep on the toilet knowing that lightweight!'

The group laughed heartily as they quickly downed their latest round.

'All this boogieing is making me bloody thirsty! Same again, boys?' declared Paul.

Gary placed his glass on the counter and checked his mobile phone.

'Well...I reckon its time me and my brother went and got ourselves another dirty woman each. What d'ya think, our Ian? You up for a bit of female company?'

Ian hung his arm loosely over Gary's shoulder and whispered into his ear.

'That's the best idea I've heard since the last time you suggested it! What about it, Geoffrey? One last shag for England, my dear friend?'

Geoff glanced at the persuasive vision of Trevor who was yawning across the bar.

'To be honest, Gaz...I think I'm going to sit this one out. I'm bushed! Ready for my pit...like fat man over there by the look of it.'

Ian announced the next part of his personal schedule to the group as the pumping music began to die down a little and the dry ice began to clear.

'Right...me and our kid are just going to see what erotic delights the night can unleash on us. We'll see you all back at the apartments, then. You all got your swipe cards? If not...it's a kip on that hard marble floor. And it is fucking hard as well! My back hasn't recovered from last night yet!'

Gary tugged on Ian's shirt to encourage their exit from the club.

'Right...come on, bro...enough talking...let's get laid. You lot can look for Curt. Though its sounds to me like he might not want to be found at this moment in time if he hit it off with some tart. See you all later.'

When Curt regained semi-consciousness, his ribs, face, and neck ached with a pain like nothing he'd ever felt before. His eyelids idly attempted to clear his vision, yet all they could decipher was a stirring blackness.

Surrounding his head, he sensed a flowing, rhythmical motion; a non-human form that appeared to have a life all of its own.

His skull pounded relentlessly, as though fit to crack under the most extreme pressure.

Then as the next thought gradually followed on from its bewildering predecessor, Curt began to realise an overwhelming sensation of constraint.

Bound and gagged.

Unable to move his arms or hands, which had been roped firmly behind his back.

Instinctively he tried to inhale deeply, yet his mouth was crammed with a soiled, vile-tasting cloth.

He then attempted to move his legs, yet his ankles were also strapped together.

It couldn't have been the case, yet the confounding truth became quickly apparent.

He was upside down. His feet attached to a length of winch cable.

The startling facts fitted starkly with a frightening absence of logic.

Yet that must have been why his head pounded with the force of his congregating blood.

That must have been why his sinuses burned in desperation for clear, clean oxygen.

And why the scene around him ebbed and flowed with a sickly, intangible, unfathomable force.

A semblance of possibility encroached. With the effects of the drug that he had unwittingly swallowed slowly diminishing, his position became all too clear.

Suspended above the River Vltava, Curt Osbourne was the central attraction in something sinister.

He thought he heard voices.

Four; maybe five people were in proximity.

Males and females.

Then he thought he detected the creaking of machinery.

Then he heard nothing, as without warning, his entire head became submerged in the freezing, turgid waters.

With his nostrils accepting the invasive influx into his lungs, Curt felt himself beginning to drown.

No energy to resist.

No voice to scream.

No time to pray.

And then he was retrieved to just above the surface.

His throat convulsing; his eyes bulging; his chest exploding.

The only thoughts he could muster at that moment were that of his friends.

Where were his friends?

What had occurred to separate the group?

Why was this happening to him?

And then, he was underneath the surface again.

Writhing; suffocating; screaming silently; weeping; dying.

This time the sufferance endured for much longer.

Twenty seconds; thirty seconds; of total breathlessness.

And then, welcome relief was administered once more as he was hoisted clear.

The voices laughed at him; discussed him and cursed him.

They jibed; derided and pitied.

They enjoyed; they celebrated.

But most of all, unbeknown to their hapless, helpless victim, they hated.

They hated with a blood-thirsty vengeance.

They had been waiting for the quarry to enter their lair.

And now they would finalise their mission as Curt was lowered into the depths for the third, decisive and final time.

And the victim could do nothing in response.

Except wait for the ultimate relief that death would bring.

And as he did so, Curt's mind raced with visions from history's palette.

His wife; his children; his home.

His work; his garden; his car.

His mother; his father, his childhood.

Every memory that had been stored for four decades was duly unravelled and paraded as a grim prelude to his passing.

And slowly but surely, that agonising yet emancipating moment of passage came ever closer.

Curt's form became limp; his mind and body now having surrendered to the inevitable.

And then, at the very final juncture of absolutely no return, he was salvaged.

With no explanation or warning, he was liberated from his shackles.

Still unsighted and without voice, Curt was then transported through the night.

And on the unforeseen moment of eventual, very deliberate release, the perpetrators were gone from the scene as furtively as they had entered.

Gone from Curt's life in the same manner they had arrived.

Without witness; without motive.

Gone; without trace.

TWENTY-EIGHT

Geoff, Trevor and Paul had all but given up on their search for Curt. The nightclub was now almost empty and had disclosed no obvious sign of their friend.

'What about asking the barman?' suggested Paul as they bemusedly trudged back upstairs.

The bar attendant had not seen Curt leave the club but did remember that his hoody was still hanging on a hook in the foyer.

'Well...we'll take that. Thanks for your help, boss.' murmured Trevor, as he checked the jacket pockets. 'There's nothing in here. He must have just forgotten it. Come on, boys. Let's go.'

The damp air hit the trio as they ambled slowly from the premises and into the street. Without any recognition of their immediate whereabouts, the three wandered aimlessly until they realised they had entered the main square.

Trevor noticed the astronomical clock in the short distance.

'Fuck me, Paul! It's nearly five in the morning! It won't be worth going to fucking bed at this rate!'

On through the square and towards the river, all three instantly noticed a pair of silhouettes loitering across the road from the bridge entrance.

It soon became obvious that the subjects of interest were female and that they were attired in very revealing outfits that presented little if any challenge to the imagination.

On detecting the approach of the three men the women began to walk directly towards them, waving and smiling as if reacquainting with old friends.

'Ayup, lads...' stuttered Trevor under his breath. '...these two look up for a good time. Seems like our luck might be in after all!'

Paul and Geoff exchanged knowing glances as Trevor opted to openly confront the ladies with a boisterous gesture of greeting.

'Hello, girlies! What are you two doing out this time in the morning? Looking for some fun by any chance?'

Both women were equally attractive and evidently held little reservation in reacting to Trevor's encouragement. He wallowed in their attention as they tried to converse with him in some vague foreign tongue.

It became quickly apparent to Paul that they were prostitutes touting for work, yet Trevor seemed oblivious to the fact as he stood between the pair, grinning with an arm now draped around each.

'I think I'm in here with this pair, boys! Don't wait up!'

It was high time for the bubble to be unceremoniously burst.

'They're hookers you dozy twat!' cried Paul from the amber shadows.

Trevor looked in astonishment at the source of the claim.

'Don't be fucking stupid! They're way too good looking to be whores. I mean...just look at the figure on this one!'

Now it was Geoff's turn to try and impart some hard truth onto proceedings.

'Well, she won't make much bloody money looking like the back end of a tram, will she? Come on Trev, for fuck's sake. Leave them be. I'm knackered and we've a long walk back.'

Having discussed the situation with his newfound companions, the subject of money suddenly arose.

With a subsequent grunt of mild disgust, Trevor removed his arms from around the ladies' shoulders and slowly but surely ambled back towards his waiting friends.

'You were right, you know! And here's me thinking I'd cracked it. Fucking typical.'

'Not had much success tonight, have you Trev?' chuckled Geoff.

With his second crushing mistake of the evening admitted, Trevor began to make for the bridge entrance.

'Where the fuck do you think you're going now?' enquired Paul.

Trevor stopped in the middle of the road and held his arms open.

'The apartments, of course! Where do you think I'm going?'

'Well, they aren't on *that* side of the river, are they!' snapped Geoff.

'Of course, they are!'

Paul shook his head as Trevor turned away once again and strode toward the bridge.

'How pissed are you? You mean to tell me that you can't even remember where our digs are?'

'Look, boys...you do as you like. But I'm telling you they're over here.'

Now more than tired with the tedious display, Geoff began to walk away in the other direction as he made a casual suggestion.

'Leave the knob-head to it. Come on, Paul. I'm falling asleep standing up, here! I need my pit.'

The pair deserted Trevor at the bridge and began to make their way back along the main road that flanked the river.

'You can't tell him anything, Geoff. He knows it all does Trev Palmer.'

After a couple of minutes had elapsed Paul took a curious glance over his shoulder to see that Trevor was indeed now following them some fifty yards further back.

'Ayup...I think he's changed his mind.'

Geoff looked at his companion and spat his vote of sarcasm into the darkness.

'Oh good...I'm so fucking relieved, Paul! You don't know how worried I would have been if he'd disappeared into the night without a trace and was never seen again!'

The two chuckled at Trevor's bold ignorance as the violet flood lamps of the apartment block became barely visible in the far distance.

'Not far now.' sighed Paul, with the chill breeze of night suddenly cutting into him, as it gradually escorted the three back to base camp.

TWENTY-NINE

Another twenty minutes had elapsed before the three finally ascended the stone steps of the accommodation complex.

'Thank fuck for that! These bastard shoes! I thought I'd brought two pairs! I'm chucking 'em when I get home!' winced Trevor as he approached the top step.

Paul pulled open the main doors of the foyer for his friends and smiled as Trevor wearily brushed past.

'Bet you're glad you didn't follow your own instincts to cross the bridge, eh Trev? You'd have been traipsing back up the bleeding cathedral spire if you'd have had your way! Then again, you might have even bumped into your boyfriend again, too!'

'Probably the real reason he went that way. He's bound to get some good luck at some point.' giggled Geoff as he entered the building last of all.

Trevor was singularly unimpressed with the commentary.

'Yeah, yeah, yeah! Okay...so I get things wrong occasionally. Even the best aren't perfect, you know!'

The weary trio staggered up the flight of the marble staircase to the first-floor landing.

'Anyone got a swipe card to get in?' asked Paul.

'Yeah...reckon I have somewhere.' replied Geoff, half-heartedly rummaging in his pockets.

As they climbed the secondary flight, a sight emerged before them that caused all three to halt their progress in genuine surprise.

Trevor was the first to comment on the wholly unexpected vision that awaited them outside the door of room twelve.

'Fuck me, boys! Look who it isn't! Captain Shagger himself!'

'So, this is where he ended up!' concurred Geoff.

'Look at the fucking state of him! Looks like his night ended up better than the rest of us put together! concluded Paul.

Curt lay outside the locked door tightly curled up in the foetal position.

Apparently asleep, he heard the sound of voices but did not register the familiar tone of his friends talking as they stood around his hunched, shivering form.

Trevor crouched down and gently shoved Curt's right shoulder; an action that caused aggressive pain to instantly shoot through Curt's arm.

Paul and Geoff then joined the pair down on their haunches as the latter attempted to wake Curt up with a firm command.

'Come on, mate! It's time for bed. You look like you need it as well.'

Paul made closer observation of Curt's wan features.

'Do you reckon he's alright? Looks a bit pale, the lad does. His hair is wet through. It hasn't rained that bad, has it?'

Trevor rose back up to his full height and duly opened the door to their room.

'You'd look fucking pale if you'd drunk as much as Curtis has. I wonder if he ever got off with that bird after all. Crafty sod! Never thought he had it in him.'

Curt stirred as he attempted to conceal his immense physical discomfort from the trio.

The earnest assistance from his friends was welcome, if woefully belated.

Yet in their misguided concerns to lift him to his feet, the three simply encouraged further agonised reaction which Curt quickly masked with a loud yet feigned cough.

Paul glanced across the floor a few feet from where Curt had lain.

One of the address cards supplied by the travel agency was by the top step and he stooped to retrieve it.

'Looks like he got a taxi back, anyway. Shame he forgot his swipe key. He could have been in the land of nod by now! Lucky we were behind him or he'd have had a fucking stiff back in the morning!'

On eventually helping Curt through the door, Geoff left them to it and returned to enter the comparative sanctity of room eleven.

Successfully positioning their beleaguered companion fully clothed under the duvet, Trevor and Paul retired to bed themselves not suspecting for one second the unspeakable nightmare their friend had endured in the previous hours.

With silence quickly falling on both rooms, it was a time for temporary peace.

A time for all to sleep.

A time for all to rest.

Aside that is from Curt Osbourne, for whom peace was now a relic of the very recent past.

THIRTY

Curt was mentally jolted from his painfully shallow and fitful slumber. Drenched from head to toe in perspiration, he quickly began to shiver as the sharp late morning air enveloped his aching form.

As he lay in the supposed security of the apartment, the indelible calling card of unknown demons soon began to plague his conscience.

His eyes felt swollen and sore; his throat raw and chafed.

He gingerly touched his lower ribs under the bedclothes. The pain was excruciating when he attempted to inflate his lungs.

His neck was stiff and unyielding to even the slightest varied movement. His right cheek throbbed relentlessly.

Acid churned within his stomach as his gut convulsed unpredictably with each passing second.

It was already clear to him that these were not symptoms of any typical hangover.

At least, nothing resembling the hangovers Curt had ever previously experienced.

He dared to peer through the half-light of the bedroom interior. The encroaching winter sunshine pierced his eyelids, causing him to squeeze them tightly shut once again. With his nose and ears blocked as though under the strain of a heavy cold, Curt had never felt so utterly dreadful in his entire life.

Nestling his head back into the pillow, he thought he detected muffled voices through the closed door.

A conversation.

Then laughter.

Then silence.

Then the repeat of the same cycle.

Ascertaining the source of the mysterious dialogues, Curt raised his head once more and attempted to pull himself clear of the bedclothes. Drawing what he surmised felt like the strength of three men, he finally positioned himself to the edge of the mattress.

His mind then began to toil with the delirious events of several hours earlier. Yet his uncooperative brain would not compute with its own memory file.

Curt searched the past for a recognisable foothold, yet it was as though a vital paragraph in a story had suddenly been withdrawn without explanation, leaving the reader desperate for all important information.

He had been through some kind of physical mangle; that much was glaringly obvious.

Yet he retained absolutely no idea as to where he had been to sustain such injuries or indeed the potential administrators that he may have encountered.

He pushed his memory further back into the history of the previous evening. There was precious little recollection regarding those he had liaised with, or the locations visited.

Or indeed, how he had managed to return to the apartment block without so much as recalling entering the building and failing to gain entry to the room.

The effort to remember was proving to be far too much of a strain at that moment. Deciding to deal with more imminent matters, he pulled and pushed himself to his feet and quietly shuffled toward the bedroom door.

Through the wall in the adjacent room, the now slightly familiar voices continued their jovial exchange.

It was the sound of his friends.

He recognised Trevor; he recognised Paul.

There were others present, too.

Gary and his brother Ian.

And the other member of the party, Geoff, who determinedly asked if anyone wanted to go out for breakfast.

This was now the appropriate time to make himself known.

Curt twisted the brass knob and quietly made his entrance.

The sound of conversation ended abruptly, soon to be followed by a highly audible chorus of cheers and shouts.

Hollers of mocking celebration at the belated sighting of the sixth and final member of the group bombarded Curt as he made his unsteady way into the arena.

'Fuck me, Curtis...' sighed Trevor. '...so *that* is what death looks like!'

Curt tried to smile his pain away as the others voted in fond agreement.

Gary laughed out loud as he ventured the inevitable question.

'That black haired bit of totty in there with you, then?'

Curt did not even begin to understand Gary's statement as he slowly reclined against the windowsill to face them all. The sunshine felt good on his back and shoulders as he responded wearily to the ever-enthusiastic inquisition.

'Eh? What do you mean...black-haired...what...which black-haired bird?'

Ian attempted to present some clarity to the evident and genuine lapse in Curt's data banks.

'Come on, mate. No point denying it. You were all over each other. Where did you both end up, anyway? She was bloody tasty, though! You copped lucky there. Can't blame you, mate. Well worth a length!'

'You're a dark horse, Curtis! Never thought you had it in you! Good lad!' teased Gary as he checked his wristwatch.

Aside his immense discomfort, Curt was now also feeling utterly confused to say the very least.

Letting them play out their empty charade, he simply said nothing and allowed the warm morning sun to enshroud him further.

Gary opted to lead the party from the front as per the norm.

'Look lads...now droopy drawers is finally awake we can all get our shit together and fuck off out of here? Its nearly midday and I could kill for something to eat. We can go and drop our bags off and find a boozer. What do you say?'

Ian rose to his feet and moved toward Curt before draping an arm across his shoulder.

'I'm up for that! It's Arsenal and Man United at four. Should see us through until it's time to leave. What about you, Curt? Up for some bacon and eggs, lad?'

Curt again tried to focus on the five friends strewn in various poses around the lounge area. His eyesight had barely adjusted since emerging from the bedclothes. However, the unrelenting desire to try and make sense of even the immediate moment was once again far too strenuous.

'Yeah...breakfast...whatever you say. But I think I need a shower first. What happened after we left that pub, anyway?'

Trevor looked at his friend in earnest disbelief.

'Which particular pub do you mean? There were about ten during the day.'

Curt scratched his forehead and tried to think back.

'The last one...the busy one...with the singer...'

Now Geoff attempted to place the missing pieces into Curt's equation.

'That wasn't the last one! Can't you remember? We left there at kicking out time. That's when Ian and Gary sorted out that fucking oddball couple who wouldn't leave us alone.'

Curt slowly shook his head, which only served to remind him of the thunderous aching in his skull.

'What couple?'

Trevor continued to reassemble the picture for his troubled companion.

'Fuck me. You weren't *that* drunk, Curtis? It was raining...we went to a nightclub...you got off with that bird...you left your jacket behind as well so we grabbed it.'

Curt suddenly recalled one tiny aspect of Trevor's story.

'My jacket...what do you mean...my hoody? I left it behind? I can't remember leaving it. Didn't I come home with you lot, then?'

'Sorry mate. You vanished. We spent nearly two hours looking for you before we found you back here. You were outside on the landing. Can't you remember anything at all?' confirmed Paul.

Gently rubbing his ultra-sensitised eyes, Curt again conceded defeat to his currently unreliable powers of recollection.

'No. Christ alive...I must have been in a right mess.'

'Yeah...' implored Gary. '...you *were*...but all in the name of fun. Doesn't matter now, anyway. You're here. Come on...get yourself sorted. We need food.'

Curt hauled himself away from the windowsill and quietly winced as he did so.

'Okay guys. I definitely need a clean-up, though. I'll be fifteen minutes.'

THIRTY-ONE

The soothing cascade initially felt fierce against his tender skin yet infinitely liberating. Curt stood motionless under the spray of hot water as he attempted to coax his senses back to barely minor responsiveness.

The nauseous sensation of earlier had diminished slightly, yet he did not feel anything resembling normal, much as though he were a snake that had recently shed its skin and was still acquainting himself with the new one.

Curt's skull was still thudding although with partially less resonance as he reached for the shower gel and began to smear suds over his feebly upright form. Brushing the soap across his body, he again received acute pangs of rebellion from his ribcage.

His neck and face also felt badly bruised, yet he could identify no obvious signature of trauma as he inspected his upper body after stepping unsteadily from the shower cubicle.

Similarly, the rest of his anatomy appeared unblemished, yet it pulsed with the tell-tale signs of some evidently harsh encounter with a far more ferocious form than his own.

Back in the bedroom he chose the clothes he would wear for the remainder of the day and packed the remainder of his laundry and belongings.

'Ready, mate?' inquired Trevor, peering around the bedroom door.

Curt bolted with surprise, not expecting the friendly intruder.

'Yeah...yeah...I'll be one minute. Then I'm with you.'

Curt retrieved his mobile phone and passport from the bedside drawer. Inserting the latter into his now dried hoody pocket, he quickly checked the former for text messages.

There was indeed a new addition to the inbox, which immediately encouraged him to open it as his heart raced with anticipation. He smiled at the content whilst distinct waves of unease pricked at his conscience.

SO GLAD ITS SUNDAY.
MISSED U
LOOKING FWD TO 2NITE.
LUV HAYLEY AND GIRLS
XXX

How Curt longed for home in that cherished moment of welcome familiarity.

A moment soon to be obliterated by more pressing matters as Trevor re-appeared and reinforced his earlier demand.

'Oi...Curtis...will you fucking come on...it's nearly one o'clock! We're all starving!'

*****

The six breakfasted in the same establishment as the previous day. There were no complaints regarding the detail of the menu this time. Everybody around the table was grateful to devour whatever they could consume to quell their alcohol-ravaged stomach linings.

Curt capably concealed his persistent discomfort as he ate and then ambled steadily along the river back to the apartment complex. The others walked some way in front as they excitedly discussed the next stage of proceedings.

No one gave a second thought to the ailing figure that lingered a few paces behind, almost feeling sick with the disorientation and the instantly regrettable intake of food.

Still he said nothing as they convened outside the rooms on the landing with their luggage. Gary took the honour in supervising the final checks.

'Right. Everybody got passports?'

The childish giggles eventually conveyed a united agreement.

'Luggage? Everybody checked for leftovers in their rooms?'

Again, the vocal affirmation arose amid the immature backdrop of laughter.

'Curtis...you kicked that black-haired piece out of your bed yet?' guffawed Trevor.

Despite the typical teasing, the intended butt of the joke barely heard his name mentioned, let alone the jibe that accompanied it.

'Eh...sorry...what did you say, Trev?'

'Doesn't matter.' interrupted Gary. 'Right...give us your swipe cards. There should be four in all, shouldn't there?'

The door passes were promptly handed back along with the information cards that were handed out by the taxi drivers on arrival. Gary offered a sarcastic quip as he picked his suitcase off the floor.

'Christ almighty...this has to be a first! What good little boys you all are! No lost property whatsoever! I'm absolutely, overwhelmingly, and fucking genuinely amazed! Right...kiss this place goodbye. Let's try and find this fucking agency office. Goes without saying I'm leading the search? Thought so!'

*****

The initially unwelcome trudge through the sunlit outskirts of Prague was proving a relatively pleasant experience for most.

As they silently tugged their suitcases and holdalls through the near deserted back streets, Curt happily placed himself at the rear of the group once more.

However, despite being resident in the area for the better part of two days, he now viewed the environment as incredibly daunting.

An inexplicable and increasing feeling of vulnerability washed over him, causing him to nervously scrutinise every shadow, corner, nook and cranny of every street and junction that the group navigated.

And whilst Curt was not physically alone, his subconscious had suddenly rendered him completely isolated. Almost as a little boy who had lost his mother in a crowd, crying out for some source of comforting respite from the threatening vicinity.

His mindset was totally erratic, yet it was concise and unyielding as he battled vainly against the unjust and perturbing anxieties.

For once he was inwardly thankful for the distracting voices of complaint and derision that accompanied the walk.

'Where is this fucking office supposed to be then, Gaz?' groaned Trevor as the group encountered yet another junction. 'These fucking shoes are getting binned when I'm home! Got blisters like fucking ping-pong balls I have!'

'Shut up about your fucking feet, Palmer!' grumbled Ian in reply.

Gary did not respond as he headed the group, eagerly studying the small map on the back of the information card.

Curt observed the disjointed stride of his companions as he struggled to keep up. Ironically on truthful reflection, it had been a very successful weekend tainted only by the deep and mysterious blackness that had engulfed the previous hours.

The shooting muscular spasms in his arms and legs indicated to him he had perhaps suffered a fall of some kind, yet it was adamantly clear that his friends could shed little light on the subject and certainly none of the other five had detected his currently debilitated predicament.

Then a pleasant thought appeared on his horizon which went some way to lighten the low-hanging midday winter sun.

Home beckoned imminently; his family were not far away now.

And despite having enjoyed the seemingly eternal trail of pubs and booze, Curt adjudged the fatigue to have finally beaten him and maybe that was the source of his current struggle.

It offered him great appeasement to conclude that his wife and children would eventually provide the sanctity he craved.

Curt's pleasant thoughts were suddenly disturbed by a voice from the front as finally Gary declared the travel agency office to be just ahead.

'Well lads...I reckon it's got to be that place across the road. Look...next to the surgery...just like the taxi driver said.'

'Well, I don't see why he couldn't just come and fetch us! Save all this fucking walking about lark! I don't use my legs this much when I'm at *work*, for fuck's sake!'

Curt managed to offer a responsive smirk to Trevor Palmer's continuing remonstrations.

Ian was rather less understanding on the issue.

'Just shut the fuck up with your moaning, Palmer! You're like an old woman at times!'

Gary knocked on the door of the office. The six were quickly greeted from a side entrance by the short balding taxi driver from Friday evening.

'Good afternoons, gentlemen. You are late, yes?'

There was little in the way of a reply as the driver beckoned them inside and suggested they store their luggage in the confines of an outhouse at the rear of the premises.

'Okays...gentlemen...you enjoy staying here in Prague, yes?'

Everybody nodded and murmured in unison as they handed their luggage over to the driver.

'Okays...you all coming back to this office for seven o'clock. Yes? Then we are taking you to airport for flights home. Yes?'

Ian obliged the group with a pertinent query.

'Okay, okay. Can you tell us where the nearest pub is, mate? You know...sport on telly...food ...fit women...the works?'

The short man pointed back over Ian's shoulder.

'Drinkings for you again? Okay. Nearest. Outside office...crossing road...good pub...Irishman's bar...especially for you Englishmen! Yes?'

'That'll do for us thank you very much, pal!' grinned Geoff as he rubbed his hands together in gleeful expectation of the first pint of the day.

'Session number three...here we come, then!' laughed Gary as he led the group back into the street.

The squat balding man followed the group onto the pavement and shouted after them.

'Don't be forgetting gentlemen...seven o'clock...back to here...then we go to airport...okays?'

There was no obvious verbal acknowledgment of the taxi driver's instructions as the six-strong party strode determinedly across the road in order to commence the final chapter in their weekend away.

And as Curt entered the lounge of the Irish themed pub with the rest of his friends, he found himself becoming gradually ever thankful that the conclusion of their foreign venture was now finally in sight.

THIRTY-TWO

The timing of their arrival could not have been better. Having entered the barely occupied *McCluskey's* Bar, the group promptly located themselves up a flight of stairs in the conveniently vacant attic room.

Whilst it was a supreme bonus to discover that they had sole occupancy of the area, the real joy manifested itself at the sight of several large empty leather armchairs awaiting use and they had monopolised singular authority over a large flat-screen television.

'Well boys...' announced Gary as he turned to his merry men. '...do I look after you lot...or fucking *do* I?'

'Absolutely fucking superb, Gareth! Couldn't have planned it better myself! Get that telly on, then!' grinned Ian as he plummeted into the plush black settee positioned against the wall.

'Right...I'll get the first ones in! What we having...as if I need to ask?' enquired Geoff, standing back up and retrieving a crisp Czech Coruna note from his wallet.

'No need for rounds...' interrupted Gary. 'We'll do what we did last night. Should keep the barmaids busy enough, shouldn't it? I'm certain they'll sort us out for a decent tip up front. Six beers to start with is it, lads?'

The cry of united approval abounded around the wooden roof beams of the building as Gary descended the stairs to make the necessary arrangements with the bar staff.

Within a minute he had re-joined the group armed with the television remote controller.

'What did the bar manager say?' asked Paul, expectantly.

Gary grinned as he bemusedly studied the TV remote.

'No problem whatsoever. She's pouring the first tray of lagers as I speak. And she's bringing up a menu as well. And the telly is ours for as long as we want it. Happy days! Eat, drink and fill your boots, gentlemen! This is your living room for the afternoon.'

Whilst extremely grateful for the arena that had been provided, Trevor suddenly hauled himself unannounced from his seat and sported a grimace of fearful uncertainty.

'You alright, Trev?' quizzed Gary as the TV screen flashed into life.

'No! I don't think so! Not at the moment. Thank God the fucking bog's up here! I think my back doors are about to blow open!'

With the statement regarding his impending bowel movement causing not a little amusement around the upper lounge, they all watched with delight as Trevor scampered frantically toward the gents' toilet door which was denoted by a vaguely stylised male symbol etched into a brass wall plaque.

Yanking it open with an undue sense of urgency, Trevor jumped through the doorframe and duly slammed it shut behind him.

'Looks like someone's got themselves a bit of a loose arsehole!' spluttered Ian as he laughed mercilessly at Trevor's impromptu misfortune.

'I'm not surprised! Fat greedy twat!' affirmed Gary. 'He wolfed his breakfast down like he hadn't eaten for a month! Serves him fucking right!'

A blonde-haired young barmaid promptly appeared at the top of the stairway carrying a tray of frothing pint glasses and happily immersed herself in an earnest smattering of applause from the thirsty recipients.

Gary helped her set the tray down on the end table as he expressed appreciation of behalf of all.

'Thank you, my love. What's your name?'

The young girl flashed a brilliant white smile to her captive audience. Her grasp of English was equally impressive.

'My name is Helenka.'

'Well...thanks awfully...Helenka.' smarmed Ian from the sofa.

She smirked at the lazily reclining figure of Gary's brother.

'I will bring your next drinks in...say...half an hour? Is that okay for you?'

'That will be totally perfect! Just like you!' purred Ian, offering her a distinctly lecherous glare as she retreated back to the area downstairs. He didn't hesitate with his verdict.

'I tell you what, boys...the things I could do to that! Right then...whose having Palmer's pint being as he's got the shits? Curt? You want it, mate?'

Sited quietly at the other end of the room, Curt shook his head as he delicately sampled the top of his own drink.

'No thanks Ian, mate. You feel free. I'm pacing myself today. I don't feel too clever either, to be honest.'

'Anybody else? Right? Mine then!'

Ian didn't need asking twice to claim the spare beer, which he forcibly downed in four large gulps before replacing it with his own full glass.

'Right you are then, squires! Here's an old-fashioned toast to my big brother and his forty years on God's earth! Bottoms up!'

*****

Five and a half hours, two entire football matches and ten rounds of sausage baguettes later, the time was nigh for the Lockley party to call an end to their afternoon of leisure.

Gary stood something near upright in front of the television and addressed his sufficiently re-lubricated companions with a definitive slur in his speech.

'Okay gentlemen...it is now ten minutes to seven exactly and I have just called the bar maid up to give us our bill. All contributions are welcome...that includes you Palmer, you tight arse! That's if you can stay away from the shithouse long enough to get your money out?'

Trevor smiled and adjusted position to retrieve his wallet from his back pocket.

'Should be alright, mate. I've had an hour of anal peace up to now. I think the lower decks have finally settled! Better not finish that drink though, had I?'

With the bar tab generously paid off and reluctant goodbyes bid to the eager and compliant staff, the six made their way back across the road to see the two drivers standing impatiently beside their cabs.

The shorter driver commanded them to hurry things along.

'Nearly late again, gentlemen! We must be quick! Cases are here next to your cars! Please check...quickly!'

With overwhelming relief enveloping Curt as he willingly climbed into the rear of his taxi, he smiled at the continuing backdrop of banter between the others who raised puzzlement at the sudden need for speed.

Watching the driver slide in behind the wheel and engage gear, Curt sighed heavily as both cars finally embarked on the route back to the airport.

Gazing beyond the window at the retreating scene of darkness that flashed by, Curt reflected on the past forty-eight hours, knowing full well that despite the jovial mood among the others in the group, his own feelings on the issue were still firmly subdued.

And even as Gary and Ian sat beside him and discussed the not-too distant future and the probability of another visit, Curt himself secretly harboured little wish to return to the streets of Prague ever again.

THIRTY-THREE

Curt digested very little of the journey back to the airport. The surrounding blackness outside and fatigued silence that gradually reigned within the taxicab allowed him a few minutes to settle his thoughts once again on seeing his wife and daughters.

After tipping the drivers for their continued assistance, the check-in process at Prague International was a little more stringent than they had experienced on leaving England, the highlight of which involving Trevor reluctantly having to remove his jewellery, belt, and shoes at the security scanner due to the various brass and gold attachments.

'You safe to take that belt off, Palmer?' mocked Geoff as he stood with the others relishing Trevor's embarrassment.

'Watch that shitter of yours doesn't open up again! You'll stink the airport out! Be a shame as this carpet looks quite new as well!' quipped Ian, as Trevor was eventually allowed by the security guards to re-dress himself and join his friends in the departure lounge.

With an hour to kill before their gate call, the six decided to encamp by a large bay window which overlooked the main runway. There was little to observe beyond the soundproofed glass aside rows of flashing lights and emergency and maintenance activity, soon leaving them bored of waiting and increasingly enthusiastic for the flight home.

Whilst most indulged in a selection of over-priced and bland looking food bought from the airport cafeteria, Curt took the opportunity to amble around the half dozen duty free shops in his search for Hayley's requested perfume.

Having spied a good deal which would just about consume the remainder of his Czech currency, he experienced a surge of inner contentment that he would soon be away from the place and back within the safe confines of home.

He paid for the perfume and regrouped with the others, who were now becoming particularly restless, yet despite his pangs of relief, Curt's mind also toiled intermittently with the ongoing enigma surrounding the previous evening.

The spasms of bodily pain seemed to be getting worse as he continually altered position in his seat whilst observing the plethora of outgoing passengers that ambled slowly past in the hunt for a vacant seat.

Gary noticed his friend's unusual change of mood and shifted chairs to place himself next to Curt.

'You've been quiet today, mate. Still not feeling too well?'

Curt forced a smile as he reservedly compiled a response.

'Yeah...to be honest, Gaz...I'm pretty shattered! Not used to this marathon partying. It's hard work. I feel like I've been run over by a tractor. I'll be glad to get some decent kip tonight. Suppose I must be getting old!'

Gary placed a firm hand on Curt's shoulder, which in itself caused some sharp discomfort along the latter's collar bone.

'You need more practice...that's all!'

'Yeah...you're probably right!'

Gary glanced over to the rest of the party before continuing.

'I just wanted to say, mate...while all these gob-shites aren't listening...I just wanted to say...well...thanks for coming with us this weekend. It's been brilliant. I've loved it! Been a scream.'

Curt again contemplated his reply quickly figuring that, for the most part, he agreed with Gary entirely.

'Yes...I've enjoyed it too, Gaz. Thanks for asking me. It's done me good.'

'Well...we all need a break now and then, don't we, Curt? Some time away from the bullshit to recharge the batteries. I think it's been a great change for everybody. The digs were smart, too. A really good choice. Not too expensive, either. Didn't you think so?'

The ensuing conversation was not particularly difficult for Curt to sustain, yet at that moment his appetite for a return to England far outweighed any wish to extol the dubious virtues of Prague.

'Yeah...nice place, Gaz. Very nice.'

Then, as if on cue, their private exchange was interrupted by the electronic tone of the departure lounge announcer, who requested that all passengers booked on flight five-oh-seven-six make their way to gate number seven as boarding was about to commence.

It was music to Curt's ears as he observed the others suddenly spring from their seats and bemusedly scan the surrounding area for a suitable direction to follow.

Typically, it was Gary who again adopted the role of chief organiser as he looked at the open-mounted vacancy of his travelling companions.

'What a fucking surprise. You lot need me to hold your hands again? What a pleasant change that is. Come on, you lot. This way!'

*****

190

It was near exaltation for Curt to eventually see the ground beneath them peel away and then feel the aircraft soar upward into the night sky.

His inner thoughts offered no solemn goodbye or a fond farewell to the country they were departing.

On the contrary, Curt felt strangely ill at ease as he watched the flickering impression of Prague airport slowly vanish behind them into the past. Again, inhaling deeply to apply some needed composure, he faced front as the captain addressed his passengers through the overhead speakers.

It was proclaimed that the flight had departed ten minutes behind schedule but apparently this would not affect the preordained time of arrival back in England.

Curt's attention hopped around the tops of the heads that occupied the chairs in front in an attempt to identify the rest of his party. They had been separated at the boarding gate and as such could not claim seats together.

The atmosphere inside the plane cabin was in direct contrast to that of the outbound journey. Everybody on board seemed tired and drawn after their weekend's exertions. Indeed, as the plane levelled off at altitude and the crew began to mingle with their duty-free wares, Curt contentedly submitted to the tempting call of slumber.

*****

For over an hour he dozed, allowing him temporary respite from his ever-swirling conscience.

The last thoughts before his immersion into a light sleep concerned the vision of his wife and the fact that home soon beckoned.

Yet unbeknown to Curt as he embraced immense inner joy in leaving Prague behind, the long shadows of his visit were still in tangible attendance.

The unseen ghosts that now stirred within his memory were untamed and restless; ever poised to strike.

Ever ready, to bring the uncertainty of the recent past back to haunt him at their will.

*****

It was a sharp nudge on the shoulder that brought Curt crashing back to reality. Jolted from his uncomfortable posture by a firm set of knuckles, Curt looked up to see Ian looming above him.

'Come on, dopey! We've landed! This plane's going back to Prague! And so are you if you don't get your fucking arse off it!'

Mild bewilderment confronted Curt as he rubbed his eyes and strived to recall where he was at that moment.

Then another familiar voice unfurled from the crowd.

'Had a good sleep, Curtis? Nice of you to join us! You should have plenty of energy for the missus when you get home now then!' laughed Trevor from some way further down the aisle.

Congregating in a very disorderly fashion around the empty baggage carousel, the six mingled wearily with the rest of the impatient travellers battling for the right to get away ahead of everyone else.

Disinterested in proceedings, Curt simply slumped into one of the chairs against the wall and put his head in his hands.

It was nearly fifteen minutes before the first suitcase was paraded before the eager crowd and more than a full half hour had elapsed until all the Lockley party had finally been reunited with their luggage.

Gathering outside the arrivals lounge, the shrill January air cut into them as Gary attempted to gain their attention for a final time.

'Welcome back to England, lads! Right, put your watches back an hour. I've just rung Phil. He's coming for us as we speak. Be about twenty minutes.'

Gary then looked directly at Geoff and Paul shivering in the semi-darkness.

'What are you two doing about getting back home?'

'It's alright...we'll grab a cab from the rank over there. Saves any titting about, doesn't it! Time to say goodbye then, boys!'

As the departing duo shook hands in a fond farewell and the group diminished from six to four, it was a veritable pleasure to observe Phil's seven-seater taxi arrive far sooner than expected.

Prompted by his growing excitement, Curt retrieved his mobile phone from his pocket and sent Hayley a text message to inform her he would be home in half an hour.

With the hour now at twenty past nine, all inside the car harboured the simple united ambition to sink into their own beds and sleep forever.

Little conversation ensued as the taxi weaved its way through the black countryside before the first drop-off allowed Trevor to bid his farewell with a final jest.

'Thanks lads! It's been brilliant! And I think Phil's timing at getting me back home was immaculate as I reckon my back tunnel's about to lower the drawbridge again!'

'See you at the funhouse tomorrow, then!' bellowed Gary through the rear passenger window.

Laughter abounded as the cab duly made for the next stop of the journey.

Curt felt a powerful adrenaline surge as the welcoming features of Leyton Close honed gloriously into view.

Clutching his carrier bag containing the duty-free perfume in one hand and his suitcase in the other, he jumped out onto the pavement and placed his head back through the open car door to again express appreciation for being invited on the trip.

'Just one thing before you shoot off, Curt...'

'What's that then, Ian?'

There was a pause before Ian sniggered in continuation.

'I bet you any money when you're on top of the missus tonight you'll really be thinking about that black-haired piece from the nightclub!'

Whilst causing the Lockley brothers to squirm in hysterics, it was the last comment that Curt wanted to accompany his return home.

Turning away from the taxi with a forced if feeble grin, he watched its red lights merge into the distance before he ambled through the front gate of number thirty-two and past the car.

Hayley pulled open the front door to greet him.

The vision of his wife was sheer bliss for Curt to behold.

To hear her voice was akin to heavenly.

'Hello stranger! Heard the cab pull up just after I found your text! Thought it must be you! Had a good time, love?'

Curt smiled in earnest and entered the hallway.

The aroma of home filled his nostrils as he lowered his luggage to the floor and embraced his wife with more intent and more feeling than he had done in an age.

He smelled her delicate feminine scent and pulled her tightly to him as emotion threatened to break his temporarily buoyant mood. Whispering softly into Hayley's ear felt like ecstasy.

193

'You have no idea how much I've missed you, love. I'm so glad to be back.'

In response, she pulled him into her and returned the sentiment.

'Christ! You're not kidding! I've really missed you as well, love. But there's something I need to know before we get too lovey-dovey!'

Inside, Curt panicked at her statement as blinding thoughts momentarily shattered his re-acquaintance with domestic sanctity. Ian's final passing comment rang in his mind like a tolling bell of doom.

Did she actually suspect in that moment that he may indeed have involved himself with another woman?

Were there giveaway signs on his clothing or on his neck?

He hadn't checked.

Were the rumours regarding the girl with the black hair in the nightclub baring any foundation?

Did this woman even exist?

Could it be that female intuition was indeed as accurate as legend had portrayed?

Curt's heart raced under the intense heat of apparent suspicion.

However, subtly maintaining a calm exterior, he cautiously invited the continuing scrutiny whilst silently crumbling inside.

'What do you mean, darling? What is it that's bothering you?'

Hayley drew away and looked deep into his eyes.

She adopted a straight, unreadable expression and spoke with a cold and untypical sternness.

'You know full well, Curt Osbourne...what we talked about...before you went...on Friday...'

She knew.

She knew that something had happened.

Yet ironically even Curt himself couldn't recall what had happened.

His palms began to clam up as his chest felt ready to burst under the strain of impending conviction.

But he hadn't done anything.

Had he?

'Look, love...I...I didn't...I didn't know...'

Then, just as his empty confession of some completely invented and unrecalled event began to spill from his lips, Hayley smiled slightly yet did not drop her very convincing facade.

'You see, Curt...I need to know...you have to be honest...I really need to know the truth.'

Then she wavered and began to giggle like a child.

Then her laughter resonated from the hallway and up the stairs as she guiltily cradled his face in her palms.

Curt's legs trembled as his features quickly drained of colour.

'Need to know what, love? There's nothing to know! Nothing happened! Honestly! Nothing at all!'

Hayley doubled up in hysteria at the sight of Curt's pleading form.

'Look at your stupid face, Curt Osbourne! Hook, line and sinker! Hook...line and bloody sinker!'

Now mildly embarrassed by the charade, he feigned a partial loss of temper.

'What then?' he blasted. 'What is it you're on about? What exactly do you need to know?'

Retaining an amused composure, Hayley again addressed her husband with an expression of seriousness.

'I need to know...if...you...remembered...my...perfume...'

The sudden release from accusatory shackles was infinitely the most liberating sensation of his life in that moment in the hallway.

Duly handing her the carrier bag as his heart rate slowly returned to normal, Hayley squealed with delight as she eagerly delved for its contents.

Then he watched her expression alter once again as she focused into his gaze once more.

'Curt...I said I wanted apple! You brought me the wrong one!'

Instantly plunged back into his personal well of urgent despair, Curt struggled to recall exactly which fragrance he had purchased.

This was an even bigger potential disaster than the one of ten seconds earlier.

'The wrong one? You are kidding...don't tell me I bought you the red instead of the green?'

Yet again, her unrelenting mirth gave her away as she ended her teasing with a soft kiss on his lips.

'No... it's okay, darling...you got me green...just messing!'

Curt now had little choice but to relax and see the funny side.

'Well *don't* mess with me! It's cruel! Though I can see you've missed having me around to pick on! Are the girls okay?'

Pushing herself close to her husband, she looked up into him and kissed him once again.

'Yes...they're absolutely fine! But they are fast asleep. And anyway, it's *this* particular little girl that needs a bit of attention tonight! In fact, she needs a *lot* of attention.'

'Really, my lady? You truly have missed me, then?'

No further words were necessary.

Switching off the hall light, Hayley took Curt's hand and led him upstairs as the sound of her amusement quickly subsided and a tender reunion ensued.

MONDAY

THIRTY-FOUR

It was not the preferred first sound that Curt wished to hear that morning, yet the shrill scream of the alarm clock accomplished its function admirably.

Curt squirmed under the duvet as he contemplated terminating the incessant whine. Reaching out from under the bedclothes caused the hairs on his forearm to stand on end as the central heating thermostat kicked in and gamely battled to warm the house through.

Temporary silence resumed allowing him to settle his head back into the pillow and perhaps dream it was not the first working day of the week after all.

Physical discomfort had plagued him throughout the past twenty-four hours and had still not subsided despite a night's rest.

Indeed, it had incurred sufficient cause for him to convincingly hide his pain whilst making love to Hayley - a distinctly odd predicament that ably served to dilute his pleasure in the act.

Fortunately, she had not detected his symptoms and despite the unwelcome five-thirty wake-up call she continued to sleep soundly beside him.

Curt observed the bedroom ceiling and contemplated the hours ahead.

He was not relishing the return to the office.

Gary and Trevor would no doubt prompt the subject of Prague within seconds of his arrival through the doors and it was a cast iron guarantee that Curt's supposed exploits would come under further scrutiny in front of other colleagues.

It was a potential scenario that repulsed him, if only for the fact that his memory could still not ably recall any event regarding Saturday evening.

And this was the most frustrating aspect.

The totally blank page.

The absence of knowledge.

The complete, absolute dearth of information.

If he could remember something to be even mildly ashamed of, then perhaps the mental torment he was undergoing would be justified to some extent. Yet the mystery purged his conscience so.

The tenderness of his back and limbs suggested something traumatic may well have taken place, yet his mind insistently refused to surrender any detail.

It was a conundrum that he did not wish to dwell on, yet the shroud of confusion was inescapable.

His thoughts were disturbed as Hayley stirred and snorted something inaudible into her armpit.

Curt gazed lovingly at his wife and spoke in a whisper.

'You alright, love? Do you want a coffee?'

She nodded without word as a smile began to form slowly on her lips. A naked Curt eased himself from the duvet and pulled on a robe. Pushing his feet into a pair of slippers he traipsed wearily downstairs.

Flicking on the radio and kettle in turn, he quickly sensed a presence in the room.

Two presences; to be exact.

He swivelled on the spot to face the visitors standing at the kitchen door, both of whom offered a simultaneous cry of joy.

'DADDY!'

Hannah and Emily bounded toward their father who duly crouched down and lifted them both from the floor in one swooping movement that encouraged a crucifying ache to travel throughout his legs, arms and back.

Grimacing fiercely at the discomfort, Curt then projected smiles and kisses to his two little girls, whose tousled and unkempt bedbug appearance was a welcome addition to breakfast time on any Monday morning.

'How are my two favourite little angels, then?'

'We've missed you, Daddy!' barked young Emily.

'Did you bring us a present back from Prague?' inquired Hannah, bluntly.

'Well...no...I didn't...because...honestly...well there was nothing over there that little girls would like. But I will get you a present tonight if you want?'

Hannah observed her father with certain suspicion before exploring the endless possibilities.

'What kind of present?'

'That's up to you two! We can go to Toys4Ever with Mummy when I finish work if you want. You can pick something nice then!'

Emily was more than contented with the deal that had been laid on the table, yet her elder sister was not so forthcoming with her approval.

'But that shop is for babies! I'm not a baby anymore!'

Curt giggled at the claim as Emily offered her elder sibling a customary scowl in defence of her own wishes.

'Oh...yes...I forgot...you're all grown up now Hannah, aren't you!' he replied as she grinned broadly at the complement.

'Did you have a nice time with your friends, Daddy?'

'Yes, thank you, Hannah. Very nice. I'm very tired though!'

Curt's eldest daughter considered her father's claim with childish honesty.

'Is that because you were drunk all the time?'

He observed the innocence in her eyes and smirked.

'What? Drunk? Me?'

'Yes...Mummy said that's all that you would be doing. Drinking lots of beer and shouting at football on television in pubs.'

Curt lowered his girls back to the kitchen floor as he laughed out loud.

'Oh, did she now? Well...your mummy's a very smart lady isn't she!'

'Why, Daddy...is it true?' interjected Emily.

'It might be, my love! I can't remember! I was too drunk! Anyway...you two are up very early for a school day.'

Emily jumped on the spot and raised her arms, inspiring Curt to lift her back up to his eye level once more.

'We wanted to see you! We were asleep when you came home on the aeroplane last night. Was it exciting on the aeroplane, Daddy?'

'Yes, darling...very exciting! A little bit scary too, though!'

'Will you take us on an aeroplane one day, Daddy?'

'Yes, my love...maybe...one day...'

As the loving conversation transpired, Hayley poked her yawning features around the kitchen door and squinted at the three occupants. Scratching her neck and rubbing her eyes, she yawned once more before unleashing her statement.

'Are you going to stand around talking all morning or do I actually get that coffee in bed that you promised me?'

'Yes...coffee in bed...coming up shortly...you go back upstairs and relax, love.'

'Well, that was the original plan, but it sort of defeats the object a little bit when I have to come down and remind you, doesn't it?'

Still cradling Emily, Curt moved toward his wife and kissed her tenderly.

'Of course, boss! Anything you say, boss! Just conferring with the two people in the house who have actually missed me this weekend! Sorry! Please forgive me! I'm out of practice with the butler role!'

Hayley looked at the girls in turn before offering a suggestion.

'You two go back to bed and put your televisions on. I'll shout you when it's time for breakfast.'

Emily could not help but reveal the plan that had already been discussed for the latter part of the day.

'Daddy says we're going to Toys4Ever when he comes home from work!'

'Oh...did he now? Well, you'd better behave at school today then, hadn't you! Go on both of you! Upstairs please! Let me and Daddy have a bit of quiet for a while before he goes to work.'

The girls gave their father a kiss apiece before scampering back upstairs.

Curt smiled after them before hugging Hayley from behind.

She leaned back into him to whisper into his ear.

'Last night...was very, very nice, sir!'

'Why thank you, madam! And may I say your perfume smells delightful! The scent is apple...if ...I'm not mistaken!'

'You are *not* mistaken, sir! A handsome man bought it for me...I can't quite recall his name...but I'm sure it'll come to me during the day.'

Man and wife giggled, tickled and cuddled as the six o'clock news prevailed over the radio.

'Christ!' muttered Curt. 'I really cannot be bothered with work today! I'd give anything to stop here with you!'

Hayley drew away from his embrace and re-heated the kettle.

'Yes...I bet you would! Anyway...you haven't told me about your weekend. You were that eager to get me into bed last night!'

Curt settled himself at the breakfast bar.

'Oh? I was eager to get *you* into bed, was I? Not really the way I remember it! I seem to recall you dragging me upstairs by the collar! Or did I imagine that bit?'

Hayley chuckled as she pulled two mugs from the cupboard.

'Well...?

'Well, what?'

'Well...how was Prague?'

She could never have guessed how much Curt did not want to divulge her on the subject. It was something he was hoping to put behind him rapidly, but it was also necessary for him to play along with the game for now.

'It was...good. Yes...enjoyable.'

'So? What did you get up to?'

'Well...pubs...obviously...lots of those...watched a few football matches...found a great Irish bar yesterday afternoon! The apartments were very nice, too!'

Hayley finished making their drinks and handed Curt a milky mug of coffee.

'So, you literally spent two days on the piss, then?'

'No! Not at all! How dare you, madam! Believe it or not...three of us went on a bit of a sightseeing expedition. We went around the castle grounds...and up the cathedral spire...nearly three hundred steps to the top as well!'

Hayley displayed a knowing grin, suggesting she didn't quite believe his story.

'You? Curt Osbourne? Looking for a bit of culture?'

'Yes! Me! And Trev Palmer, too! He couldn't get enough history down him! Though he moaned his shoes hurt him after a while!'

'Sounds more like it! Any...erm...you know...?'

Curt furrowed his brow as Hayley teased him with the next stage of her protracted inquiry.

'Any...erm...what, love?'

'You know...any of the boys sample some of the more...shall we say...local delicacies on offer?'

'You mean...like the women?'

'Well done, Sherlock!'

'Before you get any ideas...I definitely did *not*! But yes...the Lockley brothers enjoyed themselves with one or two of the ladies I do believe!'

'Now there's a surprise! The oldest swingers in town, those two!'

'Oh...and apparently Trevor thought he'd pulled a stunner...until the lads told him she was a prostitute! Oh yeah...and he got chatted up by a bloke!'

Hayley burst into a fit of the giggles as she passed Curt his drink.

'What? No! The twat!'

'Yes...funnily enough...that's what we said to him!'

'I take it the prostitute didn't look like your typical street girl, then?'

Now Curt found himself ever-so-slightly on the spot.

'Erm...well, I didn't actually see her, myself. I was tucked up in bed by then. I needed an early night! Think I'd overdone the booze. Too much too soon and all that!'

'Sounds about right for you! You look absolutely bloody knackered!'

High time to alter the subject.

Curt gazed through the kitchen window to observe the wintry scene in the back garden.

'Have we had much snow here since Friday, love?'

'A few flurries. Nothing to get the knickers in a twist about, though. I think the girls were hoping to build a snowman. Fat chance of that! Any way...time's getting on. I'd better make you some lunch for work.'

Curt observed the wall clock.

'Yes...I need a quick shower. I'll just have to get in to work late if traffic's bad. I'm sure the boss will understand! Not! Are you at work today, love?'

'Yeah...ten til two. It should be pretty quiet as well. The supermarket is always dead on Mondays! What do you want in your sandwiches, dear?'

'Oh...anything...not bothered. Right...I'll be in the bathroom if you need me.'

Placing his half-empty mug on the draining board Curt leaned across to Hayley and cheekily nuzzled into her neck as she opened a tin of tuna over the sink.

'You shouldn't do that!' she giggled.

'Do what?'

'That!'

'Why not?'

'Because it does very nice things to me and makes me feel very naughty! That's why!'

Curt laughed out loud as he headed into the hallway.

'Well...I appreciate the offer darling, but I've got to get ready for work! I can't even spare you a quick ten minutes this morning!'

The resonance of Hayley's delighted amusement as he climbed the stairway was a sound Curt relished.

Indeed, home had never felt so good.

THIRTY-FIVE

It proved to be a considerable wrench for Curt to reluctantly climb into the car, reverse off the drive, and pull away from his happy, waving wife and daughters as they wished him farewell from the front door of number thirty-two.

He cruised half-heartedly along Leyton Close and came to a stop at the T-junction, completely unwilling to face a day of predictably tedious ritual at work.

The familiar accompaniments on route were all in place as he clasped the wheel and joined the flow of early rush hour traffic towards the city.

His favourite sounds blasted from the stereo speakers and the tapping sound was still reliably in evidence under the bonnet – perhaps a little more pertinent than usual due to the nigh on three days' rest the car engine had sustained in his absence.

The unfamiliar sensation of muscular bruising also remained present; noticeably in his legs as he intermittently depressed the foot pedals.

He had hoped a shower before leaving home might invigorate him, but instead, Curt simply now felt more fatigued and beaten up than ever.

Despite the atmosphere of domestic contentment experienced just a few minutes earlier, he now found himself to be suffering a distinct change of demeanour as his destination drew ever closer.

The grey skies had begun to release a smattering of rain drops at the beginning of the journey, which had evolved into an all-out freezing downpour by the time he pulled into the premises and located a vacant space in the employee car park.

It was very rare to see colleagues running into the workplace, but the unpredictable weather had deemed such an act to be the only suitable option.

As he walked quickly past the security lodge and on through the glass reception doors to clock in, Curt instantly felt totally ill at ease with the prospect of reconvening with his workmates again.

And still none of it made any sense.

Why he should feel such insecurity in such everyday circumstances remained a complete riddle.

He could normally embrace the workday teasing, playful mockery and crude banter, yet something unspoken kept reminding him about the weekend and the possible unscrupulous acts that now eluded his memory.

And as the doubt continued to curse him, he nevertheless kept reminding himself that such an unlikely scenario could never have endured.

Not involving Curt Osbourne.

Not involving the upstanding family man who loved his wife and children more than anything in the world.

He would never willingly risk the stability of home-life for a few minutes of wanton selfishness.

Would he?

He swiped in at the time and attendance station and duly made his way to the far end of the plant where the warehouse was situated. Curt strode briskly, as if to avoid being spotted along the way and confronted with a thousand and one awkward questions about the rumoured subversive activity he had perhaps been party to in Prague.

Prague.

Fucking Prague.

Fucking bastard Prague.

He wished at that moment of entrance into the warehouse that he had never even heard of the damned place.

The wariness he had adopted proved fully justified as he walked into the first greeting of the working week.

'HEEEEY! SHAGGER'S HERE! HEY, GAZ! LOOK WHAT THE CAT'S DRAGGED IN!'

Curt glanced along the gangway to embrace the vision of Trevor Palmer sitting on his forklift truck casually thumbing a newspaper, sporting an inane smirk of amusement, and proceeding to beep his horn repeatedly to announce his colleague's arrival.

The next unwanted hurdle came in the form of Gary Lockley, who had decided to intercept Curt halfway along the pedestrian footpath that flanked a row of racking.

'How's it going, Curt? Sleep well, mate?'

'Yes, mate. Cheers. You?'

'Like a fucking baby! Missus glad to have you back, was she?'

'Yes...I suppose so.'

'Good lad!'

Curt kept walking to the bottom of the mezzanine office steps in the hope that Gary would become bored quickly.

No such luck.

Fulfilling all expectation, Trevor appeared beside the pair as if by magic and sported his typically mischievous expression.

'I tell you what Curtis! I feel totally fucked! Wish I'd have booked today off! I ache like a bastard everywhere! And my bloody blisters! Struggled to get my fucking safety boots on earlier!'

Curt was alerted to Trevor's innocuous statement which carried more than a strain of pertinence.

'Me too! Don't know why, though! Feel like I've been hanging on the cross for a week!'

Trevor sniggered and exchanged looks with Gary before sounding off.

'Well, it's alright for you, Curtis! You can sit around on your crack all day, can't you! Some of us have got to do some grafting! We can't all laze about chewing pencils and pushing buttons, you know!'

'Yeah...you looked under the cosh when I first walked in!' grinned Curt.

That was more like it. Curt began to ascend the stairway as the gentle jibing continued from Gary who followed him up the steps.

'So...did you get the Spanish inquisition off the missus then, Curt?'

'No need, Gaz. She trusts me. I told her about you and Ian spending all Saturday in the brothels, though. Oh...and about Trev's boyfriend!'

Gary laughed loudly as Trevor scowled up the stairway at Curt.

'Oh yeah...I'd forgotten all about that. You'd better watch your tongue Palmer or that little snippet of information will be all over the factory by break time! I don't think Mister Tansley would show you much mercy...do you?' warned Gary.

Curt observed the sudden flush of embarrassment growing in Trevor's stubbly features. The pair eyed one another, as his colleague attempted to strike back with a proposition.

'Well, alright then Curtis. I'll do you a deal. You don't mention the boyfriend...and I don't mention the black-haired piece in the nightclub. Okay?'

Curt unlocked the office door before leaning back over the safety rail to address his dual audience.

'Yes, mate...no problem. Even though I haven't got a clue what you're going on about! Anyway...that's the rule, isn't it? What goes on tour...stays on tour? Right?'

'Right!' affirmed Trevor, sheepishly.

'Right! Give me half an hour and I'll have some work for you. I should look busy if I were you...Smithy won't be long.'

207

*****

The remainder of the day passed without incident. The loading schedules were busier than of late and as a result Curt was spared any unwanted attention or intrusion into the office due to all warehouse operatives being fully occupied for the duration of the shift for once.

Caroline had arrived at eight o'clock that morning with her usual cheeriness and she expressed particular interest in the humorous issue of Trevor's boyfriend that had been wilfully disclosed by Gary as she navigated the warehouse footpath.

Under her casual scrutiny, Curt opted to remain coy on the matter and managed to convince Caroline that everybody in the party had behaved admirably for the duration of the weekend.

With a few general details of the itinerary having been conveyed, her interest was rapidly sated, and it was back to business as usual.

Lunch time was the part of the day that Curt was most looking forward to as it would give the opportunity to witness Colin Tansley launch one of his famous assaults on the squirming figure of Trevor Palmer.

The reality did not disappoint, with the opening gambit igniting the hysteria.

'Hey, Trevor. Did you manage to find any prostitutes that didn't laugh at the size of your dick?'

Colin's mockery was cruel and relentless for the full thirty minutes, leaving Trevor Palmer's ego tattered and torn and rendering the numerous spectators to the show nursing sore ribs from the incessant entertainment.

Finally, as five o clock approached, the knowledge that he was about to embrace the culmination of the working day was an idyllic sensation for Curt.

He walked quickly to the car park with Caroline and Gary as the harsh winter rains began to fall once more. There was little in the way of verbal exchange as the crude elements battered the trio.

In their bid to escape, it was deemed far too cold and wet for any more serious banter.

Bidding his colleagues a good night brought Curt certain reassurance as he operated the car remote.

Climbing behind the wheel and turning the ignition were similarly heavenly duties as the energising music again pounded throughout the car interior.

At last, his family awaited his return once more.
As did, the shadows of the very recent past.

THIRTY-SIX

Curt felt he must have made the journey home in record time. Less than twenty minutes had elapsed between leaving the car park and pulling to a stop on the driveway of number thirty-two, Leyton Close.

Hayley greeted her husband at the door as she often did and allowed him to locate himself at the kitchen breakfast bar with a newspaper. She dutifully placed a mug of tea in front of him and an un-opened packet of chocolate digestives.

'How was your day, love?' he mumbled as he wrestled with the biscuit wrapper and dunked the first one into his drink.

Hayley was standing by the sink and gazing through the window as sleet tapped against the glass from an ever-blackening backdrop.

'Oh...all right, I suppose. You?'

'Yeah...better than I expected, actually. There was no traffic at all coming home, either! It's not a bank holiday, is it?'

'No, love...not today. You must have caught it lucky.'

There was a pause in conversation before Hayley opted to relay a discovery of earlier.

'By the way...there's been a phone call for you. From the bank. They've left a voice message. It said you have to get in touch with them immediately as it's very urgent.'

Curt was now absorbed in his tabloid read and barely acknowledged his wife's words.

'Really, love? I'll do it tomorrow. Can't be bothered tonight. Are the girls okay?'

'Yes. They're fine! Both looking forward to choosing a present each!'

He threw Hayley a glance which suggested an element of surprise.

'Oh shit, yes! I forgot about that! We'll eat out for tea as well if you like?'

'Yeah! Great! What time?'

Curt looked up at the kitchen wall clock.

'Erm...about half an hour, okay? We'll leave here about half-six? Alright with you?'

Hayley moved toward Curt and kissed him on the cheek.

'Brilliant! I'll go and get the girls ready and re-do my make-up. No doubt they'll both be down to see you once they've realised you're home!'

*****

It was no secret among the family that Curt loved browsing around toy shops.

Especially the largest toy shop in the district.

As Hayley supervised the girls among the various aisles, Curt was temporarily at liberty to fully immerse himself back into childhood.

Robots; super-heroes; action figures.

The infantile fascination for such things had never waned for Curt Osbourne. In fact, he readily declared that perusing through such fantastical worlds was something he appreciated more now as an adult than he ever did as a child some thirty years ago.

He was just about to exercise a practical demonstration of a voice-changer mask when Emily and Hannah came rushing along the aisle towards him, with their choice of gifts clutched tightly in their hands.

'Daddy! Daddy! Look what I've picked! Can I have this? PLEASE?!'

Curt replaced the toy helmet back on the shelf and turned to engage with Emily's ecstatic expression. She was carrying a colourful box that on closer inspection was seen to contain a tiny figurine playset that represented a farmyard scene complete with every animal imaginable.

Hayley followed on close behind adorning a wide grin.

'It'll keep her quiet for days! Cheap at the price as well!'

Hannah was contented to play second fiddle to her younger sister, mainly because her personal choice was twice as expensive. Curt looked slightly puzzled as she held aloft a slip of paper.

'It's for a new console game, Daddy! For my handheld. You have to fetch the game from the counter over there! They swap it for this ticket! See?'

Again, Curt gazed to his wife for approval.

'How much is this little lot going to cost me, then?'

'It's what she wanted, Curt! Don't start moaning about the price. This was your idea! Remember?'

'I haven't said a word, have I?' he giggled.

'No! And don't forget we want burgers and fries after this! We're all very hungry, aren't we girls!'

'YEAH!' they cried in unison, with Hannah leading her parents eagerly to the electronics' collection point.

With two contented children in tow, Curt fetched the console game and accompanied the girls to the first available till as Hayley stood by the exit flicking through a store catalogue in silent amusement.

The cashier swiped in the items and unveiled the final tally.

'That will be sixty-two pounds forty-four please, sir.'

Curt gulped in fearful surprise as he delved into his jeans pocket.

However, the even bigger surprise soon became apparent.

He checked all the compartments of his wallet and then his coat as embarrassment quickly encroached.

Hayley soon noticed the hiatus in progress and wandered across to ascertain the problem.

'What's the matter, love?'

Curt continued with his fruitless, frantic search as he unveiled the mystery.

'It's my card! My debit card! It's not in here! I've got no cash, either! You're going to have to bail me out, darling. I don't believe it! How embarrassing is this?!'

Hannah and Emily looked on as their puzzled expectation gradually began to falter.

'Does this mean we don't get our treats after all? enquired Hannah, evidently on the verge of disappointment.

Hayley was quick to intercept the verging disgruntlement.

'No, my love! Of course, you can have them. But it looks like Mummy's going to be paying! Very shrewd of your father that, isn't it!'

Curt was however genuinely dumbfounded and looked at his wife with a sheepish expression.

'I haven't done this on purpose, you know!'

'No, dear! Of course not! Well, you can pay me back! I'm telling you now! I don't get paid for another fortnight! And you'd better get on the phone when you get home! I bet that's what the bank wanted! I bet someone's found your card and handed it in! You dozy bugger! You should be more careful!'

As Hayley paid for the toys, Curt endeavoured to triple check his wallet as growing frustration began to cloud the moment.

'But I never take it out of my wallet unless I'm at a till paying for something! I mean...there's no point having a debit card just to leave it at home, is there?'

'No, love...whatever you say. Come on, girls. Looks like Mummy's going to be paying for tea as well!'

Now somewhat perturbed by the unprecedented disappearance of his card, Curt dejectedly followed the rest of the family out of the toy store and directly across the car park towards the restaurant.

'Darling...' he muttered whilst trudging behind, somewhat guiltily.

'Yes...darling?' replied Hayley, smiling in feigned disapproval as she held her daughters' free hands.

'...can I have two quarter pounders and a large chips with coke?'

Two little girls and their mother stopped their stride and turned to face the source of the humbly toned request.

They looked at one another in turn before declaring their verdict, which Hayley duly voiced.

'We have decided that if you're not paying then you're not invited to eat with us! You have to go and sit in the car on your own until we've finished!'

On conveying their unsympathetic declaration, the trio of female Osbournes continued onward to the restaurant.

Curt shuffled behind, now helplessly laughing out loud as the cold January air caused everyone to increase their pace.

THIRTY-SEVEN

The central heating offered welcome respite from the seasonal chill as the Osbourne family entered the hallway of number thirty-two. Curt hurriedly locked the front door behind them.

'Crikey it's damned nippy out there! Get that kettle on, love!' he proclaimed whilst attaching the safety chain to the door.

As the girls bounded upstairs to play with their new purchases, Curt was still in the process of removing his coat and shoes when Hayley called through from the lounge.

'The bank's been on the phone again! Same message! You'd better ring back and tell them you've lost your card.'

Curt shook his head as he inserted his feet into his slippers and wandered through into the kitchen.

'I haven't lost it! I just don't know where it is! That's all! I'll have a look upstairs in a minute. Are you making coffee, or shall I open that bottle of white that's in the fridge?'

Hayley joined her husband in the kitchen and lovingly pinched his bottom.

'Why darling...are you trying to get me tipsy by any chance? Wine then, eh?'

Curt smiled without response as he retrieved the bottle from the fridge door, uncorked it and poured most of the contents into two large glasses Hayley had readily pulled from the cabinet.

'Right, then...suppose I'd better ring the bloody bank, hadn't I!'

'I should do it now before you look for your card. I'd say it's for your own benefit, love. They obviously need to talk to you about something important.'

Curt slumped into the sofa and picked the receiver up from its cradle.

'Probably only a bloody call centre! Pains in the arse, they are! And they'd better not charge me for this, either!'

'Oh, stop moaning and get on with it!' giggled Hayley.

'Can you just play me that message again, dear? I need the number.'

Hayley grimaced as she swallowed a mouthful of wine.

'Don't be so bloody lazy! You're sitting right next to the bloody thing!'

'I know, love...but it's technological...and I don't do technology, do I?'

With a sigh of mirthful frustration Hayley depressed the phone memory button and the voice message replayed for them both to hear.

'This is an urgent contact for Mister Curt Osbourne from Bartrees Bank. Please call this number immediately to discuss your account status with one of our staff. Thank you.'

Man and wife looked vacantly at one another.

'Well...that doesn't give much away, does it?' Curt snorted.

'Well, you won't get to know very much by sitting there guessing, will you? Go on, then! I've just pressed the dial button! All you've got to do is talk when someone answers at the other end. You can manage that bit on your own, can't you?'

'Very funny, dear! And I hope they're not trying to sell me life insurance or anything stupid like that! Cos I might just get annoyed!'

'That's a shame...I bet you're worth a fortune dead as well!'

Hayley departed the lounge with a titter and moved back into the kitchen to empty the washing machine.

Curt observed her disappear from the room as strains of bemusement began to etch into the forefront of his mind.

There was little time to ponder the situation however as his concentration was abruptly engaged by the voice at the other end of the line.

'Hello, this is Bartrees Bank Customer Protection Services. Rachel speaking...how may I help you?'

'Oh...hello...this is Mister Curt Osbourne...I have a current account with your bank. You've left me two messages to phone you back urgently. Can you tell me what this is about?'

'One moment please, Mister Osbourne.'

Without being given any concrete clue as to the nature of the imminent business, Curt remained totally puzzled and sampled some more wine as the hiatus endured for several seconds.

Hayley peered at him through the doorway to receive a listless shrug of the shoulders from her husband, whose attention was suddenly drawn back to the phone conversation.

'Yes, Mister Osbourne. Sorry to keep you waiting.'

'No problem.'

'We needed to contact you with regard to your current account. Do you have your ATM debit card to hand at all?'

'No, funnily enough! This is a weird coincidence! I only discovered about an hour ago that I seem to have mislaid it somewhere. Has it been found?'

'So, you don't have it in your possession at all?'

'No...that's what I'm saying. I must have dropped it somewhere. Or it might be at home. I haven't looked properly yet though.'

'Are you currently situated in the United Kingdom, Mister Osbourne?'

'Well...yes. Where do you think I'm calling from?'

'Have you been located abroad at any time at all in the last few months?'

'Well...yes, actually. I just got back from the Czech Republic only last night. Why?'

Hayley had now become more than a little intrigued by the content of Curt's responses and his notable shift of tone. She moved closer to him and crouched at the end of the settee.

She studied the expression on his face which suggested the business at hand was puzzling him at best.

And concerning him at worst.

'Did you have you debit card with you on arrival back in this country, Mister Osbourne?'

'I'm not entirely sure to be honest. I know I took it to Prague with me just in case I needed any more currency changing. Look...what exactly is the problem here?'

'So, you can be absolutely sure that you are not in Romania?'

'Romania? What are you talking about? I just said...I was in Prague only yesterday!'

'And you are definitely not in Poland either at this current time, Mister Osbourne?'

'Right! Listen! Can you start talking some sense, please? I don't understand at all why we are having this conversation!'

Hayley now perched herself next to Curt and depressed the speakerphone button to allow her to listen in to the exchange. She could see that he was quickly becoming impatient and placed a hand on his knee as a gesture for calm.

'I have to tell you that we have enforced a temporary freeze order on your current account, Mister Osbourne.'

'A what? A *freeze* order? Why? Why have you had to do that? I'm not overdrawn, am I?'

216

'No, sir. It is because in the past forty-eight hours your ATM card number has been utilised in attempting to make payments in the Czech Republic, Romania and Poland.'

'You are bloody joking with me...right?'

'Unfortunately, no sir. This is no laughing matter, Mister Osbourne. This is an official security measure to protect both the card holder and card provider. If you are willing to confirm that you have not been in either Romania or Poland today, we can follow our procedure.'

'No! I'm not there and I never bloody have been! I'm here in bloody England in my lounge talking to you!'

'Okay, sir. That's fine. Our procedure is very simple. I need you to either confirm or deny the following series of transactions and locations, Mister Osbourne. Please state either 'yes' if you are responsible for the transaction or 'no' if you are not the person that attempted to make these transactions in these locations during this calendar month.'

A shroud of exasperation had descended over Curt as he exchanged a brief glance of bewildered anger with Hayley.

'Right, okay...go on then.'

'Sunday morning; the tenth of January. One hundred and forty-seven pounds...Lola's Revue Show Bar...Prague.'

Curt's heart began to beat like a bass drum as he registered both the information being conveyed and the understandable instinctive reaction of evolving annoyance in his wife.

'No...not me! Definitely not! No!'

'Sunday morning; again the tenth of January. Two hundred and seventy-four pounds. Orlando's Casino...Prague.'

'No...not me, either!'

'Tuesday afternoon; the fifth. One hundred and eight pounds eleven pence.'

'Yes...I did that one! That was me! That was the weekly shopping.'

'Sunday morning; the tenth. Seventy-five pounds. High Sierra sauna and massage rooms...Prague.'

Curt eyed Hayley's evidently growing fury before stammering his reply.

'N-NO! NOT ME EITHER! JESUS CHRIST! ANY MORE OF THESE?'

'Wednesday; the sixth. Three hundred pounds. Bank ATM.'

'Yes! That was for my currency for Prague. I changed it at the airport on Friday night.'

217

'One more, Mister Osbourne. Monday morning; the eleventh. Vattern's Private Show Stage ...Prague.'

'No! That's definitely not me, either! I have been home since last night, like I just said. Is that it?'

'I believe so Mister Osbourne. I am happy to discount the attempts in the other two countries made today. Thank you. Could you now give me the first four numbers in your date of birth sequence?'

'Erm...yes...erm...one-five-oh-two.'

'The fifteenth of February. That is fine. We have good reason to conclude that your ATM debit card has been stolen and the details have been cloned. The fraudulent holders have attempted to use the physical card in Prague and the details have been scanned for use in other countries.'

'Is that why you asked me about Poland and Romania?'

'That is correct, sir.'

'So...how much money have these bastards taken, then?'

'None, Mister Osbourne. Your funds remain untouched and intact.'

Curt noted the worrying mask of disapproval that Hayley had now adorned as he attempted to decipher the puzzle that had just been conveyed to him.

'So... how did you know to suspend the account?'

'It is our company's security policy to request that all customers inform us if they are taking any of their cards outside of the UK and whether they are going to be utilised or not. As we had received no contact from yourself regarding this, our protection system was immediately alerted simply by the locations of the attempted transactions.'

'So...if I *had* told you I was in Prague beforehand...my account could have been fleeced and there's nothing you could have done?'

'In theory, sir, yes. But it seems the fraudulent holders did not have a correct personal identification number in any case. There was little chance of the funds in your account being touched.'

'So, what happens now?'

'I have just authorised cancellation of your current account ATM debit card. That one is now rendered obsolete. A new card is on order and should be with you within the next five working days. Your PIN number will remain the same.'

'Okay...yeah...fine. So, what do I do?'

'You need do nothing further, Mister Osbourne. Rest assured your account is secure. Do you have any questions regarding the procedure we have just administered?'

'No...not really, I don't suppose. It's just a bit of a shock...that's all. I never used my card in Prague, you see. I don't understand how it could have been cloned or stolen. I hardly had my wallet out of my pocket for two days!'

'It matters not now, sir. The issue has been resolved. On behalf of Bartrees Bank I thank you for your cooperation in this matter.'

'No...thank *you*. Really...thank you. The service has been excellent. You've obviously saved me a few quid. You just caught me by surprise. Sorry if I was a bit narked earlier.'

'Quite alright, Mister Osbourne. Please direct any future queries you may have to your local branch.'

'Yes...thanks...I will...goodbye.'

Curt gently dropped the receiver back into the cradle and stared vacantly at the lounge carpet. Confusion filtered his mind as he tried to recall where and how and when his card may have disappeared.

However, his contemplative silence would not be allowed to reign for long.

'You are quite sure you didn't visit any brothels over the weekend?' asked Hayley, vexation now burning in her eyes as she stood over him with arms folded.

Curt could sense her reaction of distaste and quickly moved to douse any misguided conclusions.

'No! Absolutely positive! You've just listened to it yourself! My fucking card's been nicked!'

Hayley offered a dismissive sneer before the sound of her voice rose audibly.

'Well, the tarts that took your money might have cloned your fucking card! Did you ever think of that when you were putting your fucking trousers back on?'

Curt remained seated as his own voice raised an octave to match his wife's.

'I'm telling you here and now I never went to any places like that! You've got to believe me, Hayley! I swear on the girls lives! It never happened!'

219

He watched as his wife moved quickly toward the lounge door; her eyes moistening and voice now trembling as if she were on the verge of tears.

'You can swear on whose ever life you fucking like! I might just still struggle to think you're telling the truth!'

'Oh, for fuck's sake, Hayley! Grow up and get real!'

With that serving as Curt's final parting shot, the lounge door was duly slammed shut as Hayley stormed upstairs to the bedroom.

His mind now fully acquainted with desperation on several fronts, Curt remained slouched on the settee and finished his drink before grabbing the bottle and emptying its remnants into the glass.

TUESDAY

Curt reached across and illuminated the alarm clock. Its digital display read as 03:17. He had not slept a wink since pulling himself up from the settee and cautiously joining Hayley in bed some two hours earlier.

Still the relentless mystery continued to taunt his memory banks.

The issue with the ATM card had become something of a secondary consideration under the emergence of Hayley's upset. So far as she was concerned, her suspicions were justified, and he dared not to wake her as he slipped under the duvet.

His mind toiled with the events of the recent past and the aching chasm of emptiness in his head became more and more frustrating by the hour. He was feeling on the verge of madness.

Staring upward into the darkness he again attempted to revive Saturday night in his conscience, yet it was pointless; almost as though he had never been in Prague at all such was the fog of nothingness currently surrounding the weekend.

It was some small crumb of comfort to learn that the bank had responded with supreme efficiency to the problem with his account. That particular issue could have cost him dearly.

Yet he still rankled with the fact that despite feeling fully assured about his own integrity, his wife had now sided with ideas to the contrary.

As he pondered and worried by turn in the dead of night, it came as something of a shock to hear her muffled voice through the bedclothes as he silently contested with the dilemma.

'Can't you sleep?' she murmured into the pillow.

'What do you think?' he replied, blankly.

Hayley lifted her head to allow her voice to carry more clearly.

'How do you expect me to react, Curt? The evidence is all there! I don't want to believe it...but what am I supposed to think? I trusted you!'

Curt turned over on to his side and placed a tentative arm around Hayley's midriff. Facing away from him, she continued to convey her worst fears in a trembling whisper.

'I love you, Curt. How can I believe you about anything, now?'

He took the unexpected opportunity to try and bolster his defences.

'Listen to me, Hayley. Those places...where my card was used...it could have been anyone. My details were cloned! You heard the bank say it yourself! I was fast asleep in bed at the hotel when it all happened!

223

I was pick-pocketed. We even saw kids doing it in front of our very eyes! You've got to listen to me!'

A silence ensued before Hayley responded.

'It's too difficult, Curt. I can't get the image out of my head of you being with...well...being with anyone but me!'

He pulled her closer into him; a calm desperation now lacing his voice.

'But I haven't *been* with anyone else, Hayley! I'm totally sure of it! But I am worried. Something's really wrong with my mind. I can't remember Saturday night at all. I can recall the football match we watched at teatime in the pub and then going back for a shower. But nothing else until Sunday. I don't know what's the matter with me. It's like someone's took my memory away.'

Hayley swivelled position to face her husband. He could just about visualise her features in the murk of the bedroom. It was considered inappropriate at that moment to offer her a kiss.

Yet her next words at least suggested a slight shift in mood.

'Look...Curt...okay...just forget it, please. What's done is done. Whatever it was that happened. I don't want to hear any more about fucking Prague. Okay? I just want to forget you ever bloody went.'

A strangely satisfying hiatus preceded his earnest and heartfelt reply as he lay back and resumed his futile study of the ceiling.

'So do I, love. Believe me. So do I...'

*****

The atmosphere remained uneasy at breakfast time although Curt was secretly amazed that Hayley was willing to be even mildly sociable. The girls didn't pick up on the friction that had ensued from the night before and Curt bid them good day as normal before venturing off to work.

On pulling open the car door, he glanced back to the lounge window to see her staring at him through the glass with an unreadable expression. With arms defiantly folded, she looked every inch the disapproving spouse. It was not an image with which Curt was accustomed to seeing.

He offered a casual wave of the hand; her response to which was to immediately disappear from the window altogether.

There was little incentive for hearing music on the morning's journey. The aching in his joints and muscles had eased slightly, yet his increasing mental agony was ably eclipsing everything else on the routine agenda.

Even parking the car at work was achieved with apparently little in the way of concentration. Swiping in at the clock through reception, he dejectedly wandered through the plant acknowledging nothing and nobody as his brain rankled with the search for vital missing pieces.

It was Curt's full intention to avoid any in-depth conversation with the warehouse operatives, yet as per normal, he was veritably ambushed as he made his way to the transport office.

'Hey, Curt...'

'Ayup, Gaz. You okay?'

'Yes, mate. Got an invite here for you and your missus, mate!'

Curt's heart rate suddenly skipped to a rapid beat as he suspiciously eyed the envelope in Gary Lockley's hand.

'Really? What's that for then?'

'My birthday party, you dope! A week on Saturday! I told you about it, didn't I?'

'Erm...yes...I think so.'

'It's at the Red Lion! Everyone's coming. All the lads from Prague will be there. I've tried to put Palmer off, but he insists he can make it!'

Curt giggled at the jest.

'Right! Great! Cheers, Gaz!'

'You'll come, won't you? Bring your little girls along if you want. There'll be other kids there. There's one of them play barns round the back of the pub, now. They'll be sorted for the night! It's all properly supervised! Free grub, too!'

Curt cautiously took the envelope from Gary's grasp. His legs felt like jelly as he began to mount the steps to the office.

'Erm...yeah...thanks. We'll be there...of course we will.'

'Good lad. See you later.'

It was an unpleasant sensation, yet at that precise moment as he navigated the stairs, Curt Osbourne wished he had never ever met Gary Lockley and wished he worked anywhere but in that warehouse.

Unsurprisingly, his somewhat glum demeanour did not go unnoticed as a friend's concern carried up the stairwell after him.

'Oi...Curt...'

It was emotionally painful for the object of address to even turn around and acknowledge Gary's call, but the game of civility had to be played.

'Yes, Gaz?'

'You alright, mate? You don't look with it today, at all!'

Curt considered umpteen replies to the statement as he gripped the handrail.

In the end, he opted for the most convenient response.

'Yeah...I'm fine, Gaz. Thanks. I'll sort you guys some work out as soon as I'm set up. Just need a drink. That's all.'

The remainder of the working week saw Curt Osbourne reeling in a state of almost nauseous and angered agitation.

Relations with Hayley had retained the unwelcome under-current, although things were becoming increasingly amicable. It was more the thought of possibility that purged her mind with doubt, as opposed to the bemusing reality of the situation that her husband now found himself immersed in.

It was Friday afternoon when he returned home from work to be confronted with a sudden downturn in her approach. He entered the hallway to find her busily tugging the vacuum cleaner through from the lounge.

Dropping the suction tube, she cast a disparaging glance in his direction and kicked the machine into silence with her right foot.

Curt took a deep breath before forcing a smile and a first word.

'Hello, love. You okay?'

Hayley simply nodded without offering any greeting.

'There's a letter for you on the kitchen worktop. Reckon it's from the bank. And take your work boots to the outhouse, will you? I'm trying to clean up!'

'Right...cheers. No problem, love.'

Sidling past his wife without testing the potential chance of a welcome home kiss, Curt entered the kitchen and picked up the white envelope adorning his name and address.

For what felt like the thousandth time in the past few days, his mind transferred back in history to the previous weekend.

The plaguing, gnawing uncertainty.

The baseless denials.

The lingering and eternal quest for the facts.

Had he dreamed the whole thing?

Yet in his hand he held irrefutable evidence that something had indeed occurred and that someone had indeed decided to cause interruptive havoc with his contented and happy life.

He pulled the new ATM card from the letter, promptly signed it and slipped it into his wallet. The remaining correspondence went into the bin once registered, almost as if Curt was symbolically banishing any further reminder of the event.

He heard the vacuum cleaner roar back into life at the top of the stairs. It was time to broach the party invitation with his wife.

For most of the week he had deferred consulting with Hayley about Gary's official birthday celebration, yet somehow the time now seemed right despite the evident renewal in hostility.

He trudged wearily up the staircase to locate her.

She was in Emily's bedroom, rearranging teddy bears and DVDs to clear a path of access for the hoover.

Standing behind her as she crouched on all fours, Curt opted to switch off the contraption himself with his foot, which caused her to immediately stand upright and swivel on the spot.

'What did you do that for?'

Before speaking, he looked deeply into her eyes which now displayed raw evidence of real hurting.

He wanted to hold her and make the recent days disappear from her mind, yet instead he retrieved Gary's invitation from his back pocket where it had remained since Tuesday morning.

'What's that?' Hayley enquired, as the small cream-coloured envelope was waved under her nose.

'Read it. It's for the family. It's from Gary.'

With an expression of confused curiosity befalling her features, Hayley ripped open the seal and cast her eyes across the hand-written wording.

Curt held his breath as she deliberated upon her verdict.

'Yeah...okay...fine. The girls will enjoy that. A week tomorrow! Look forward to it! Thank him for me.'

Curt exhaled with overpowering relief and searched for something even slightly potent and positive to say, yet instead he verged on the side of incredibly sensible and mundane.

'Do you...erm...want me to make you a coffee, love?'

Hayley tapped the hoover activation switch with her toe inviting the contraption to recommence its din. In answer to her husband's offer of a drink, she simply smiled and presented a thumbs-up.

For that moment as Curt retreated downstairs and into the kitchen to oblige with the task, a miniscule yet most welcome injection of optimism fuelled his veins.

As he filled the kettle and switched it on at the wall, the fleeting thought occurred that perhaps normality was about to make its return to number thirty-two, Leyton Close, after all.

*****

With over a week having elapsed since his return home, Curt continued in vain to both analyse every aspect of the time in Prague and then by turn attempt to obliterate the trip from his brain altogether.

Yet an unexpected development had come to prominence. His sleep pattern had become disturbed by deeply sinister and unfounded visions. He awoke on both Saturday and Sunday during the early hours, drenched in perspiration, staring into the darkness of the bedroom, and silently clamouring for help.

Unseen demons chased him into the recesses of his imagination and tormented him for most of his waking hours.

He had briefly discussed the matter with Hayley, and she had been sympathetic to a degree but did not let the issue of her husband's growing insomnia bother her unduly.

During the daytime both at work and home Curt would be caught in the belief he could hear voices at his shoulder, yet the words they spoke were indecipherable and meaningless.

He felt as though he was being watched by unseen observers, as if something terrible was about to be unleashed upon his form.

As if a conspiracy were about to unfold and envelope him.

Echoing messages would reverberate around his head as he drove the car to and from work, leaving him grasping for any partial connection to reality.

Paranoia had quickly become his constant companion.

It came as something of a surprise to discover that the workplace had become a temporary refuge from the elusive presence that had begun to shadow him. Giving the option serious consideration, Curt had decided not to raise the subject of his distress with either Gary or Trevor.

Justifiably wary of ridicule from his peers, he preferred to keep them in ignorance and investigate the problem for himself.

As a bonus to temper his festering insecurity, the attempts by his workmates to stir up the memories of Prague had all but faded for good. The trip quickly seemed something of a distant event and Curt did not wish to ignite the dying embers with any mention of his personal struggle.

Having harboured severe reservations regarding dealing with his psychological battle, his fears quickly proved themselves to be well founded.

Indeed, it was the little everyday things that were becoming increasingly difficult for him to confront.

A visit to the bank's cash point to test his new debit card had fuelled him with a jolting attack of nerves. The sensation of vulnerability was uncanny and completely unsettling.

He felt eyes all around him as he waited his turn by the hole in the wall. The woman using the machine before him offered Curt a curious parting glance and half smile before retrieving her card and cash.

Curt felt oppressive trepidation as he moved forward to make his transaction. Yet it soon became clear that the source of his disharmony was merely another customer standing by politely awaiting his own turn.

Curt quickly eyed the elderly man with suspicion and hunched over the keypad, being overly prudent as he punched in his PIN number. His gaze switched intermittently from the display screen to the waiting customer behind, as though the stranger was about to unleash his wrath and pounce.

It was satisfying to see that the card worked and after ordering a mini statement it was confirmed that his finances all seemed in order.

Furtively replacing the card back into his wallet felt like some futile gesture of victory.

Yet to whom the gesture may have been directed remained a complete riddle.

The recent unrest with Hayley had not helped his mindset regarding the domestic scenario. Even sitting in the lounge with the girls to watch television had proved to be a task requiring an unwarranted amount of courage.

It was a ridiculous situation for a loving father and husband to find himself in and the entire week had left him feeling empty, exhausted, and restless.

Yet he was also finding himself to be increasingly scared.

Scared of the known; perhaps scared of the unknown.

However, as the dawn of a new weekend began to rinse the skies of early Saturday morning, Curt endeavoured to approach matters with a confident frame of mind.

The day's itinerary would hopefully relax his mood.

Food shopping with Hayley was on the agenda in the morning, before taking Hannah and Emily to the local swimming baths in the afternoon.

It was also the date of Gary Lockley's birthday party.

With such a positive agenda planned, it now seemed to him high time to exorcise the unwarranted presence of ghosts and make assured steps to leave the past well and truly behind.

FORTY

Curt, Hayley and the girls had opted to walk to the Red Lion public house. The early evening air carried a milder feel than of late, but it was a refreshing change for the family to walk anywhere together considering recent events.

Despite best efforts to calm his stirring demeanour in the previous hours, Curt found himself squeezing Hayley's hand as the trepidation inside him began to loom ever more potent with every step toward their destination.

The Red Lion was situated just over a mile from Leyton Close.

Hannah and Emily skipped off in front with their minds firmly attuned to the prospect of two or three hours immersed in the promised joys of a child's play-barn.

Content that his daughters would be more than happily occupied for the evening, Curt felt free to concentrate his energies on maintaining his wife's currently fragile contentment.

'This is nice.' Curt commented as his lightly frosted breath billowed upward.

To his pleasant surprise, Hayley's response was immediate and gentle in tone.

'Yes. I can't remember the last time we even held hands in public, let alone went anywhere together without the car!'

Hayley continued the dialogue, having seemingly recovered from the unnecessary upset caused a few days earlier.

'Have you ever been to this pub before?'

He thought about the question for a few moments, pondering the answer with some consideration.

'Don't think so, no. Not since we've been married, anyway. You?'

'Never.' came Hayley's adamant confirmation before she became distracted by events in front. 'Hannah...Emily...don't run too far ahead! Come back here with us! It's too dark for your dad and me to play and hide and seek. Are you listening to me?'

Both daughters ignored the call of their mother and continued to scamper into the distant amber-hued murk of the street that stretched away as far as the eye could see.

'GIRLS!' reinforced Curt. 'Do as your mother asks, please! Come back here!'

Having recognised the rather sterner vocal of their father, the game was suddenly up, with two junior silhouettes stopping their stride and patiently awaiting their parents amid a streetlamp's orange pool.

As they crossed the road, Curt eyed the swinging coat of arms that denoted the location of the party venue. His heart began to race, and his hands became clammy. It was an unfounded reaction and only served to confirm to him that since returning from Prague his entire disposition had altered radically.

Despite still having little memory of that fateful and mysterious Saturday evening of two weeks ago, Curt had subsequently been subject to a shroud of unsubstantiated fear.

A deep-rooted mistrust of his surroundings had manifested very rapidly, rendering him with a sensation of persistent exposure.

His night sweats had continued, yet the frightening visions that continued to plague his sleep still offered little clue as to their orientation.

'Your palms are sticky, Curt! Are you heating over?' noted Hayley as they approached the front doorway of the pub.

'No...I'm fine. Ready for a pint, though! Let's get the girls signed into the play-barn and then we'll get a drink.'

And so it was, with a heavy heart and tension thudding through his skull, that Curt Osbourne finally entered the fray.

*****

As events transpired, the party did not bring forth its expected endless tales of mischief and mayhem associated with the trip to Prague. In fact, the jaunt abroad was not mentioned even once.

The usual suspects were present, with everybody making Hayley and Curt feel relaxed and welcome.

Gary Lockley himself was in fine form and played out the role of birthday boy with a surprising amount of civility and noticeable absence of profanity. The banter with his brother was ever-present, yet evidently under stricter control in such a convivial setting.

Even Trevor Palmer was in a buoyant mood for the most part, but when the subject of work arose its ugly head, it was Curt inevitably who took the brunt of the carefully barbed jokes.

As the intake of drink and food increased, Curt felt sufficiently at ease to invite Hayley for a dance, which endured for at least three records.

Whilst not generally one for a boogie himself, Curt made sure to be attentive to his wife's needs, whilst keeping one eye on the intermittent approaches of his one-time travelling companions.

In truth, the evening passed without hindrance or further cause for anxiety.

The girls had utilised most of their energy in the play area when Hayley called time on their adventure in the enormous climbing frame and ball pool.

Curt smiled as he observed his two red-cheeked daughters return to the lounge room table and each in turn breathlessly consumed lemonade through a drinking straw as they silently observed the surrounding activity.

Departing the party came at a timely moment.

Curt was tired and ready to escape from the throbbing disco. Having shook hands and exchanged goodbyes with the relevant personalities, he found himself very comfortable in the knowledge that whatever had occurred on their trip, Prague was seemingly now firmly at the back of the minds of the participants.

The walk back home in the shrill winter air served to invigorate Curt to the point of semi-contentment. The demons that had ravaged his mindset were seemingly vanquished for the time being.

The distorted memories of the recent past were apparently gone.

The future now beckoned, and Curt mentally embraced the fact as his family entered Leyton Close and shuffled through the front gate of number thirty-two.

He watched as Hayley inserted the door key and instructed Emily and Hannah to get ready for bed as it was nearly midnight. As the girls scampered upstairs in a fit of mutually teasing giggles, Curt approached his wife from behind and pulled her into his embrace with a whisper.

He smelled her hair and placed his lips to her ear.

'Fancy playing around for a while?'

Hayley instantly smirked as the idea registered.

She deliberated for a fleeting second before turning to face him.

In a quiet tone, she expressed her support for the suggestion.

'What a good idea, sir. Go and get that bed warmed up for me, then!'

The subsequent days formed into short weeks and developed into rapidly passing months. The general financial picture at work was very positive considering the strife that many small businesses had suffered nationwide due to a calamitous recession.

Indeed, employment for Curt Osbourne had barely been better as spring became slowly eclipsed by the empty expert promise of a warm summer.

An annual pay rise had supplemented his income to the point whereby the family car was upgraded to a newer model with nothing under the bonnet that rattled.

Hayley had taken to the blue colour instantly and when it came to keeping a smile on his dear wife's face, Curt rarely passed up the opportunity to do so.

A holiday to Devon was also in the pipeline for August and as time ticked ever closer to the schools' six-week holidays, the girls' excitement for a vacation on the coast was steadily reaching fever pitch.

Life within the walls at number thirty-two, Leyton Close was very rewarding once again. The year's developments had fuelled Curt with much needed enthusiasm and the passage of supposedly healing time had adequately distanced him from the source of his relentless winter troubles.

In short, he had found fresh perspective. And it felt familiarly good.

It was a glorious sunny start in early July that accompanied his Thursday morning journey to work as the latest favourite tracks pounded through the new surround-sound speakers. Hayley bemoaned his reliably rocking choice of music, but Curt could not bear the repetitive chart tunes that she was accustomed to favouring.

As normal he parked the car and ambled toward the main entrance of the plant, retrieving his clocking card from his wallet as he did so.

He waved at Carl the security guard, who was surprisingly awake in his chair and responded accordingly.

After swiping his card through the clocking station, Curt walked briskly through the complex and nodded to various recognisable faces along the way.

On reaching the warehouse entrance, he glanced at his wristwatch.

Seven-thirty-eight.

He was slightly later than normal.

Curt made his way along the pedestrian walkway as a familiar vision honed into view.

Trevor and Gary were poised leaning against a pallet with mugs of tea in hand, no doubt discussing something trivial and irrelevant concerning some poor unfortunate soul somewhere.

Their mutual laughter disguised Curt's approach, affording him a surprise attack.

'You two look flat out again!' Curt smirked, observing the picture of inactivity that paraded itself before him.

Needless to say, Trevor Palmer obliged the opening verbal gambit with his usual gusto.

'Why don't you just go and get Smithy's coffee made, Curtis. And if you've run out of sugar, I've got something I can squirt in it!'

Gary chuckled as Curt returned volley.

'If you mean what I think you mean, Trev, you haven't got a prayer of achieving that!'

'Why's that then?'

'Because you'd need an erection first!'

Now Gary exploded with laughter as Trevor's complexion reddened.

'Yeah? Well, your missus doesn't seem to have too much trouble getting me up!'

Curt merely smiled and continued walking toward the office steps.

'You are one sad man, Palmer. One sad man...'

*****

Following a relatively busy morning of logistical problem solving, lunchtime reared its welcome head unusually quickly and as was the norm, Curt opted to join his colleagues in the crew mess room.

The associated noises and aromas emanated from the vicinity as he stood outside the partially closed door.

A mixture of shouting and swearing combined with the multiple fragrances of soup, coffee and bacon. Curt entered the canteen and perched himself opposite Colin Tansley, who as per normal was hidden behind a newspaper.

'Mind if I join you, Colin?'

The elder statesman of the warehouse team wearily glanced over the top of his read and grunted an amusing reply.

'Suppose you're a better option than that tosser over there!'

Stirring his cup of noodles as he settled at the other end of the room, Trevor Palmer acknowledged the commentary with a mimed profanity. Curt retrieved his lunchbox from his bag as the scent of powdered chicken wafted through the air, again prompting a contribution from Mister Tansley.

'What have I told you, Palmer...eat that shit somewhere else! It stinks the whole fucking room out!'

'So do you when you've been in trap two!' jousted the willing opponent.

With the eager audience poised for a continuation of insults and banter, Colin disappointed and merely turned the page of his newspaper with a disgruntled shake of the head.

The canteen remained unusually silent for at least three or four minutes before everyone again became annoyed by the sound of Trevor slurping the dubious constituents of his meal as he hauled it mouth-ward with a plastic fork.

The surrounding occupants looked at one another and then centred attention on the ignorant perpetrator. Giggling commenced in earnest as the oblivious cause of disgust continued to gorge himself like a pig at a trough.

Finally, the voice of authority, Colin Tansley, could bear it no more.

'Right...Palmer...put that crap in the fucking bin before I ram that fucking mug down your throat and stick that fucking plastic fork up your arse!'

As a measure of partial compliance, Trevor resorted to raising the cup up to his mouth and drinking the remnants in one swift gulp.

Then of course came the ritual round of belching, which duly served to infuse the sense of fun that was to be found when Colin Tansley became properly annoyed.

'ONCE MORE, PALMER! JUST ONCE FUCKING MORE AND YOU'LL BE PICKING YOUR TEETH UP OFF THE FLOOR!'

Seemingly content with his empty victory, the agitator sat back in his chair with a broad smile stretching from ear to ear.

Curt reached for a second limp ham sandwich as Colin slowly leaned forward in his seat and rested his newspaper on the table.

He seemed engaged by a particular story; the headline of which Curt could not fully decipher from his upside-down perspective.

However, the salient details of the feature were soon revealed as, without invitation, the reader openly conveyed his findings.

'Now why couldn't this have happened to fucking Palmer? I tell you what lads...there's no luck in this world is there?'

Gary Lockley glanced along the dining table and gestured for an explanation from his elder colleague.

'What you on about now, Colin?'

'This story I've just read here! There are some mentalists about these days. It's about some long-lost nutcase from the rural wilderness of Romania who police have been after for three years. They've only just fucking found him at last!'

'What's so interesting about that?' barked Trevor. 'Everywhere you turn these days there's another fucking murderer or child molester. The world's fucking full of 'em!'

Colin Tansley rustled the pages of his read as he continued with the disclosure.

'Yeah...but this one's taken a few out with him along the way by the looks of this.'

'How do you mean?' Gary enquired.

'Apparently this joker is an ex-member of the communist party. A real fruit-loop! An official psychopath! He had been locked up for crimes against humanity and escaped some while back.'

'So what?' replied Trevor. 'Like I said...they're everywhere!'

Colin lowered his newspaper and glared at the source of the last comment.

As he pulled open a bag of salt and vinegar crisps, Curt noted the unusual grimace that the elder man displayed.

'Yes...but this particular nut-job has been pretty busy lately. Left a few silly clues about. And you'll never guess where police eventually tracked him to!'

Trevor bolted upright in his chair and grinned inanely.

'Don't tell me! His grandma's wardrobe!'

As the laughter rippled around the room, Colin simply stared back at his most favoured opponent and remained silent for a few contemplative seconds before issuing an unnerving statement.

'I'm glad I *didn't* come on that trip to Prague with you lot, now!

Gary was the first to place two and two together.

'What? Not Prague! Really? Was Jack the Russian Ripper hanging around there, then?'

Colin simply nodded as Trevor Palmer contributed to the growing reaction.

'You mean to tell me that this maniac was running round Prague whilst we were there?'

Colin sat back in his chair and offered the page down the table for Gary to scrutinise.

'Yep! And not a bloke you really want to cross judging by his record. He's suspected of murdering fifteen people since his escape from the loony bin! And all of them have been tourists that have disappeared in the last few years! You know...foreign visitors. Some have been found floating in rivers...hung by the neck in disused buildings. And their bank accounts have been raided! And that's just the ones the coppers *know* about! How many other poor fuckers has he bumped off? You lot were fucking lucky if you ask me!'

Gary re-read the story before announcing his own conclusions.

'Look...this kind of thing goes on every day somewhere. You've really got to be unfortunate to fall into a trap like this. Is this his picture, then?'

Trevor left his seat and moved in to scan the photograph before quickly concurring with his colleague.

'Bullshit! Can't say I recall that face. What about you, Curtis? Come and have a butchers at this ugly bastard.'

Mildly intrigued by the discussion, Curt grabbed his last sandwich and shifted position to afford himself a better view of the tabloid.

MADMAN CAUGHT AT LAST!

The wording of the headline meant very little.

Curt quickly absorbed the gist of the text before swallowing a morsel of food. As he chewed, his eyes transferred attention to the face of the man in the photograph.

He studied the features; the hair; the glint in the eye.

A pang of familiarity set his heart racing uncontrollably.

Curt's stomach began to buckle as he became transfixed by the grainy black and white print.

There must have been some incredulous mistake.

Yet a link in his memory bank that had been missing for months, was suddenly replaced.

239

He had reached the conclusion only recently that his imagination must have been playing cruel tricks for most of the year.

Yet the immediate involuntary mental and physical response to what he had just seen shook Curt Osbourne to his very core.

He knew instinctively.

He definitely recognised the suspect.

From somewhere in the past.

Somehow their paths had crossed.

And as the droning bell signalled the end of another lunchtime, Curt slowly but surely found himself confronted with the commencement of another nightmare.

Yet he continued to scan the copy and said nothing.

He waited until the room had emptied.

Colin left the newspaper on the table, and left Curt staring into the face of death itself as flitting acknowledgement haunted him to his very soul.

It was a face he knew but it needed a place.

A frame of reference.

Some situation that would allow him to join the dots.

A time and location that would enable Curt to convincingly deduce where he had viewed this person within history.

And as Gary Lockley appeared at the door to remind his colleague that David Smith was on the prowl, Curt Osbourne's painful conundrum finally unfurled its agonisingly real solution.

Under a lashing storm of intensive horror, Curt's mind slotted the relevant details into order.

The man: stern features, curly hair, a rucksack on his back.

The situation: a nightclub; a crowded dance floor; a beautiful girl.

The time: very early hours. Anyone's guess.

The time and location: Prague – Sunday the tenth of January.

As he eventually emerged from the mess room and back toward the warehouse office, Curt Osbourne realised that all those weeks ago when he refused to accept his own mindset and its tormenting distractions, he should indeed have listened carefully to the crying echoes of his clinging yet unknown past.

Climbing the steps to the office, he firmly held both banister rails to retain his balance as once more, Curt found himself enveloped in nothing less than utter, terrifying turmoil.

FORTY-TWO

The sensation was completely debilitating. The very notion of possibly being rendered unto the clutches of the monster depicted in the newspaper was unthinkable.

Questions purged Curt's mind for the remainder of the working day as a cloud of abhorrence served to extinguish any hope of concentration on normal duty.

Caroline enquired as to his wellbeing when she found him at the coffee machine staring into space in contemplation of his discovery. Thoughts bombarded his psyche like poisoned darts.

Had he actually become an intended victim of the killer, only to be offered some last-minute reprieve?

And why did the full memory of events still elude him?

Why was the jigsaw still missing so many obvious and vital pieces?

But undeniably, the face in the newspaper mirrored the latent image in his mind and was reliably in tune with the bare spark of reminiscence that Curt had managed to retain. But now the unspoken truth began to gnaw at him relentlessly.

Had he come into direct contact with a convicted killer?

That much was still uncertain.

But if so - then what happened?

And how; and when; and why?

The dense fog remained, yet now the quest was clear.

The lid had to be lifted on the ongoing riddle.

And Curt Osbourne did not relish the premise one iota.

*****

The rush hour traffic throbbed and choked. Curt was just over halfway through the journey home when he felt the need to pull over into a bus stop.

Turning off the engine, he reluctantly studied at the vision in his rear-view mirror.

And he saw a frightened man.

A cowering man, desperate for the next step to present itself and guide him through the mental maelstrom.

He stared intently at the man's eyes, and they stared back at him.

And without warning, the man in the mirror began to weep.

A bursting release of pent-up emotion which quickly gathered momentum and developed into a howling crescendo. Curt thought of his family and how close they might possibly have come to never seeing him again.

The incredulous premise of being stranded abroad and left for dead wrenched at his very fibres and turned his stomach inside out. Occasional passers-by did not notice the man in the metallic blue car who let his moistened gaze wander through the windscreen and lazily analyse the mid-summer early evening sky.

The tears continued to wash his face and fall onto his lap as Curt searched for direction.

What move should he now make?

Perhaps the police could assist, but the absence of detail would render them virtually toothless from the outset.

Should he burden Hayley with his suspicions? Perhaps his parents might assist with his plight? But these options would surely lead only to observing theirs and his further anguish in response?

And what of his companions who unwittingly travelled with him to that fiendish place? His colleagues, who innocently and yet willingly plunged themselves into that maw of hidden peril and who as yet still have no indication of their friend buckling under the weight of his sufferance.

No.

He needed his wife and children at that moment.

Not to share his trauma or wipe his emotions clear or sooth his aching brow.

But for them to offer him unconditional protection without questioning the motive or reason for doing so.

To be home.

To be safe.

*****

He arrived back at Leyton Close at just before six-thirty to be greeted by the welcoming sight of Hayley in the kitchen.

She offered him a kiss and flicked on the kettle to boil.

'You're very late, love.' she commented as he smiled and perched at the breakfast bar.

242

'Yeah...accident caused bad traffic jams everywhere.' he sighed.

Curt felt numb inside. His usual desire to communicate and interact with his wife had all but disintegrated in the previous hours, leaving him feeling strangely uneasy in her company.

Thankfully, he was adept at hiding the symptoms of his woe and he responded to her interest in his day with a faintly applied coat of optimism as she prepared his drink.

'Work okay, love?'

'Yeah...no real news to tell you I don't think. You alright at the supermarket?'

'Yes. Fine. Although the store's computer system crashed, and we had to estimate every customer's shopping for an hour. Christ knows how much money the place lost!'

Curt sipped some coffee and smiled.

'Shame it never happens when *we're* shopping!'

The exchange was interrupted by the sound of two pairs of feet thumping down the stairs, followed by the kitchen doorway opening to reveal the dual smiling faces of his daughters.

'Hello girls. You both okay?'

Hannah and Emily immediately rushed to their father's side and offered him the tightest of hugs. Curt felt his emotions lurch once more as the reality of what he had learned came back to the forefront of his thoughts.

He fought for a semblance of composure and adopted a facade of daily routine, when in fact it was the most abnormal day of his entire existence.

'School okay, ladies?'

Both girls looked up into his eyes and nodded with partial grimaces which in turn caused Curt to smile broadly.

'Well...as okay as school can be, I suppose. I know what you're saying! Still, you break up on Friday, don't you?'

The simultaneous squeal of relieved excitement reverberated around the kitchen and the girls began to jump up and down on the spot. Emily was first to express her happiness at the prospect.

'Yes...and then we go to the seaside soon, don't we Daddy?'

'Yes, darling. I can't wait. Can you?'

'NO!' came the cry from both girls as they vied for their father's attention.

However, unbeknown to them, both daughters were chasing a lost cause in trying to engage Curt in anything remotely connected with fun. His head continued to spin with what had transpired that afternoon.

He glanced across to Hayley, but Curt could only see the man in the newspaper. She caught his stare and smiled in response.

'Chicken, salad and chips for tea, love. Is that okay?'

Curt felt he could not confront food at that moment but nodded in appreciation.

'Yes. Great, love...sounds really good!'

*****

The girls were eventually tucked up in bed by five minutes to ten, with Hayley upstairs trying to placate Emily's continual buoyancy with a reading book.

Curt observed the time on the lounge wall clock and idly picked up the television remote. He slumped on the settee and ignored the boring and protracted weather forecast.

Then the opening credit sequence for the ten o' clock news paraded itself across the screen. The volume was on a low setting as Curt forced himself to look at the presenters and the brief overview of the main headlines.

And the man from the pages of the newspaper appeared once again.

Only this time in clear, disarming, electrifying colour.

The photograph was clean-lined and in focus.

The eyes of evil brimmed from the screen as Curt interlocked with the story and turned up the sound with the remote control.

The story would be the second lead of the evening bulletin following a slot on the latest row in Westminster.

The delay offered Curt opportunity to check that Hayley was still occupied with Emily. He listened at the bottom of the stairs and confirmed his wife's whispered tones conveying a bedtime story.

Retreating to the lounge, he pushed the door to nearly completely shut and knelt by the television.

His heart began to thump as the newscaster honed back into view and commenced introduction to the next item.

The item that Curt Osbourne never thought he would ever need to hear.

With grim reluctance and a fearful fascination, he immediately became transfixed by the stark revelations that ensued. The serious expression of the news presenter only served to heighten Curt's overbearing tension as the report opened in earnest.

'Police in the capital of the Czech Republic have finally recaptured the man they believe to be responsible for the deaths of at least fifteen tourists during the last four years.

Fifty-six-year-old Romanian exile Alexandru Damitri was diagnosed with serious mental dysfunction in 2005 and sentenced to medical incarceration. As the founder and subsequent leader of the European neo-communist organisation known as 'Invingator Vigilente' or I.V. - translated roughly as meaning 'Watchful Victor' - his adjudged crimes against the state of Romania utilised a network of unscrupulous agents throughout the former Eastern Bloc.

From Prague, Michael Turner brings us this report:

Originally an anti-capitalist and resounding anti-Westernist, Damitri was well educated and quickly became a devotee to the principles of Karl Marx. An avid political activist, he stood for Romanian parliament in the nineteen-eighty-two elections at the age of twenty-eight and quickly amassed a large band of followers.

However, his allegiance to orthodox communism began to take a sinister turn in the mid-eighties during which he championed a series of violent demonstrations in Yugoslavia and Poland among others.

With the rapid weakening of communism's stranglehold in Eastern Europe in the early nineties, Damitri became obsessed with the concept that western civilization and its inhabitants had become poisoned to the point of evil by greed and their need for wealth.

This obsession evolved into an inherent and unfounded desire to hunt down all perceived representatives of capitalist culture using his covert network of political associations.

Unfortunately, what was initially a purely political and peaceful operation, the I.V. emerged with increasingly violent tendencies and were suspected of several acts of wanton terrorism.

The most notable incident arose at a neo-communist rally in Warsaw in nineteen-ninety-three, where Damitri refused to accept blood on his hands when twelve innocent people were shot dead. The Polish authorities claimed the victims had been specifically hired by the I.V. organisation to commit atrocities at the rally.

This was never proven however, and Damitri's thirst for bloodshed was effectively permitted to gather momentum. His political beliefs were becoming of seemingly secondary consideration and regularly failed to eclipse the fact that his main ambition was to decimate any strand of anti-communism within his home state.

His notoriety became a burden that the Romanian Government found impossible to bare, and Damitri was officially exiled from Romania in nineteen-ninety-seven and immediately classed as a confirmed enemy of the state.

This was a mantle that he was, it seems, quite content to adorn.

More blood was shed two years later when he interrupted armament talks at the British Embassy in Romania when officials were besieged and held hostage for forty-eight hours until the government agreed to postpone the conference.

By the new Millennium, Damitri was a dangerously loose cannon in the political circles of Eastern Europe and his state of mind was brought under scrutiny when he allegedly turned a shotgun on one of his own teenage supporters and murdered him without explanation or mitigation.

An act that has never been proven or explained to this day.

During the murder trial, Damitri fell ill and was subsequently quarantined from public life for ongoing medical examination. He was subsequently sectioned under the UN Mental Health Act and consigned to life in an open prison, the location of which was never revealed.

However, his imprisonment was to be a short-lived affair, with Damitri making his escape whilst on a supervised day visit – again, the precise time and location of his disappearance was never exposed.

With the subsequent fragmentation of the I.V. organisation, Damitri found himself increasingly short of pro-active supporters. However, the police are convinced that his trademark then became all-out atrocity, with several tourists being found hanged or drowned simply because they originated from capitalist countries.

Damitri has in the past suggested to the police that he intended to make killing his business and he has since admitted to murdering people from France, Spain and the Americas.

Now it appears his wrath is all but quashed.

He was suspected to be residing in Prague at the beginning of the year by police intelligence.

Elusive and accustomed to living a life fortified by intense stealth, Damitri evaded capture for as long as possible.

Until now, that is, where police tracked him down and bided their time whilst closing the net.

Back behind bars tonight, Alexandru Damitri's reign of terror is finally over for good. The only disappointment for many will be that his mental condition will likely render him immune from prosecution for his crimes.

This is Michael Turner reporting from Prague. Back to the studio.'

*****

Curt remained completely still as the image of his tormentor faded from view and the next headline story played out.

He was hardly breathing, yet his mind felt suddenly diluted of all doubt and fear. The reality of his good fortune would likely never fully register.

It would likely take a dozen lifetimes to fully comprehend just how close he came to his demise.

Yet Curt Osbourne made his decision there and then as he crouched in front of the television.

He didn't have the luxury of a dozen lifetimes to understand his ordeal.

There was only one lifetime; the one he was now happily living with the family he cherished and the sanctity he has earned within the walls of number thirty-two, Leyton Close. There was no further need to deliberate on the mystery.

It had been solved so far as he was concerned. There would never be the chance for explanation or opportunity for retribution.

And it mattered not one iota. Not anymore.

Curt pulled himself upright and turned off the television at the wall socket, content that he could now draw a line under the past and continue with his future.

Maybe he would confide in somebody, someday, but the actual details of his own experience were still enshrouded in the fog of that near-fateful night back in January. And as he entered the hallway and began to climb the stairs, a thought entered his head which was both perversely amusing and strangely placating.

How could two days of supposed fun with friends result in nearly a year of such personal indecision and anxiety?

The scenario was totally implausible and would be destined to remain so for the foreseeable future.

Turning off the landing light and entering the bedroom, Curt could only hold the hope in his heart that the traumatic chapter was now closed for good.

EPILOGUE

Tuesday the ninth of November.

Curt glanced at the office wall clock before reverting attention back to the computer screen. Not long until lunch time now.

As he scrutinised the display, he barely noticed the arrival of two figures who had ascended the steps to the mezzanine office and stood expectantly in the doorway.

Gary Lockley and Trevor Palmer attempted to remain composed, yet their childish sense of humour overwhelmed them as they both launched screwed up pieces of paper at the target to get his attention.

Finally, Curt was persuaded from concentration and enquired as to the motive for the interruption.

'What do you two reprobates want? Smithy will be back in a minute, you know!'

Gary simply smirked in response.

'Just a quick word, Curt. Well, actually, it's Trevor that wants a word.'

Curt waited whilst the portly, ever-unshaven features of his colleague straightened into something resembling serious and civilised.

'Well, you know it's my birthday next February, Curtis. I know you've got family and all that, so I'm giving you the heads up early. I'm organising a bit of a bender in the New Year. It's not a special birthday, just my forty-fourth. But any excuse now, eh? You know the score…just like we did in Prague…but perhaps somewhere else. Somewhere similar, though. You fancy that?'

Gary intervened before Curt could offer his thoughts.

'Yeah! Be a right laugh! Our Ian's already said he'll look into sorting it out again. So...you in...or what?'

There was no need for deliberation.

Curt's answer was short and polite.

'No thanks, guys. I appreciate the invite and all that. But count me out this time.'

Trevor Palmer was not happy to be faced with a refusal at any time, but this one he classed as an insult.

'What do you mean fucking '*no*'?! You *loved* Prague! You were in your fucking element! What is it? Is it the missus? Are you scared she'll *really* say *no* this time? You are, aren't you? You're too shit scared to even ask her.'

Curt swivelled position in his chair to face his colleagues squarely.

His heartbeat increased with every passing second.

His gaze centred on Trevor and his expression did not waver.

Again, Curt Osbourne's adamant reply was concise, courteous and above all, completely honest.

'Like I said...I'll give this one a miss...and yes...I'm scared...in fact... I'm so frightened you wouldn't *believe* it...'

ACKNOWLEDGEMENTS

I wish to thank the following people for their invaluable expertise and support in helping this book gain wings:
Samantha Thornton; Hannah Bliss; Charlotte Wilson; Robbie Wilson; Carole Thornton, Chris Bliss; Charlotte Bliss; Jeanette Taylor Ford; Sue Hayward; Ford Wood and last but certainly not least, David Slaney for his superb cover design.
I couldn't have done it without any of you.
I am forever indebted.
RJT

Printed in Great Britain
by Amazon